# *Loving Betrayal*

## Marjorie Hemans

# Loving Betrayal

# TABLE OF CONTENTS

# ACKNOWLEDGMENTS

**Brynn, my Editor, who read this several times without complaint.**

**Chuck, for his love and support.**

**Marty, for her excellent editorial skills and friendship**

Loving Betrayal

# Prologue

The moonlight came to settle on the sleeping girl as if it had been seeking her. The wind was picking up its strength, turning the night cold at its touch. The leaves fell from the trees, rustling along the ground. The sounds of the night streamed into the girl's mind becoming part of her dreams. She began to shake with the cold; unconsciously she drew the cover over her shoulders. The sleeper began to toss and turn as her dream became more vivid. Finally the wind settled and stopped. A mist encircled her. The moonlight moved from her window; the dreamer quieted down.

The girl awoke with a start. Sitting up in her bed with a pain so strong, she found it hard to breathe. Gasping for air and swallowing it as fast as she could, her sobbing cries came from deep within her soul. She wrapped her arms around herself, rocking back and forth. The covers enfolded her as if someone was holding her, soothing her. Still she cried, her pain increasing. This pain was recognizable. It was the pain of a broken heart, the loss of something dear. Her dream was in fragments; her memory was lost to her. All that was left was her sense of loss. But what had she lost? The girl had no idea but still she sobbed. After a time, the girl laid down with the cover wrapped around her. From exhaustion sleep found her; it did not allow her to hear her grandmother enter their home.

The old woman stumbled in and found her cot. She managed to lie down and breathe deeply, attempting to relax and forget the night's events. Her mind retraced her steps as she thought about what she had done. The wise woman shook her head in disbelief. Why had she done this unkind and cruel thing? She held all responsibility. Staring into the dark, Lillium determined to reverse this curse. She thought she saw her unsmiling daughter, Finola, standing by her bed. The old woman felt her life ebbing away as she fell into a deep sleep.

# Part I

## Chapter 1

The young mother went about her morning chores with her daughter following her closely. After the morning meal, she cleaned up, went to her garden to weed and water. The child watched her attentively asking her many questions.

"Why do you wash the plants every day?"

"It is a form of feeding the plants, child. They need water to help them grow. If I do not water them, they will begin to shrivel up and die. They need the sun as well. The sun shines on them; then they turn to the bright light and smile."

With that explanation stated, the girl began to look closely at the leaves. She pointed things out to her mother. She began to speak to the plants, naming them as she went. Sometimes she would sit listening intently.

"This one has a worm on it, Mama. This one looks yellow, not green. This one has white specks on its leaves."

Finola began to look at the plants Maeve pointed out. The more they worked in the garden together, the more the mother noticed the child's acumen for gardening. She observed that it was an instinct within the child. Soon the little girl took over her mother's garden; she requested types of plants they could grow. The learning did not stop there. Her mother taught her the use of the herbs, instructed her how to use them for various cooking, illnesses and wounds. The child absorbed the information quickly and surprised her mother almost daily.

Soon the little girl began to instinctively move about the plants; that knowledge increased to study of the trees, flowers and then to sky and the sun. She began leaving her cot at night to observe the moon and the stars. She chanted to the moon in beautiful little songs that she made up herself. She extended her arm as if to touch the magnificent wonder in the sky.

One evening her mother woke to her songs and quietly went to see what her daughter was doing. She stood in awe of her child, for the dance and song she performed was a ritual of worship that Finola had not passed on to the girl. The child's black hair was the same color as Finola's, but Maeve's hair was abundant with curls, flying about as she danced. Her deep blue eyes were the shade of her father's. As her mother watched, she was moved by Maeve's grace and went to worship with her. Together they finished the ritual.

"How do you know this, Maeve?" Finola asked the child as she drew her into her arms.

"Your mother taught me, Mama." Tears swelled into her mother's eyes and made it impossible to speak.

Maeve released herself from her mother's embrace; she began to dance and sing again. Finola just watched her noticing the arm movements reminded her of her mother.

"Yes, you have been taught by my mother, Tiny One; but how can that be?"

"I dream of your Mum often, Mama. She tells me stories, teaches me songs and dances."

"She comes to you in your dreams?"

"Oh yes, she calls me Little Girl and she laughs when I call her Mum."

Finola realized it had been far too long since she had met with her mother. She mixed her incense to burn prior to travel. Finola loved the smell of Dittany of Crete as she burned it. Colm came in to help her as she anointed her body with her special ointment. She had designated this particular evening a few weeks before the actual event, with instructions to Maeve to tell Mum to prepare for her visit. Colm covered her with a woolen blanket as she laid down by the hearth. Soon her body became warm; it appeared she was asleep by the fire, but she was actually flying to her mother to discuss Maeve. Colm waited patiently near his wife by the fire. If anything went wrong he would not know what to do but he felt more at ease waiting for her.

Finola and Mum's meeting was loving and fruitful. The old woman promised to continue her instruction of little Maeve in the rituals of the seasons. Finola was grateful for her mother's ability to meet with the child through her dreams. Before they had finished Finola whispered to her mother that she was again with child. The old woman embraced Finola, wished her well and after a time they both returned to consciousness.

Waking, Finola awoke to find Colm sitting near the fire. He came to her, then holding her in his arms to welcome her back. Fi whispered to him that she loved him dearly. He held her closer whispering to her. They laid down by the fire but Colm gave her a questioning look. Fi quietly said, "Maeve is dreaming of my Mum right now. She will be with her for a time." They smiled at each other then as he began to undress her.

The following day, Finola worked in her garden reminiscing of her childhood. She had been her parents' only child; her mother had taught her all she knew about herbs and healing. Finola was taller than her mother with beautiful black hair and green eyes. Spending her days with her Mum had been all she knew in life. When her father contracted the long illness that eventually killed him, her mother grieved for years. Finola stayed by her mother's side attempting to cheer her. Meeting Colm had been an accident. Finola had gone to town to visit a friend when Colm saw her. He immediately asked about her. He was told that she was the daughter of the wise woman. As she began her walk to her home, he introduced himself. There was an immediate attraction between them. Colm did not live in the village; he told Finola that he worked at a manor house miles away. He came to visit her as much as he could before finally asking for her hand in marriage. Finola did not want to leave her mother since she was alone but eventually both Colm and her mother persuaded her to marry him and move.

Finola and Colm moved to a cottage on the grounds of the manor and commenced to live happily together. The birth of Maeve was a blessing as they adored their daughter. She was quick to learn; their pride was evident as they watched her grow. Colm would grab Finola's hand as their eyes followed their daughter's adventures. Maeve brought her parents to laughter many times. Her hugs were precious. They felt their happiness could not be more than it was.

Now Finola was pregnant again. She felt the child move within her. Maeve loved feeling her mother's belly as the child kicked within her. Colm would hold them both as Finola sang a soft lullaby.

Colm had grown up on the manor grounds. His father and mother worked for the Lord and Lady so Colm knew no other home or life. He was a handsome young man so many of the maids had hoped to marry him. They were surprised when he married someone not from the manor.

# Chapter 2

The months passed as the family moved about their lives waiting for the birth of the new child. Maeve cared for her mother with herbs for her health and strength. Finola laughed daily at the new motherly instinct in her daughter. Her father encouraged Maeve to care for Finola while he worked, instructing her about coming to him when the baby was ready to be born.

Her father did not escape her kindness. When he arrived home she questioned him about his health and if he had injured himself during the day. He allowed her to treat his cuts and wounds with laughter as she cleaned them and bandaged him. When she finished she would kiss him and tell him she loved him. Then she would run off as her parents observed her next endeavor. Their looks of love for their child would transfer to each other as they walked together to their cottage.

One day Maeve's father brought her to the stables where he worked as a farrier to show her the horses. One of the horses was lame and Finola had suggested that Maeve might be able to help. This, of course, was a tall order for the child who so far had taken care of only her mother and father. When the child saw the horse, she was saddened to see it suffering.

"What do you call him, Da?"
Her father was occupied with brushing out a horse when he heard his child's query.

"Oh, he's an old fellow; we have been calling him Grandpa but his real name is Flame."

Maeve began to coo to the horse calling him Flame and he responded to her. She spoke softly, telling him she was going to change his bandages because his were dirty. She talked and talked to him but her father could not hear her words. After his bandages were changed, Maeve began brushing him as he stood tall and majestic. The other men at the stable watched in awe at the change in the horse who they thought was near his death.

Her father told Maeve it was time for her to go home to her mother and she began picking up her things all the while talking to her horse. She stood for a time petting the animal as he nudged her and whinnied.

Maeve turned to go and said to her father, "Please don't call him Grandpa anymore. He does not like it. Call him Flame."

The men around nodded in agreement and she asked them, "Why was he named Flame? Is it because of his red coat?"

One of the men answered her, "I was there the morning he was born. He was standing, testing his legs when the sun rose in the sky. The sun shone on him; he turned bright red like a flame in the fire. We have called him Flame ever since."

Maeve smiled, nodded and said, "Thank you, Sir. Flame is a beautiful horse with a beautiful name. Keep him safe and happy."

She kissed her father and headed toward their home. Flame turned to watch her go as he held his head proudly.

When Maeve arrived home, she told her mother the story of Flame. She told Finola what the horse liked, why he was feeling ill and that he felt better when she left him. Finola asked her daughter how she knew everything about the horse. Maeve became very serious, "Mama, he told me. Have you never spoken to a horse?"

Finola said that she had never spoken to a horse. She suggested that Maeve ask her father when he returned home if he could communicate with a horse. Maeve nodded somberly.

When Colm arrived home, the first thing Maeve did was to ask her father if he could understand what a horse was feeling. Colm was taken aback by the question. Finally he answered his daughter, "Tiny One, I can tell when a horse is in pain because it whinnies a certain way. But I do not know if they like their names or not."

Maeve listened, shook her head, kissed her father and said, "I will teach you, Da."

Although Maeve wanted to accompany her father to work in the following days, he told her that she would not be able to come. The daughter of the manor had been coming to the stable for riding lessons. Maeve's eyes grew bright when she heard this; she imagined herself riding one of the beautiful horses. Her father told her he would see about her coming back to see Flame but she had to be patient.

# Chapter 3

One morning her father woke Maeve very early telling her to dress because they were going to the stable. On the way, Maeve was told that Flame was doing poorly again; the men had asked for her help. Maeve saw Flame and ran to him. He seemed sick again so she began to coo to him, feeding him treats as she changed his bandages. While she was tending to Flame a little girl approached her.

"How is he this morning?" she asked.

"He does not seem himself; he is not eating as he should." Maeve answered.

The little girl watched and listened as Maeve talked to Flame, petting him.

"He likes you. He likes your voice," said the child.

"He just needs attention. Do you come here every day? If you do, you could talk to him." Maeve told her.

A voice from behind them interrupted their conversation and the children turned around to see who was speaking.

"Miss LaLa, please come away from there. See to your pony." The speaker was a young man who appeared to be dressed for riding rather than handling the horses.

"I am coming, Thomas. I am sorry to keep you waiting." The young girl then turned to Maeve and said, "I must go to ride. Would you care to ride with me?"

Maeve's eyes lit up but she said very softly, "I cannot ride, Miss."

"Thomas will teach you; I'm just learning."

The child ran to Thomas speaking with him quietly. Thomas went into the barn and spoke with some men, one of whom was Maeve's father. Maeve's attention had been drawn back to Flame. She was unaware of what was taking place behind her. Eventually there was a call from her father to come to him. Maeve answered her father's call, going to him.

"Would you like to learn to ride, Tiny One?" asked her father.

"Oh, could I? I would love to ride," answered Maeve smiling so brightly she lit up the dreary, cloudy day. Her father chuckled to himself, nodded; he gently touched her shoulder moving her in the direction of a young horse that had been saddled for her.

Thomas gave Maeve instruction on the saddle, reins and mounting the horse. By the end of this brief lesson, Miss LaLa was already mounted on her horse and Maeve mounted her horse. Thomas then held the reins of both horses and took them to the paddock where they rode as he continued to instruct about their posture and the way they sat the horses. Maeve was so earnest in her learning that she caught on very quickly.

Once the lesson was over, it was determined that Maeve would come daily to ride with Miss LaLa. The smiles from both girls showed how happy they were as they said goodbye to each other.

"Thank you so much, Miss LaLa, for allowing me to ride with you today," Maeve said.

"You're welcome, Tiny One," said Miss LaLa, "but call me LaLa," and she scampered off to catch up to Thomas as he walked back to the manor house. Maeve could hear her singing as she went.

Maeve ran back to Flame to whisper goodbye to him, promising she would see him the next day. She bid her father goodbye and started for home. He could hear her laughing and giggling on her way.

The friendship between Maeve and LaLa grew rapidly. Maeve's attention to Flame was not lost on LaLa and she began to pick up on the ways Maeve treated the horses. Sometimes they would have lunch together and Maeve would tell LaLa about her garden at home. LaLa told Maeve about what she was learning from her tutor and how she had to learn to do needlework. Maeve found it interesting to learn how different their lives were, but she was not envious of LaLa in any way.

Both girls excelled in riding. Maeve's father would watch her, marveling how she had grown but yet she was so young. He would tell Finola of Maeve's interest in the horses and her riding.

"Come to see her tomorrow, Finola. She is wonderful to watch," he said one evening after Maeve had gone to sleep. Finola promised

she would walk over with Maeve in the morning; the exercise would
do her good.

# Chapter 4

Finola woke in the morning with a sense of excitement since her labor had begun. She woke Colm to tell him but although the pains were coming, they were slow; they decided Finola would walk to the manor to see Maeve at her riding lesson.

Finola's walking was not as quick as it might have been since she had to stop on occasion for the pain to pass. Maeve ran ahead at the behest of her father so she would not be late. Her parents came along a little bit later in time to watch her ride. Finola could not believe her eyes. Maeve was elegant on the horse. She looked beautiful as did Miss LaLa. Finola's smile lit her entire face as Colm laughed at her reaction.

"Love, I am so glad that I came to see this. Our daughter is beautiful; fit to be the wife of a prince."

This remark made Colm laugh, "You are not biased are you?"

Finola turned to her husband and in her best straight face replied, "Absolutely not."

Then they both laughed together as their eyes traveled back to Maeve. Finola's labor seemed to stop. She had not experienced any pain for a time so when Maeve was finished, they all walked back to their cottage. Colm wanted to be sure Fi was comfortable before he returned to work.

As they walked home, Finola told Colm that the steady pains had ceased. She felt fine and was glad that she had not stayed home. The walk was not far but Finola was slow. She suddenly stopped; putting her hand on Colm's arm she said, "Wait here a moment."

She walked behind a tree blocking Colm's sight of her. After a moment she returned to the path, quietly she said, "I am bleeding. Please fetch the midwife."

Colm called to Maeve who was quite a bit ahead of them. Maeve ran back.

Her father looked at her speaking these words, "It is time to go to Maura. Please run to her and ask her to come to the cottage, for your Mama needs her."

Maeve smiled, running in the direction of Maura's cottage. Finola looked at her husband with a questioning look.

"A few weeks back I brought Maeve to Maura so she would know where to go when you needed her. She has been waiting for this chance to help."

Finola smiled, "My little girl seems to be beyond her years. Thank you, dear Colm. Help me home."

The couple finished the walk to the cottage. Colm helped Finola to settle in a comfortable position but she was more comfortable walking. After some time had passed Colm spoke sternly to her, "Fi, you continue to bleed. Please sit or lie down."

She did as he asked, falling into a swoon. He ran to her then, placing a wet cloth on her forehead to bring her out of it. At this moment, Maeve and Maura entered the cottage. Maura sent Colm and the child on their way so she could examine Finola. The two waited outside until Maura came to them.

"Colm, this doesn't look like it will be easy. I fear the child is turned. I will sit with her and do what I can. You should go about your business."

She turned then to Maeve, "Child, please pray for your Mama. Go to your garden. Your Mama said you know what to do."

Colm kissed Maeve goodbye. Maeve went to the garden. Colm went to the manor; he was going to ask for help. He was afraid, but he was going to do all he could to save his wife and child.

As Maeve sat in the garden she thought back to just a couple of days ago. Her parents had been happy about the birth of their child and talked many hours to Maeve about the responsibilities of an older sister. She listened quietly, enraptured by the thought of a tiny being she could love. As time went on her mother seemed to become quieter and weaker.

Now that the labor had begun her mother was ill; the midwife seemed grim. Maeve heard the woman tell her father that her mother did not have the strength to survive the birth. Maeve did not understand what this meant. She sat in the garden, praying as she was told to do, but her mind wandered over what had recently happened. Then she saw her father come back with a person she did not know. She left the garden running to her father. He saw her but told her to wait outside. She did as she was told.

Colm entered the cottage with the older gentlemen who had accompanied him from the manor. Both Maura and Colm waited outside the room where Finola labored as the gentlemen went inside.

Maura looked at Colm, "I would have told you to bring him if I thought he would come."

"He came willingly as soon as the Lord said he could."

"I only hope he can help. Poor Fi is suffering."

Colm shook his head at this and ran his hand through his hair. Maura led him to a seat, pouring him tea. "Drink this, Colm, try to relax. It is women's work."

Maura left him then to see if she could help with Finola.

The physician and Maura managed to get the bleeding to stop but all maneuvering of the position of the child did not go well. Poor Finola would scream as they tried to turn the child. Her screaming sent chills down Colm's spine as he held on to Maeve. Maeve would cry when she heard her mother's painful screams.

The sun set but still they waited outside. Maura came out after the moon was up to beckon them back inside. She had prepared them a small meal. Once they ate, Maura told Maeve to go outside to pray. Maeve did as she was told calling to the moon for help.
Maura and the physician sat beside Finola's bed waiting the night to pass. Finola was able to sleep a bit but the pain would wake her. Maura would let Colm come to sit with her during the night. He held Fi's hand, speaking to her softly.

When the sun arose, the physician thought he saw a glimmer of hope. He and Maura prepared to deliver the child. Hours passed but they had nothing to show for it.

Colm sat despondently on a bench outside the cottage waiting. He held Maeve's hand and told her all would be well. She had no reason to doubt his word. But all was not well. They could hear her mother moaning. She had not enough strength to do more. Maura busied herself inside; after a time she called Maeve's father. Maeve ran to the garden; she sat in her favorite place then commenced to commune with her grandmother. After a time she came back to consciousness; she went about the garden gathering herbs. Maeve went to the cottage and crept inside where she mixed her herbs with water singing a very quiet spell.

Maeve went to her mother and insisted she drink from the cup she had prepared. Finola was delirious but she drank the liquid for her daughter.

The physician and Maura explained to Colm that this birth was killing Finola. They were unable to deliver the child in the normal way. The physician insisted that he would need to remove the child by cutting the mother. Colm looked at him in shock. The physician shook his head, "Your wife will not survive this. It has gone on too long."

After hours of pain and bleeding, Finola whispered to her husband and begged him to do as she bid, "My love, I will not survive this child. It has gone far too long. I have lost so much blood. Please when this is over, take Maeve to my Mum for her further instruction in the ways of th e healer. She has a gift…must learn more."

Just this much was far too hard for her to say. Her husband knelt at her bedside with tears running down his face. He shook his head, "Fi, you will survive this and you will teach her. Please do not give up."

When the midwife appeared beside him, she made him leave the room. Closing the door, she and the physician commenced the delivery of the child. Finola lost consciousness; then was still.

Later that night Maeve was brought to the bedside of her mother while she slept. Her father and Maeve each held her mother's hands as they quietly waited. Finola did not wake but slept quietly. Maeve did not notice when Maura crept from the cottage.

Finola's breathing ceased. Maeve and her father both noticed the quiet. Her father cried; Maeve sensed that her mother was gone. The tears began to stream down her face; her father held her tightly. All seemed lost.

# Chapter 5

There was a quiet in the cottage so unusual that Maeve quietly walked about searching for a living person. There was no trace of her mother nor her father; the new baby appeared to be missing as well.

The girl dressed to go to the garden, watering the plants with her tears slowly falling down her cheeks. She felt so alone. She did not know where her family could be. She heard a horse on the road and turned to see her father leading the horse to their cottage. Her father never brought horses to their home so she ran to him to question him.

"Da, where is Mama? Why did you bring the horse? Why are you so sad? Da?"

Her father stopped in his tracks; he wrapped his arms around the child. He stood there holding her for what seemed like many hours. Eventually, he cleared his throat, speaking to Maeve, "I am taking you to your grandmother, your mother's Mum. You will stay with her until I come back for you."

With his words beginning to make sense in Maeve's mind, she began to tremble and cry. He held her closer stroking her hair.

"Tiny One, do not cry. It is not forever. I will come back for you."

Maeve did not understand why her father decided it would be best to visit her grandmother. Maeve stood watching as her father gathered some things together for the journey. He closed the cottage door. She did not understand his grief and torment. Maeve ran to the garden to pick some plants. She wrapped them in her cloak as she spoke to them about having a new home soon.

"We will be leaving here now, Tiny One," he spoke softly to the child, "we will travel for a few days; you will soon meet your grandmother."

"You have told me about grandmother but I do not know her; I have only seen her in my dreams."

"You will soon enough. She is a good woman who will love you dearly; you will love her," his smile gave her reassurance.

He lifted Maeve onto his horse and soon they were on their way. The child could not help the tears streaming down her face as they set off down the road. Up until this time she had been very brave but now her little heart broke as she began to understand. Her small hands brushed back the tears as she silently decided not to cry. Her father noticed and placed a kiss on the top of her head. She did not cry any more. She promised herself she would not cry. She became strong in her resolve and accepted whatever life had to give her.

Father and daughter traveled together quietly. When they stopped for the night, Maeve looked at her father for a time. Finally she spoke but his attention was elsewhere. Maeve went to him then taking his hand, "Da, please talk to me."

Colm started as if he had been a million miles away, "Oh, Tiny One, I am so sorry. I have been lost in my thoughts."

"Yes, but I just need you to be here with me now. It is fine while we are riding but now … I want to know what happened to my mother."

Colm cleared his throat as his eyes filled with tears, "The birth was difficult this time. When your Mama had you, it was an easy birth. I do not know why she bled so much or why she could not deliver the child. She knew that she would not survive it while it was taking place. Your Mama told me to take you to her mother. She thought you could learn so much from her."

Maeve looked at him before asking, "Did she always know she would die with the baby?"

"No, I do not think so. If she had known, I think she would have told both of us."

Maeve hugged her father then. She laid against his chest falling asleep. He laid her down and then prepared a makeshift bed for each of them on the ground. After moving her to her bed, he made a fire for the night.

Colm sat awake for quite some time watching over his daughter and the fire. He spoke softly to Finola as if she were present. Colm had never believed in spirits as his wife did. He did not understand how she and his daughter managed to communicate with Fi's mum. But he spoke with Finola hoping she was listening, guiding him and watching over them.

Once he had fallen asleep, Fi came to him in his dream. She assured him that he was doing the right thing by Maeve, taking her to her grandmother. When he awoke, he stared at the fire thinking about Finola and her words to him about their daughter. Colm had never experienced anything like that before. His heart was not so heavy. He knew that he had been talking with his wife and that the whole dream was real. It was not like any dream he had before; he could still feel her presence. Colm quietly spoke to Finola again and laid down falling back to sleep.

Their journey took a few days. Colm placed his arms around Maeve as they rode the borrowed horse. After the evening conversations, Maeve's heart was lighter during the day so she sang along the way. Her singing managed to lift her father's spirits as well. Sometimes he would join her in song which made them both laugh.

Finally the journey was over. They arrived at Mum's cottage in the afternoon but she was not at home. They watered the horse, fed him oats and let him rest. Maeve and her father sat outside the cottage waiting for Mum to return.

They saw her walking down the road after a couple of hours. When Mum noticed them, she stopped where she was, just staring at them. She resumed her walking. As Mum stood before them, she began to cry. Her sense told her why they were there. Colm embraced her as did Maeve. This began a long time of grief as they all cried together. Mum spoke at last looking at her dear family, "Finola did not come to tell me. I did not know."

Colm spoke then, "Fi did not survive the birth. She bled for hours; it did not stop. She told me to bring Maeve here to you for instruction. The midwife, although she tried, could not save my Finola."

Mum nodded her head drawing her granddaughter to her. She held the child, crooning to her.

They moved into the cottage then. Mum prepared beds for them, began a meal and listened as Colm spoke of Finola's last days. He then told Mum of Maeve's knowledge of plants, gardening and her ability to care for people and horses. This perked Mum's spirits as she watched her granddaughter who had fallen asleep by the fire. Colm also told her about Finola's visit to him in his dreams.

"That will help you to live better without her then. I am glad she visited you. If she comes to you again, please ask her to visit me," her eyes twinkled at this.

Colm smiled, "Lillium, I have never experienced anything like that. It was so real. We spoke for quite a while."

"It was real, dear Colm, never doubt that for a moment."

They woke the child when supper was ready; then the three sat together to enjoy the meal.

Maeve spoke to her grandmother about the plants she had brought with her from the garden at home. Lillium encouraged her to plant them in the morning in her own garden. Colm enjoyed listening to the discussion between the child and her grandmother; this also made him feel better about leaving his daughter behind.

Colm went to his cot sooner than Lillium and Maeve. As the moon rose, Lillium took Maeve to the garden to greet the celestial body. They sang quietly so as not to disturb the sleeping father.

They tiptoed back into the cottage seeking their own cots. Maeve fell asleep quickly. Lillium laid awake thinking of her daughter.

# Chapter 6

Having arrived at Finola's mother's home Maeve's father was able to relax for a time. Mum listened to his sorrows trying her best to quiet his grief and give him strength to continue. It became evident that looking at Maeve only increased his pain. She looked so much like her mother that he began to spend his days away from her.

Mum rebuked him for this behavior, "You cannot blame the child for your loss for it is her loss as well. You must look at her for the person she is - Maeve, your daughter, not Finola, your wife. Think, son, what Finola would want you to do. She expected you to care for her child, not abandon her. You are being selfish."

"Your words are somewhat true. But Fi begged me to bring her to you. I cannot help what is in my heart. I love the child with all my soul but to look on her is so painful; it breaks my heart for the loss of both Fi and Maeve. I must go for a while, if only to find that what I am looking for is right here. Please care for my darling daughter; I will come back as soon as my heart is lighter."

Mum looked at the young man and quieted, "What about the boy?"

Maeve answered from behind them, "Mum, Mama took him with her."

And in a day's time Maeve's father left. He held his daughter to his breast promising his quick return. Maeve did not cry. She smiled at him, hugged him, told him she loved him.

Maeve investigated her grandmother's garden then. She was looking for a place to sit, sing and be by herself. Lillium noticed her speaking with the plants, stepping carefully so as not to disturb them and finally sitting among them. She went to the edge of the garden and quietly said, "Your Mama used to sit over there," as she pointed to a small corner of the garden. Maeve turned to look at the spot. She noticed that the plants were the same as in her favorite spot at home.

"Mama made me a corner just like that, Mum. She did it from memory then?"

"Aye, from memory and love."

"Mum, may that be my corner?"

"Of course, child.  It is now yours."

Maeve looked at the garden, moving quietly to the corner which now belonged to her. She sat among the plants, speaking to them and then singing.

Lillium moved away from the garden thinking to herself how lovely it was to have a child in her home again. She would care for her as she had her own daughter, Finola, but she would teach her more than she did Fi. Young Maeve would be very special in her up-bringing; she would be a great healer.

# Chapter 7

With her father's departure, Maeve turned to her grandmother for love and guidance. They developed a close relationship in a short time; at her grandmother's knee Maeve learned much. Old Lillium was considered a white witch or wise woman among the folk in the vicinity of her home. She knew the ways of herbs and potions but used them only in the care of the sick and dying. She was not an evil woman. She cared for and loved the people. They loved her.

Her grandmother began teaching Maeve about the herb garden almost immediately. Maeve planted her herbs in Mum's garden as her grandmother watched. She took the girl on her visits to the sick, showing her the way around her new home. In one of their visits to the village, Maeve discovered a hill which overlooked the whole meadow and village. Her grandmother took her to the bottom of the hill. Lillium pointed out the path that was worn.

"That path will take you to the top of the hill and you will be able to see all around. All roads in and out of Grashner can be seen if you stand on the North side of the hill. I cannot accompany you; I am much too old to walk that far. I will go home and when you are finished, come along," the old woman grinned as she walked away. It was time the little girl spread her wings a bit; she was always at her grandmother's side but she needed some freedom to do what children should do.

The child began the walk up the hill, all along the way discovering wonderful flowers and small animals which made her feel happy because they were so beautiful. She wished the animals were not frightened because she would have liked to pet them. On she went following the path all the way to the top. The view from the hill was more exciting to her than she thought it would be. The valley spread wide and the lakes seemed like tiny pools of water. The sunshine made the picture sparkle before her and she sat down on a large rock to enjoy the scene. Presently her imagination became active; she was the queen of the land, this was her kingdom. The rock became her throne as she surveyed all she owned.

Maeve watched the road into the village most of the time she sat on the rock. She began to wish fervently for her father's return. Again and again she voiced the words in her head, "Please come back. Please come back for me." Her eyes closed, she held her hands together tightly and whispered the words out loud. Only the trees, the animals and the rest of nature could hear her, or so she thought. She was unaware of the eyes watching her from the bushes.

The watcher found her to be quite fascinating and just stood watching for a long time. Maeve laid her head down closing her eyes. The warm sun made her feel secure, so after a time she fell asleep. The eyes continued to watch.

As the afternoon wore on, the little girl woke. At first she did not know where she was but then she remembered. She sat up quickly then searching the road before she jumped from the rock. Perhaps her father had already come back to her grandmother's; she must hurry. He would be waiting for her and wondering where she was. She ran as fast as she could down the hill. Her little heart pounding in her chest, she ran on and on until she arrived home. But her father's horse was not outside and her grandmother was working in the cottage. She stood in the doorway trying to catch her breath.

"Who is chasing you, Tiny One?" asked her grandmother as she looked up from the kettle on the hearth.

A smile broke on the child's face and she laughed, "No one. I just thought Papa might be home so I ran."

"Ahh," was all her grandmother said as she placed the girl's meal in front of her.

The child and her grandmother sat down to a pleasant supper; as they conversed about the wondrous things that Maeve had seen on the hill, the girl forgot her disappointment.

# Chapter 8

The child had slept well. She had a good appetite for the morning meal. Her grandmother was pleased that Maeve had decided to return to the hill again and explore her new home.

"I have packed you a small basket so you can stay there for the day if you wish," her grandmother smiled.

"You will not mind if I stay there all day?" questioned the child with her eyes growing wider.

Her grandmother laughed at the look on her face assuring her that it would be fine to stay the day.

"I will do my visiting this morning, return early in the afternoon if you want to come back before the day is out. Now go along with you."

She followed the girl out of the cottage. They waved goodbye to each other as they both went in their separate directions.

Maeve took her time climbing to the top of the hill. She picked some flowers, examined a butterfly, watched a squirrel. All this made her forget about watching the road. When she reached the top, she clambered onto the rock and watched the birds flying. She felt happy on top of the hill, happier than she had since her mother died. As she reclined on the rock, she became lost in her thoughts. She recalled her mother singing a song about a bird; she tried to remember it. Gradually the melody came into her head, the words tripped off her tongue. Her sweet little voice raised in song astonished the watcher. The girl had not talked loudly enough for her voice to be heard until now. The watcher began to listen intently to the words of the song and quietly sat down so as not to disturb the singer. When the song was finished, the girl laughed at a special memory of her mother, contentedly pulling her knees to her chest encircling them with her arms. A slight breeze ruffled through her curls tickling the back of her neck; the child giggled again.

The watcher had become fascinated with this little stranger so decided to continue to observe her. Suddenly the child stood up on the rock and seemed mesmerized by something she saw. She jumped from her perch to begin running to the bottom of the hill. It all happened so fast that the watcher had no time to move. By the time the watcher reached the bottom of the hill, the girl was nowhere in sight.

Maeve ran breathless toward the cottage she shared with her grandmother. She was certain that the rider on the road had been her father. She would try to reach home before he did. The cottage was quiet when she finally arrived. Her grandmother had not returned as yet; there were no horses outside. She sat on the bench outside the window, waiting. By mid-morning Maeve realized that she had made a mistake. The rider had not been her father and her grandmother would not be returning very soon. She decided that she was hungry, remembering the basket her grandmother had given her. Where was it? She realized that she had left it on the hill. She decided she would return to the hill to eat her lunch on her rock.

Full of energy she headed back to the hill to whatever adventures she might encounter. As she climbed up the path, she came upon a boy who seemed to be dueling with imaginary knights.

"Who are you?" Maeve inquired.

"I am a great knight. Beware, or the dragon I am fighting will eat you."

"I do not see a dragon and you are not a great knight."

"My men have started to laugh at your folly!" said the boy.

"Let your men laugh all they want to, you are the only one who can hear them."

"Stand aside, the dragon is about to set you on fire. I must slaughter it with my sword."

"But you do not even have a sword!" replied Maeve.

With that the boy put down his imaginary sword and turned to look at Maeve. She immediately changed her attitude and yelled, "Pick up your sword, Knight, or the dragon will kill us both."

The boy grabbed his sword, fighting a courageous battle, as Maeve screamed and ran from the dragon. When the battle was finished, the boy looked at the girl, both began to laugh.

Finally he said, "All right. I am not a knight yet, but someday I will be Lord of the Manor. You will be my servant because you are a peasant."

"What is a peasant?"

"You are one."

"Oh?" Maeve was not quite sure if this was true but she could tell from the way he talked about it that she did not like being one.

She decided to impress him with her imaginary game. "I am Queen of this Hill and everything you see before you is my kingdom."

"This is not your kingdom; it is mine."

A clash of wills and childish play, but Maeve smiled and wisely put forth, "Can we share it?"

The boy looked at her suspiciously. She was still smiling. The boy was quite taken with her smile and replied, "Well, I guess we could share." But so she would not misunderstand he added, "That is, we can share now while we play. But someday I will be Lord of the Manor."

Maeve did not know what all this meant but she said, "I think you will."

When they reached the top of the hill, Maeve found her basket and offered some of the contents to the boy. He was quite hungry and willing to share her food, as well as his kingdom. They sat on the great rock together as they ate.

He looked over at her asking, "Where do you live?"

"I live with my grandmother, Lillium."

His eyes seemed to get wider as he asked, "The witch?"

"She is not a witch. She is a wise woman; she takes care of the villagers."

At this the boy seemed disappointed, "You mean she does not cast spells on people and turn little boys into dogs."

Maeve began to laugh; she laughed so hard she held her stomach. The boy stared at her and said, "It is not polite to laugh at people."

"It isn't?" she gasped, "I'm sorry. But grandmother is a good woman and she would not harm little boys or anyone else."

Reassured by this information, the boy began to ask her more questions. Maeve told him of her mother's death, how her father brought her to live with her grandmother and then left.

"Where did he go?"

"I am not sure. My grandmother said he is looking for something."

"Oh, then he is on a quest."

"Quest? What's that?"

"All great knights go on quests."

"Really? Is my father a great knight?"

"He must be if he is on a quest."

The little girl smiled at the boy. This information made her very happy. The boy was very proud that he had been able to explain what her father was doing. They sat for a few moments without talking.

Finally the boy asked, "What are you called?"

"My name is Maeve."

"Maeve, my name is Brian."

"Hello, Brian." They smiled at each other.

"Let's play knights," said Brian.

Maeve nodded in complete agreement; although she had no idea how this was played, she was willing. Off they went to adventures all over the hill.

# Chapter 9

This was Maeve's first friend since she had left LaLa and she enjoyed being with him. It was the beginning of many happy times for her; she seemed to forget to watch the road for her father. Now that she knew he was on a quest she understood this might take him a long time. Brian had a wonderful imagination and their games were full of kings, queens, knights, dragons, elves and witches. They always won the battles and their games were great fun.

Maeve's grandmother noticed the change in her granddaughter and asked her about what she did on the hill every day. Maeve told her grandmother about the boy she had met.

"He plays on the hill every day, Mum. One day he will be Lord of the Manor. He told me so."

"Ah," said her grandmother, "you have met the young lord, Brian."

"Yes, Mum, have you met him?"

"I know his parents, Tiny One; they are the Lord and Lady of the Manor."

"Oh, Grandmother, am I a peasant?"
Lillium chuckled slightly answering, "Yes, you are, Maeve."

"But what does that mean?"

"It means that you are not high born as Brian is. Someday he will be a Lord. You will always be a peasant."

"Not high born, I am a peasant. Is that bad, Mum? Brian made it sound bad."

"No, child, it is not a bad thing to be a peasant. It is a more difficult way of life, that is all. Your life will be harder than Brian's."

"Oh, I see," but the child did not see. At the moment she could not imagine her life being any different from what it was. She and Brian playing on the hill, that was her life and she did not really believe that would ever change.

Days later, Lillium headed home after her errands and mulled over the news in her mind. People were talking about her granddaughter's friendship with the young lord. They said she looked like an urchin with her hair loose, blowing about. They said that when the Lady heard of this friendship, she would put a stop to it. This talk had been told to her by an old woman whose daughter was a maid in the Manor. The servants talked about the disgraceful appearance of the young lord's friend. Lillium mulled this over and over in her mind. She would not let anything hurt her granddaughter. What could she do to shield the child from further pain in her life? She came upon a plan and quickly turned back to Pavral's cottage. Pavral was sitting at her loom when Lillium stood at the door. Lillium did not take much time. She explained her plan to the woman and once she obtained the agreement she required, left quickly.

Maeve was at home when she reached the cottage. She sat the girl down and spoke with her a long time about what she and Brian did all day. Did they go to the manor house? Whom did they see all day? Maeve explained that they never left the hill but sometimes on the way home, a manservant would be waiting to escort the young lord home.

Lillium smiled at the child and said, "Well, Maeve, you are getting to be a grown-up girl and when girls grow up they begin to wear their hair in plaits. So I thought we should begin to braid your hair every morning before you leave for the hill."

At this proposal, Maeve was very excited because she loved the way braids looked. So her grandmother showed her how to plait her hair and she practiced. Soon the child was able to accomplish this on her own, feeling very clever. Next her grandmother mended the little garment the child wore daily and noticed that it was beginning to grow small. She showed the child how she could mend her own tears in the frock.

A couple of days later Lillium came back to the cottage with two more frocks for the child. She explained that one was for visiting and the other for playing. Maeve began every morning and ended every evening by washing her face and hands. If necessary her clothes were washed and hung to dry. Gradually she began to take pride in her appearance. She would always be a peasant but she was now a neat, clean peasant. Lillium ceased to hear the talk of the servants from the manor and believed the gossip had stopped. She thought no more about it.

# Chapter 10

Brian looked at Maeve the first morning she arrived with her hair in braids. He did not understand why she looked this way. He finally asked her after staring with his mouth open for a time,

"Why did you do that to your hair?"

"My grandmother said that I am a grown-up girl now so I should wear my hair neatly."

Brian looked at her for some time before continuing the conversation, "I like it but I like it without the braids best."

"Oh?" Maeve pondered this information. She had not thought Brian would care how she wore her hair.

They played through the morning with her hair in braids before Brian finally said, "Can you do that yourself?"

"Oh yes," she answered proudly, "Grandmother taught me to fix it myself."

His eyes got brighter and he said, "Then put your hair down while we play and put it back in braids before you go home."

Maeve did not understand why any of this should matter. She did not want to lie to her grandmother.

"No, I better leave the braids. Grandmother said I should."

Brian said nothing further until after lunch and then grinning, he asked, "Will you teach me to braid your hair?"

"I am not sure if I should. Grandmother never said anything about you braiding my hair."

"Well, I think it would be fun to know how to do that."

Looking at it as a game, Maeve agreed to teach Brian how to braid her hair. He learned quickly even though the mass of curls could be unruly. He enjoyed the fun of it. When he was finished, he yanked on the last braid to let her know he was done. Maeve giggled.

This became their secret. As soon as they met in the morning, Brian unbraided her hair, then off they went to play. Before it was time to leave, he would braid it back up for her and tug on the last braid. Then they would leave the hill. No one ever saw the girl without her braids, only Brian.

Maeve learned again that life does not remain the same. Months of the same playful routine with Brian came to an end abruptly one morning. Brian had not shown at the hill; it was nearly time for the midday meal. Maeve missed him and could not understand what had happened. She wondered if he were sick, thus needing her grandmother's care. She wondered if he would ever come to play again. Three days passed; she did not see him.

The morning of the fourth day as she was finishing her chores a horse trotted near the cottage. She and her grandmother went to the door as Brian's manservant met them there.

"Good day, Lillium," he greeted her grandmother.

"Good day to you, Festus," her grandmother replied.
Maeve's eyes grew wide. They knew each other by name. Grandmother never mentioned that she knew this man. How strange!

"My Lady of the Manor house asks that you and your granddaughter come to visit this day."

"We accept the kind offer, Festus, we will leave now."

"She will see you when you arrive," replied the manservant as he rode away.

"Grandmother, what does it mean? Is Brian ill? Does he need you to care for him?" The child was so distraught that her grandmother quickly bent to her and put her arms around her to reassure her.

"There, there, my child, I am sure it is nothing of that nature. If Brian were ill they would have their physician care for him, not me." The woman soothed the child's fears but her mind was moving fast over the strange invitation.

"Maeve, since we are going visiting, you must wear your special frock and braid your hair carefully." The child smiled at her grandmother, she lost all her fears and ran to dress for the visit. Shortly they were on their way to the manor, the little girl with her hand in her grandmother's for reassurance. Neither spoke along the way.

When they arrived, they were brought into the manor house and told to wait in the sitting room. Maeve looked around the room but could not envision Brian living here with the huge windows, large chairs, rugs. She was lost in the chair in which she was sitting. He must be too.

Brian's mother, Lady Mirima, entered the room. She was an attractive woman. Her hair was golden and her eyes were very blue. Maeve was surprised how much Brian looked like her. When Lord Lintel entered the room, Maeve marveled that Brian looked like him also. Although Lord Lintel had brown hair and brown eyes, there was something in his expression that reminded her of the young lord. Maeve was so enthralled by this that she did not hear very much of the beginning conversation. The mention of her name brought her attention around.

"We, therefore, wondered if you would consent to have her come here daily for class with Brian."

What were they talking about?

"I never thought you would ever consider such a request, My Lord," replied her grandmother, "this is a wonderful opportunity for Maeve."

"Brian has taken a fancy to the girl. He seems to miss her company."

"His tutor said that he cannot get the boy to concentrate at all. We felt that if your granddaughter were here with him, he might see that learning is not such a bad thing. Since you would be doing us a great service by letting her come, we would see that she also received more traditional training for a young lady."

Lillium's mind was racing. Exactly what this education would do for her granddaughter she was not certain. It would certainly be a wonderful occasion for the child; she would be with her friend whom she had missed so much for the last three days.

As the lord spoke, Lillium watched Lady Mirima's reaction to her granddaughter. She could tell that the Lady found the girl to be pretty, not such an unpleasant creature to have around. A smile grew on the Lady's face as she watched the little girl. Lillium knew that her granddaughter would be treated kindly.

"I am very honored for this opportunity, m'Lord, m'Lady." Lillium curtseyed, "If I can ever repay you, do not hesitate to call upon me."

They were shown to the door by another servant and walked slowly home. Maeve did not understand what had just transpired. Her grandmother was smiling a wonderful smile, so the child knew that something good had happened.

"Mum, please tell me what they said. Tell me what you said."'

"Darling girl, you will begin having lessons with the young lord, on the morrow. You will learn many wonderful things plus you will spend your time with your friend. This should make both of you very happy."

"I will be with Brian again?"

"Yes."

"Every day?"

"Yes, darling girl, you will be with Brian every day."

Oh this was wonderful news for the little girl. She began skipping down the path; she started to sing a lovely verse her mother had taught her. Her grandmother smiled as the child sang the melody about the prince who fell in love with the maid.

# Chapter 11

Brian met her at the gate on the first morning their lessons together started. They were very excited to see each other. Brian told her quickly what would be expected of them during their instructions. Maeve was absorbed by the classes of that first day. She had never heard such wonderful tales nor such funny sounding words. Together they caught on quickly competing with each other on assignments. The old tutor, Melchiarc, was pleased with their progress and gave them an occasional afternoon to themselves. When this happened they headed for their hill and the ritual began. Maeve's braids would vanish and play would commence. When it was time to go, the braids would reappear and home they went.

After a while it was arranged for them to ride horses. This became their favorite thing to do. Maeve had missed riding with LaLa but now riding with Brian was even more enjoyable. This came about when their tutor found out that Maeve knew how to ride. The first riding lesson was done secretly but once Maeve's skills were observed, Melchiarc arranged it with Lord Lintel that they ride every day.

Time spent together went quickly; as they grew they became more and more inseparable. With such a friendship came secrets and signals which only they knew. One word could cause them to break into gasps of laughter. The adults considered the relationship brother to sister. They always stressed this when speaking to the young people. Neither Brian nor Maeve considered it more than a brother-sister relationship; they thought the adults acted rather strangely.

Brian's lessons began to expand to his running the business of the manor. His lessons with Melchiarc continued long after Maeve went home. Some days the lessons began long before Maeve arrived. Brian and his father would ride throughout their holdings with instruction being delivered by his father. Brian quickly absorbed these lessons.

When it came time for Brian to learn the art of sword fighting, he insisted that Maeve also be included. At this Lord Lintel and Melchiarc gave resistance. A girl should not know the use of the sword they stated. Girls should be protected from aggressors not be the aggressors themselves. Brian would not hear of her being excluded. The men reluctantly agreed but Brian and Maeve were pressed with secrecy. No one else should know of this.

Again competition ensued. The two of them loved wielding swords, practicing with each other, the sword fighting tutor and sometimes even a young knight or two. Laughing was heard while lessons were in session. Many people at the manor were curious but the doors of the hall were locked all the way around so no one knew for sure what was happening.

When Brian reached the age of eighteen, his father explained that it was now time for him to begin actively taking part in running the business of the manor as a lord. Brian knew what this meant, as had been expecting it for about a year. He ran to find Maeve as soon as he was able to get away. He found her gathering flowers on the hillside and sat beside her. The smile that came to her face at the sight of him vanished quickly when he began to talk.

"I know we have spoken of this time often but we never considered what it really meant," he said as he played with one of her braids, "I am to leave at first light; I do not know when I shall return."

Maeve sighed and began to think about the consequences of his leaving her. "I met you while I waited for my father's return; you helped me through that time. My father never returned to me; Brian, but you must promise me that you will return."

"Oh, Maeve, I will return. I will return to leave again. We both know this. Parting from you will never be easy but we will learn to accept the separations."

Brian suggested a game of lords and ladies. This suggestion brought Maeve to life and they fell to playing. Maeve shouted that she was the lord and Brian had to be the lady captured by an evil knight. This brought laughter to both of them as Brian did his best to cry like a woman and Lord Maeve deepened her voice instructing Lady Brian to be still, he would save her. This game went on for some time until they rode off into the sunset with Brian sitting behind Maeve on their imaginary horse.

They tumbled onto the ground with laughter, trying to talk at the same time. Brian began to notice that late afternoon was upon them. He stood as he pulled Maeve to her feet, he said it was time for them to go home.

Maeve smiled and spoke, "Brian, take care. Remember me often; I will be here when you return."

With a swift tug on her braid, Brian smiled, "I will not be gone long. I promise." He left her standing then on the hillside.

Both of them felt suddenly lonely as they walked to their respective homes. They did not turn to look at each other.

The first separation was not long. Both had missed each other desperately and could not wait to be reunited. On the afternoon of Brian's return, he met long enough with his father to impart his news, give his father the missives he carried and then fled to the hillside. Lady Mirima came to the Lord's chamber asking for her son. When told by the manservant that he had departed the manor, Lady Mirima looked to her husband whose eyes met hers.

Each separation was longer than the previous one which caused Brian and Maeve to become used to the time apart from the other. Although Maeve enjoyed reading the books Brian loaned her, she began to realize that she needed some other type of interest to occupy her time so she began to spend more time in the garden learning of herbs from Lillium's wise counsel. However, Lillium would not tell Maeve the reason why some of the herbs were growing in the corner of the garden; she warned the girl not to touch the leaves of these plants.

On each return Brian would tell Maeve of his adventures when they did see each other. He wanted her to visualize everything he had seen and done. He told her stories of the hunts he had been on and the people he had met. Maeve enjoyed these tales; they would sit for hours while he described everything to the smallest detail. Brian always brought Maeve different books as she returned to him the ones he had left before. On one of his visits, he whispered to her, "I have brought you something. You should not tell anyone that you have it, not even Mum."

Maeve looked at him questioningly, "What is it, Brian?"

He then produced a sword, "This should be yours now that I have a new one. You can defend yourself if necessary. I did not insist that you learn to fight for folly. I think you will need this in the future."

Maeve looked at the sword. She took it from him. She was familiar with it, for this was the one with which Brian learned to fight. On occasion he had let her use it. The one she learned with was a sword that the tutor had but no one had ever given her a sworn of her own. Her smile was bright; then she frowned asking, " For what will I need it, Brian?"

"I do not know for sure but I dreamed that one day you will need to defend yourself. Please take it so I know you are safe."

They were in agreement. Maeve had a place to hide it so she was quite comfortable with her new gift. She went home before her grandmother returned, placing it in a hiding place where no one would ever look.

Maeve went to the village daily with her grandmother to care for the sick, to distribute food to the poor, and to visit the elderly. She began to bloom in the love of her neighbors. The time between visits with Brian no longer seemed to bother her. She was busy and occupied and time drifted away. She remembered stories to share with Brian upon his return.

Once Mum was asleep at night, Maeve would produce the sword. She would practice wielding it in the moonlight. She also began the seasonal devotions that Mum had taught her. She practiced these at night as well; Mum felt too old to stay out to participate so she asked Maeve to pray for her as well. If Mum heard her at night, she would not think anything untoward was happening.

Brian enjoyed his travels. He wanted to make friends with the noblemen he met. He tucked away his adventures in his mind to bring back to Maeve when he went home. Brian did not suspect that his father had other plans for him beside doing the work of the manor. He did not know that his mother was wracked with worry about his future choice of wife. But his parents did not know that Brian and Maeve had never spoken of marriage. They did not know that the two friends considered themselves children who were only continuing what they had been doing all the years they spent together. They were just growing up together in their expanding world.

# Chapter 12

Brian's latest journey took him several weeks. He was sent to Lord Aengus where he dealt with his father's business but enjoyed staying at the manor, hunting and taking part in the general life of the household. Many evenings were spent in the great hall with feasting, music, dancing and much enjoyment. It was during this time that Brian was introduced to Lady Catherine, the daughter of the manor. She was beautiful with blond curls often tied up on top of her head. Her dancing skills were excellent; Brian enjoyed watching her while she danced with several young men from the surrounding homes. Sometimes they were seated next to each other during dinner. Brian liked their discussions of hunting, music and the business of politics in the area. Catherine was very intelligent as Brian found her to be educated as he was. Although she was trained in the normal skills of a woman, her education exceeded that; he found that her father had trained her to be the Lady of the manor once he had passed. This was highly unusual but it seemed to be the case.

Brian found himself thinking of Catherine more and more. They were becoming friends and they were often paired for dinner and dancing. Lady Catherine's father kept an eye on them; he took to writing a missive to Brian's father which the young man would deliver when he went home. Soon he was summoned home and gave his farewells to the Lord but he could not find Catherine to bid her goodbye.

His horse had been saddled; he was outside in the courtyard when he heard a sound from above. Standing close to the clip of the curtain Catherine glimpsed the man. Never before had she experienced this feeling. Her pulse quickened; her palms became moist. The palpitations of her heart urged her to breathe deeply. Her eyes closed with the weight of this moment but she forgot well where she stood. Her head leaned against the shutter pushing it aside, causing the sound to travel to the yard. His gaze turned toward the window catching Catherine in the instant. Her cheeks burned with the shame of her longing, her lips parted for the cool air to enter her and become part of her being. Still she did not open her eyes, being oblivious to his gaze. She thought her culpability was her own but he had witnessed it. Her weakened circumstance caused her to forget that he was within sight.

He mounted his horse, turning it toward the road. His inclination was to return to the manor, to postpone the errand but it was most urgent that he complete the journey. He remembered her hand in his on their introduction, the current that bolted through his body. He thought of her widening eyes when they realized that each had felt the sensation. He thought of the look of her in the window, her moist lips as she opened them to the breeze that swirled about the courtyard. Her hair, braided and tied in a ribbon, held his thoughts for miles. He longed to release the locks from bondage and feel the soft tresses through his fingers. As the horse steadily parted him from her, his longing shattered when he glimpsed a peasant girl in a shepherd's embrace. He was on his errand; he would never see the maiden again. His life would not incline him to be her husband, lover and friend. No, he would never see the Lady Catherine again; that was just as it should be.

# Chapter 13

Whenever Brian came home it was always the same. He would stop to see his father at the manor house, then run to find Maeve.

Mirima looked straight into her husband's eyes and declared,

"You must do something. Stop looking askance at the matter. He loves her I tell you. It is his intention to wed her."

Lintel said nothing, causing Mirima to become exasperated. She walked to the other side of the room pacing, then quietly spoke, "She is nothing but the witch's granddaughter, not to be considered of importance. Her feelings, her life mean nothing. But your son is my son; my son will not wed a peasant girl. He will marry nobility, as is his birthright and destiny."

"But, Mirima, I think we must not force this matter or it will certainly cause hardship with our son's love. I have had some counsel on the subject with old Melchiarc and I know the way to proceed is through subterfuge." A smile coming to her face, Mirima questioned his plan.

"It seems he fancies the Lady Catherine of Parrisal, daughter of Lord Aengus. They were seen with their heads together over a meal and her father has sent word that he would welcome their coupling. Brian just returned from there bringing the missive that Aengus sent me. I am planning to send him back as soon as I take care of other issues."

"What a lovely plan, dear, dear Lintel, however I believe this is incomplete."

"Exactly! For it will be his decision to marry the girl to stifle his lust for her and never think of what he has done until he again arrives home to us. Of course, our messenger will seek the aid of a maid in Lord Aengus's kitchen to ensure that young Brian has the love potion from our very own Witch grandmother."

With this twist in the plan, Mirima's face grew pale and she whispered, "Old woman will know what we are about. She may change the potion to kill the Lady Catherine. She will see it in our plans."

Lintel stroked his chin shaking his head slightly. "No, my darling wife, we purchased the potion from the chambermaid. She has used a small portion for herself but gave up the rest willingly. The deed is done, my dear, do not fret. That part of the plan is complete."

Mirima raised her eyebrow and looked piercingly at her husband, "What more?" she said quietly.

"Now is time to send for Lillium once more."

# Chapter 14

Padraig was sent to deliver the message to Lillium that she was to come to see Lord Lintel at once. Lillium feared she understood the reason for the summons to the manor. When she arrived she was led directly into the sitting room where the Lord and Lady were waiting for her.

The Lord did not bother with niceties in his greeting to Lillium; he began as soon as she entered the room.

"When we asked you to allow Maeve to be educated with Brian you said you were indebted to us. We now need to ask you for the favor that you pledged."

Lillium's eyes filled with tears as she looked at the floor. She nodded her head knowing full well what the favor would be.

"We fear they are falling in love. Although we feel great affection for Maeve, as you well know, we have another match in mind for Brian. It is a match that will increase his wealth." The Lord watched Lillium as he said these words.

Lillium raised her head turning her eyes to the Lord, "What would you have me do, Sir?"

"You must do whatever necessary to ensure that they do not fall in love and expect to marry. We do not want either of them hurt. We must protect them."

Lillium sighed and then she spoke, "I will take care of this dilemma. You need not worry further. Brian will marry whom you wish. All will be well. Everyone will be happy." At their dismissal she left them then; making her way home she stopped in the woods to gather what she would need to fulfill her vow. On her arrival home, she visited the corner of the garden that she had forbidden Maeve to touch. She proceeded to her cottage and began mixing the herbs with her tears.

Brian found Maeve at her cottage; together they went to their hill. They both had so much to tell each other that their conversation was complete with interruptions and much laughter. They were comfort-

able with each other as they told of people they had met and anec-
dotes that were both humorous and sad. Maeve told of the passing of
an old man from the village whom they both had known. Brian told
of a hunt he had been on and how he had fallen from his horse. Both
laughed at this since Brian was an excellent horseman.

While they sat and talked, they both heard a rustling in the brush
and turned to see Padraig trying not to interrupt although that was
why he was there. They looked at him questioningly which brought
him back to his message.

"Lord Brian, your father requests to have you home. He has a
message for you to deliver."

Brian shook his head in knowing agreement. He sent Padraig on
his way. Turning to Maeve, his smile was sad. She questioned his
look with her eyes as they both arose from the ground.

"I must go, Maeve. But I will return as soon as I am able."

"I understand, Brian. It is the duty of the Lord of the manor,"
with this she smiled her brilliant smile and backed away from him a
step.

Brian turned from her and began toward the path to the manor.
His head was bent as he watched where he walked, but he suddenly
stopped and turned back to Maeve. As she stood watching, she questioned his strange behavior. Brian was always quick to report to his
father, always leaving her quickly with a brief smile and a promise to
return soon. Brian stood looking at her; then he moved toward her.
As he looked down at her, Maeve realized how tall he had grown. He
reached for her then, pulling her to him in an embrace. His lips found
hers as he held her tight. Her arms moved around him; they stood for
several moments in their first kiss. This sensation was new. Neither
of them had felt this way before and each held the other more closely.
When they pulled away, their faces were joyful yet sad. They knew
then. Both of them had felt the passion of their first kiss. As they
looked at each other, they knew they loved each other deeply. It was
more than friendship. They kissed again. This time the kiss was deep.
Brian's tongue explored Maeve's mouth as her tongue touched his.
Her knees began to weaken so he held her tighter to keep her from

falling. Their kisses became more passionate. Finally Brian pulled away from her, holding her at arms' length. His eyes explored her face as she looked at him differently than she had ever looked at him in the past. No words were spoken for quite some time.

"I will return soon, I promise," he said as he tugged her braid. Maeve watched him leave; then turned toward home with tears streaming down her cheeks.

# Chapter 15

When evening came Lillium laid awake on her cot waiting for Maeve to come in from her worship. Time seemed to pass slowly as Lillium realized that Maeve stayed outside for a great length of time. Mum became concerned; since the moon was full it was perfect for her ritual but it would take her time to climb the hill. Maeve had to fall asleep before Lillium could leave the house.

Finally the girl came in as Lillium pretended to sleep. This was not an ordinary night for Maeve. Her thoughts were full of Brian, their kiss and her feelings. The moon seemed larger than usual. Her prayers to the goddess were full of love for Brian, the people of the village. She laid on her cot but she could not sleep. She was restless so she moved about constantly. She rose and went back outside, lying down near the garden.

Lillium could wait no longer; she went in search of Maeve.

"Child, all this moving about woke me. Please come in. Go to sleep."

"Mum, I'm sorry I disturbed you, but you do not usually wake in the middle of the night."

"It must be the full moon, Maeve. I feel restless. Now come in so I do not have to worry about you."

Maeve followed Mum to the cottage; she sat on her cot for a time before lying down. Lillium laid on her cot waiting for Maeve to sleep. After a time Lillium heard the steady breathing of the sleeping Maeve. She rose, leaving the cottage as quietly as possible.

The old woman had difficulty climbing the hill but her way was illuminated by the full moon and the stars. She had not ventured out like this in many years; if her errand had not been such a difficult one, she would have enjoyed the beauty of the night much more. She uncovered her basket, removed the contents and placed them on the top of the rock. She slowly spread the herbs proceeding to stir them into the small vessel that she had carried with her.

Then she made a small fire to help her with the enchantment. Once the fire burned she softly said the words but she had trouble pronouncing them. She repeated them several times. When she was sure of the spell she began to chant.

She had worked on the spell for a very long time, and had thought out what she must do. She could not betray the Lord and his Lady but neither could she betray the love of her granddaughter and Brian.

Swirling mist encircled both Brian and Maeve in their separate places of sleep. Their dreams became dim so no longer would they remember what they had dreamt. Tears flowed from their eyes as they slept.

They could hear the enchantment while they slept but did not understand it. The mist continued to encircle them, the tears ceased to fall; as Maeve quietly shuddered, Brian shook violently.

Sparks of ice embraced their hearts. Then the incantation changed. The ice encased all but one corner of their hearts. Lillium fell into a deep sleep at the bottom of the rock.

The moonlight came to settle on the sleeping girl as if it had been seeking her. The wind was picking up its strength, turning the night cold at its touch. The leaves fell from the trees, rustling along the ground. The sounds of the night streamed into the girl's mind becoming part of her dreams. She began to shake with the cold; unconsciously she drew the cover over her shoulders.

The sleeper began to toss and turn as her dream became more vivid. Finally the wind settled and stopped. A mist encircled her. The moonlight moved from her window; the dreamer quieted down.

The girl awoke with a start. Sitting up in her bed with a pain so strong, she found it hard to breathe. Gasping for air and swallowing it as fast as she could, her sobbing cries came from deep within her soul. She wrapped her arms around herself, rocking back and forth. The covers enfolded her as if someone was holding her, soothing her. Still she cried, her pain increasing. This pain was recognizable. It was the pain of a broken heart, the loss of something dear. Her dream was in fragments; her memory was lost to her. All that was left was her sense of loss. But what had she lost? The girl had no idea but still she sobbed. After a time, the girl laid down with the cover wrapped around her. From exhaustion sleep found her; it was a deep sleep which did not allow her to hear her grandmother enter their home some time later.

Padraig heard a strange chanting as he walked the path back to the manor. He had gone to visit his family earlier and was on his way back. He stopped and listened intently to hear the direction of the sound. He finally determined it was near the large rock at the top of the hill. He waited quietly considering whether he should keep walking or go to investigate. He had been taught as a small boy never to go near the rock, for the magic there could transport you to places unknown. Eventually Padraig moved up the hill and found the Wise Woman lying unconscious at the bottom of the rock. He checked to see if she was alive and gently woke her. After a few confused moments, Lillium remembered where she was and who Padraig was, allowing him to help her, they moved slowly down the hill to her home.

They arrived before Maeve awoke and the old woman stumbled in and found her cot. She managed to lie down and breathe deeply attempting to relax and forget the night's events. Her mind retraced her steps as she thought about what she had done. The wise woman shook her head in disbelief. Why had she done this unkind and cruel thing? She held all responsibility. Staring into the dark, Lillium determined to reverse this curse. She thought she saw her unsmiling daughter, Finola, standing by her bed. The old woman felt her life ebbing away as she fell into a deep sleep.

# Chapter 16

Brian had no reason to suspect any deception as he began his return to Lord Aengus. This time a messenger was sent with him so he had a travel companion, which he appreciated. After the men stopped conversing, Brian became lost in thought. He remembered the dream of the night before. He remembered his physical reaction to it but not the dream itself. His bedchamber had filled with mist and the moon shone brightly in his window. He had felt a loss so strong that he did not understand it. He did not know what had been lost to him. Still there was pain in his heart.

As they traveled, Brian thought of his last meeting with Maeve and the story she told of old Malcolm's death. He remembered Padraig's interruption and that Brian had left Maeve on the hill; but he did not remember their embrace nor did he remember their kisses.

Brian arrived to a lighted hall and merriment. The music reached him in the courtyard as he beckoned the stable boy to see to their horses. Brian's travel companion immediately moved into the manor to find the kitchen maid. He imparted to her the small vial and gave her the instructions. The girl panicked, asking what the vial contained. The messenger smiled as he spoke quietly, "Lord Brian has a painful headache but refuses any type of remedy. His mother asks that you place this in his goblet so his pain will decrease. I assure you, it is to help His Lordship, not harm him." The girl was still unsure but took the vial; she said she would do as she was bid.

As Brian entered the dining hall, the Lord personally strode up to meet him as he entreated him to sit at the family's table. Brian thanked him for his hospitality as he handed him the missive from his father. The Lord received the message and removed himself from the hall. He walked to his library to open the missive. There it was; all he'd hoped for…Lord and Lady Lintel approved of a wedding between Brian and Catherine. He smiled broadly and returned to the festivities.

Brian waited for the Lord's return and the Lord motioned him to a place at the table. Catherine was seated to his left; she blushed crimson as he sat beside her. Brian nodded to the Lady bidding her a good evening. Her answer was a smile. The Lord continued his conversation about the hunt they had enjoyed that day and how Brian would have enjoyed himself. Another hunt was planned and the Lord invited young Brian to join them on the morrow. Brian agreed as he continued to listen to the pleasant music and conversation of the Lord. The only communication between the Lady Catherine and him were stolen glances between them.

The servant maiden came by the table filling the goblets with wine. As she poured the liquid into Brian's cup, she released the potion from its vial. With his first sip from the goblet, Catherine turned to Brian shyly asking him if his journey had been pleasant. He turned to her then and their eyes met. All he could see before him was the lovely Catherine; all he desired was her.

After a while Brian entreated the lady to dance so they joined the merry guests on the dance floor. As he whirled her around the floor to the lustrous sound of the pipes, Brian began to feel the potion moving through his veins. He wondered if he were becoming ill. He escorted Lady Catherine back to their seats and drank from his water goblet. Brian asked the leave of the Lord and Lady Catherine as he made an excuse of exhaustion from his journey. He excused himself, going to his bedchamber.

As Brian moved about his room, he began to feel lightheaded and nauseous. He laid down on the cot closing his eyes. His body was reacting in a way he had never felt before. He fell into a troubled sleep. Dark shapes echoed through his subconscious. The shapes came in waves with different messages screaming into his mind. Some told him he could not love. These waves repeated over and over, making Brian sick to his stomach. The next wave of shapes were different. They were gentler and whispered, he must love. He became consumed by fever.

When he did not wake in time for the hunt, the Lord sent his physician to him. The man found him unconscious. After a brief examination, the physician became alarmed. He went to Lord Aengus imploring him to send for the Lord and Lady Lintel, Brian's parents. He told Lord Aengus that he feared Brian would not survive.

A servant was sent to watch over Brian. The man had some training with the care for the sick. He stayed with his patient the entire day. That night the physician came back to examine Brian again. There seemed to be no change in his condition. Another servant was sent to stay with Brian through the night.

# Chapter 17

Maeve had a feeling of foreboding all day long. Her dream the night before was something she could not grasp. She knew she had awoken with a feeling of loss but she could not remember her dream. During the day she began to worry about someone. She did not know who was in danger. Lillium slept later than usual that morning. Maeve went to check on her and found her awake.

"Mum, you are feeling well?"

"No, not this morning, I have no strength. I will sleep more."

Maeve got her something to eat and drink but Mum was not interested. She did drink the water after a time. She found she was extremely thirsty.

Maeve began to think her grandmother was in danger when Padraig came to check on the old woman. He explained to Maeve that he had found her at the bottom of the rock early in the morning and helped her home. Maeve was concerned as to why she had been on top of the hill. Padraig pulled a small packet of herbs and a vial from his shirt. He handed it to Maeve saying it belonged to Lillium. Maeve took it but did not examine it in front of Padraig. She thanked him for his concern, leaving him at the gate.

Maeve went inside to examine the contents of the vial. She did not recognize the scent nor was the taste anything she had experienced. Her grandmother had fallen asleep again, so Maeve went about her chores. She had not known such sadness since her mother died and her father left.

Maeve began her maturity of loving her neighbors and taking care of their old and their young. She found the work so rewarding that she no longer thought about having a family of her own but remaining the good woman of the village to care for her people until it was time to leave the world. Selflessness grew in Maeve at a startling pace and the people noticed the change in her ability to console them and care for them.

Daily she would rise early, help Lillium to rise and settle her into her garden from where she watched the villagers pass. She would pack her basket and move to the village to care for the latest people with ailments. Some days she would arrive home with tear stains on her face, and a conversation with her grandmother would console her and give her new instruction into an illness she had come across.

It had been a week since Brian had come home but she hardly noticed the days that passed. Padraig came often, ostensibly to visit Lillium, but his eyes would travel to where Maeve worked in the garden or moved about the cottage. Young Padraig sat and visited with Lillium, asking about her health since the night he helped her home. Lillium enjoyed his visits, assuring him that she was well but tired and weak. She would fall asleep gently in the afternoon and feel the breeze across her face but her dreams were of dread and guilt. Sometimes she would start and wake and look quickly around to be sure all was well. On the days when Maeve was about she would let the tears fall as she watched her granddaughter. She would pray for death to come for her and clear her conscience of her sad memories. Maeve had questioned her grandmother about the contents of the vial but Lillium feigned ignorance. Maeve told her Padraig had helped her home one night; Lillium said she did not remember such an occasion. The girl felt ashamed that she did not believe her grandmother. She knew something was wrong.

When news of Brian's illness reached his parents, Lintel rushed to Melchiarc to ask his advice. The old man looked at his former pupil asking for his interpretation of the events. Lintel sat and explained that they had entreated the witch to break the connection between Brian and Maeve without hurting them. Then he explained that he sent Brian back to Lord Aengus with a missive that they welcomed their son's union with the Lord's daughter.

Melchiarc looked intently at Lintel and knew instinctively that he was not telling all. The old man waited, watching the man. Lord Lintel did not add anything further.

Finally Melchiarc spoke, "Lord, I have known you since you were a small child. I know when you are not telling all the truth. Continue your story or I might be of no help to you or your son." Lintel looked at his hands which he was wringing in his lap.

After a long moment he stated, "We sent a messenger with Brian. This man was to deliver a potion to a kitchen maid to place in Brian's drink."

"What kind of potion?"

"It was a love potion."

"A love potion? Where did you find a love potion?"

"It was from the old woman but she had given it to Lotty. She gave it to us after she used a portion of it."

Melchiarc rose from his chair with a look of terror and anger, "Sir, you may have killed your son."

Lintel started, "How, Master?" reverting back to the pupil of the man who had educated him.

Melchiarc took a breath and said, "The first spell needed time to be absorbed by the children. It was very powerful magic with an evil bent to it; the old woman risked her life to conjure the spell."

He began to pace the room. He shuffled his feet as he held on to furniture to help him encircle the room. He started to speak but it developed into a coughing fit. He had to stop walking and Lintel ushered him back to a seat. Lintel poured him a goblet of water to ease the cough.

Finally Melchiarc looked at his pupil and began, "The love potion was delivered too soon to its mark. The spell and potion are at war within Brian. He cannot fight them because they were the potions of the same sorceress. The old woman is ill I've been told, but this combination of her work will make her weaker. She may realize what is happening to her but not understand why. Did she know you had her love potion?"

Lintel shook his head, "No, we never informed her of our plans. She only knew that we required Brian and Maeve to cease their relationship."

With great sadness and deference to his student, Melchiarc asked his pupil to leave him so he could think on this dilemma.

Lintel left and went to his chamber refusing to see his wife. Mirima was confused by Lintel's behavior and stood outside his door, whispering frantically that they must get to Brian. Lintel did not answer her.

# Chapter 18

Padraig spoke to Maeve quietly in the garden as Lillium slept. He spoke of his concern for Lillium who looked weaker and paler than yesterday and her body shook as she slept. Maeve looked at Padraig with alarm then ran to her grandmother. Maeve could see what the young man was speaking of and she knelt at her grandmother's side to speak to her. She whispered quietly asking if all was well or if something else was wrong.

Lillium opened her eyes to her granddaughter's inquiry and spoke, "Something has changed. I recognize the dream and I am sorry, Maeve. I have hurt you. Be well, my daughter, find love, protect yourself from my foolishness."

She stopped speaking, falling into unconsciousness. Maeve began to cry and Padriag said he would seek a physician. Lillium opened her eyes to Padriag and spoke so softly the boy had to put his ear to her mouth. She whispered, "Brian is saved. Melchiarc."

Lillium looked over Maeve's shoulder and smiled, "Dear Finola, I am ready." She died then as her face held a peaceful repose. Maeve cried inconsolably. Padraig stayed and held her. Finally he left and went to the manor house for help.

Padraig ran immediately to Melchiarc, unsure of the message. Melchiarc called him to enter as Padraig called for him outside the door. Padraig thought the teacher looked ill and asked if he was all right. Melchiarc shook his head and asked Padraig what he wanted.

Padraig explained where he had been and why.

"The old woman has died. She has been ill and today she seemed weaker and more aggrieved than yesterday. We were at her side; she whispered to me that Brian was saved. She said your name; she died then. Maeve is deep in grief. I thought I should bring you this message."

Melchiarc thanked him and sent him on his way with instructions to return to Maeve and assist her in preparation for burying her grandmother.

Melchiarc sent for Lintel and imparted the news to him. "Brian is better. The old woman gave her life for him."

Lintel was confused by this message and looked at his teacher. "How can this be? How do you know?"

Melchiarc told him of Padraig's visitations daily to the old woman, saying she gave him the message before she died.

A silence fell between the men until finally Lintel said, "How did she know about Brian? How could she save him?"

Melchiarc cleared his throat. "When she became ill at first it was from the spell she cast on the boy and girl. When she did not revive, she felt something was amiss. She began to recognize that her further meddling, or should I say, your further meddling was due to some potion of hers that came back on her. This combination of magic caused her worsening health because her magic was sent to the same person, Brian. Without his knowledge she has cast spells on him. This concluded her ability to use magic ever again, thus shortening her life. She chose to finish herself and save Brian."

Lintel felt his strength leave him. He sat for a moment before he spoke, "I have killed the wise woman, Lillium. I have taken all the love from Maeve's life. My wife encouraged me by saying her life did not matter; Brian mattered more. I am so ashamed. I can do nothing to change this. I am so ashamed."

Melchiarc replied, "You must stay away from spells and potions. It could kill you too. It is nothing you understand and you have meddled in your son's life. It is time for you to do some good for people to whom you are responsible and try to right the wrongs you have created."

Lintel nodded and left the room with Melchiarc's words running through his mind.

# Chapter 19

After Lillium's death, Brian's illness did not last, a few days at most, but he awoke with a start to find the Lord's physician at his side. The man seemed very surprised that Brian awoke with such a clear head. He remembered where he was but was surprised to find that he had been ill for so long. Food was sent for and Brian rose to walk about the room to regain his strength. Brian told the physician that he had troubling dreams and wondered what they meant. When asked if he could tell his dreams, Brian realized that he could not recall them at all. Upon finishing his meal, he felt much better with renewed physical strength and a desire to return home. The physician told him he should not travel again for a few more days and Brian agreed. He felt as if he needed to go home for something but did not know what it might be.

Lord Aengus was happy to hear of his recovery, sending word that if he felt well enough, to join his family for dinner. Again the hall was lit with torches, music and dancing taking place in the hall. Brian laughed as he entered the hall taking his seat next to Catherine. She smiled at him asking how he was feeling. He smiled in reply and they spoke from time to time throughout the dinner.

The next morning found Brian and Catherine walking in the garden, enjoying the warmth of the sun. She sent her servant for refreshments to help Brian in his recovery. He laughed at her attentiveness, assuring her that he was fine. This ritual continued for the rest of Brian's stay. He spent the evening in the great hall with the Lord and his family. Brian felt that his earlier desire to go home was diminishing; he was quite content to stay where he was.

One evening after he felt completely himself he asked Lady Catherine to dance. They joined the other dancers whirling about the floor laughing and smiling. He stopped midst a twirl whispering to Catherine, "My lady, please tell me if you would accept my proposal of marriage, if your father agrees to the match?"

Catherine stopped mid-step. She looked at Brian, "I know my father will agree to our marriage for he has already asked me the same question you have put to me. When I first saw you, I knew that I could love you until I die. When you left the palace on your errand, I thought that I would die never to see you again. I will not be foolish enough to play the coquette. I love you, Brian. I want to be your wife."

The smile that came across Brian's face made Catherine's mind ease in her uncertainty. He lifted her to the sound of the music as they fell into step with the others. Both faces shone radiant; the Lord chuckled as he watched.

The two managed to leave the hall together without anyone noticing. They stepped outside into the cool night air. Brian pulled Catherine to him. His whisper was close to her ear, "May I kiss you, Lady Catherine?"

She turned her face to his as their lips met. When they broke apart, Brian managed to say, "We should ask for a quick wedding, my love."

Catherine giggled, falling back into his embrace.

Although the couple was anxious for the wedding to be planned quickly, it did not happen that way. They were betrothed for a year and a half before the serious planning began. Lord Aengus determined that the couple should get to know each other before they married. Brian went about his business for his father but did not travel home as often as he once did. When he went home he spent time with his father discussing the management of the manor but his departure was always the next day. He also began to learn the business of Lord Aengus, as he and his wife would inherit this manor as well.

# Chapter 20

The death of Lillium brought villagers to Maeve to console her. They brought some food for her; anything they could spare. Some of the women helped Maeve prepare Lillium for burial. Maeve cried for the loving attention to her and her grandmother. She became more resolved in her choice to care for these people always.

When all was quiet, Maeve would attend to her garden, her worship and her sword. She determined that she needed a way to carry it without drawing attention to it that it was a sword. She designed a case for it that was easy to carry.

As she worked on her design she wondered why she felt it was necessary to have it with her. No answer would come but she proceeded with the idea that she needed this.

Lord Lintel traveled to Maeve's one morning. He came with Padraig to convey his condolences at the passing of Maeve's grandmother. They brought supplies for her with the instruction that if she did not need it all, she should share it with the people. Maeve accepted this with gratitude but wondered at this turn of events. Nothing like this had ever been done. She looked at the Lord noticing his pallor. He needed Padraig's help to walk. He did not ride his horse but came in a small carriage. After Padraig conveyed the Lord to the carriage, he turned to Maeve. She looked at him but he shook his head. She could see that Padraig was unsure of what was happening also.

Padraig came with supplies every couple of weeks as ordered by the Lord. Maeve distributed the goods to the villagers ensuring their health for quite some time. Time passed but Maeve very seldom thought of Brian. She found it difficult to live alone; never having a conversation, never sharing a meal. Maeve started conversing with the people in the village more than usual. She would talk about the weather, their plants, the health of all. This helped her because when she arrived home she enjoyed the quiet. She would laugh at herself the way she adapted to her new life. When nightfall came, Maeve would venture outside for her seasonal rituals and practicing with her sword.

Padraig did not visit as much as he had when Lillium was ill. He finally decided that it did not matter if he had a specific reason, just checking on Maeve should be enough. He began to visit whenever he could leave the manor. He stopped to see his family; then he would travel to Maeve's cottage. Their conversations were friendly; she could see he was concerned for her. He asked about people in the village, offering on occasion to help her visit with them. Their friendship did grow after a time, but he noticed that she no longer asked about Brian as she had in the past. Padraig found this odd since they had been such friends growing up.

One afternoon as Padraig accompanied Maeve home from the village he asked her, "Do you mind living alone, Maeve?"

Maeve's expression became contemplative before she spoke, "I miss Mum that's for certain. I talk more to people so I do not mind the quiet when I am in the cottage alone. I am not afraid to be by myself. When I work inside, I try to sing so the quiet does not distract me. I must get used to living alone though, since I have decided this is the way it will be."

At this, Padraig stopped walking. "Do you not intend to marry, Maeve? You have decided to always live alone?"

"No, I do not intend to marry. I am happy with my work; it takes time. Some days I do not arrive home until late if someone is ill. I cannot imagine doing this with a husband and possibly a family."

"Do you not want children, Maeve? I believe you would be a wonderful mother."

Maeve laughed, "Children take so much time."

Padraig was sad at her answers but did not show it. Once they arrived at her cottage, he said his farewell. He walked back to the manor house thinking of what she had told him. How could this have happened, he wondered? She was beautiful, loving and talented. What in her life made her come to this decision?

Lady Mirima was thrilled with the betrothal of her son to Lady Catherine but the decision for them to wait before they wed made her nervous. What if Brian came back and visited Maeve? What if he regretted his promise to Catherine? What if the spell was broken? Lillium could not make it right since she was dead. Mirima put these questions to Lintel who would promise her that all was well.

When the announcement of the wedding day arrived, Lintel and Mirima were pleased. They planned their journey to be there for the nuptials.

Before leaving, Lintel visited with Melchiarc. The old man took a look at his pupil, surmising the reason for his visit, but he remained silent until the lord spoke.

"Melchiarc, I am traveling to the wedding of my son but I am afraid I will not survive the journey."

"Looking at you, I can see that you are not well. Does your wife not notice your ill health?"

"I have been spending much time in my own chamber. She is chatting with her ladies about the wedding, her gown and the journey. She has not really seen me."

"Hmmm, I see. I will make some potions for you to take but I think they will only alleviate your pain from time to time. I have nothing to cure you."

Lintel nodded, "I have had much time to think about the way of things. I have many regrets for my son, for myself and …."

The old man turned to see his pupil looking at him intently. "What more, Lintel, what more?"

"All those years ago, I should have heeded your advice."

"What advice was that?"

"My marriage to Mirima was a mistake. I tried to please her along the way. I tried to make her happy. She was never happy. She only cared for herself and her son. She wanted him to stay away from the witch's granddaughter. She could not conceive of his life with a 'peasant'. I had to do what she wanted for she made me miserable."

"There is nothing to be done now. Brian will marry Catherine. He will be happy with her. You will leave this world thus you too will be happier."

Lintel looked at Melchiarc. The old man had a wry smile on his face as they both laughed quietly. "I guess you are right. Thank you for the pain remedy. Do you have anything to hurry death along?"

The tutor laughed again, "No, my son, you must wait your time."

Lintel left. He went to his chamber to rest. He took the pain potion which enabled him to sleep. His death would look like natural causes but his meddling in witchcraft had killed him. It had killed Lillium; it almost killed his son. He was ashamed. He prayed for forgiveness. He slept.

Lintel and Mirima traveled to Lord Aengus' home for the wedding of his daughter, Catherine and their son, Brian. Mirima chattered the entire trip; her attention was on the scenery, her thoughts about the wedding and the dress she had chosen. Lintel often fell asleep in the corner of the carriage but this did not dissuade her from talking.

Once they arrived they were brought to their room by several servants. Mirima marveled at the beautiful chamber. She mentioned to Lintel that her chamber at home was nowhere near as beautiful. Her thoughts began to swirl at her ideas to redecorate her room at home.

Lintel chose to rest until dinner but Mirima went in search of her son. She found both Brian and Catherine in the garden discussing the evening festivities. They were very gracious to her as she and Catherine met for the first time. Mirima was enchanted by Catherine. She was a beautiful young woman; her personality was warm as she brought Mirima around the manor. Mirima knew Catherine loved Brian, making her happy at her son's choice. As the two women went arm in arm, Brian went to his father.

Brian knocked on the door several times before he heard his father's voice. He entered then and stopped immediately inside the room. He was astonished at the difference in his father's physical being. Lintel lay on the bed. He managed to prop himself up with some pillows but his illness was obvious. Brian seemed to be in shock as he stood staring at his father.

"My son, come in, sit for a bit."

Brian walked to the bed, sitting on the edge but never taking his eyes from his father's face.

"Father, you are ill. You should not have traveled this far. We could have postponed the wedding until you were up to traveling. Why did you not let us know?"

His father spoke quietly. His voice was not the voice Brian remembered from his boyhood. "I am fine. I did not want you to have to wait for me to recuperate."

"What ails you then? Is it a brief illness or something more serious?"

"No, it will be gone soon. Hopefully, it will be gone by the wedding since we have a week or two until the ceremony."

Brian nodded, then he said, "Mother did not tell me you were ill. It might not have been such a shock had she warned me."

Lintel smiled, "Your mother is excited about your nuptials. That is all that seems to matter to her."

Brian frowned at this; his memory went back many years as he recalled his mother's frivolous behavior regarding entertainment, gowns, the proper people to invite.

He stood then and spoke, "I'll let you rest now, Father. Will you feel well enough to come to dinner or should we have dinner brought to you?"

His father's laugh brought Brian a bit of peace, "Brian, have you ever known me to miss a meal?"

They both chuckled at this and the son left his father to sleep.

Later Brian spoke briefly to Aengus and Catherine about his father's health. It was decided then that Lady Mirima would be moved to another room so Lord Lintel could rest.

Upon being told she would have different accommodations, Mirima did not seem the least bit surprised. She was moved to a chamber in the vicinity of her husband and found it to be charming and more suited to her tastes. However they noticed that she only used it for sleeping and preparation for the next event. She spent her time wandering the manor, spending time with Brian and Catherine and a few of the other ladies who were there for the wedding.

Mirima was disappointed to learn that Catherine's mother had passed away two years prior. The Lady of the manor had become very ill but there was nothing to be done for her. She suffered a few months before her life was spent. Catherine did not like to discuss it. It was one of the ladies who told Mirima the story. Lady Siobhan was the widow of a lord in the neighboring village. She was a beautiful older woman with gray hair and dark brown eyes. Although her manners were impeccable, she tended to be gossipy, which drew Mirima to her.

Siobhan whispered to Mirima, "Aengus did all that he could. He sent for the best physicians but no one could save her. He stayed at his wife's bedside day and night. Finally the poor woman passed. Aengus grieved as did Catherine. They were just glad that her suffering was over. They buried her in the family plot on the grounds. Both of them visit her grave daily. For all the smiles on their faces, they still grieve for her, missing her terribly. Especially now that Catherine is to be married; she wants her mother with her."

"What was her name?"

"She was Aisling. Beautiful woman, she was. Catherine looks like her."

"I see. Sometimes Catherine seems to be far away. I wonder if she is thinking about her mother."

Siobhan smiled, "I am sure that she is, but Brian has brought her back from the depths of her grief. He is a remarkable young man, a very caring sort."

Mirima smiled as she thought that Brian was very much like his father. She had best warn him not to be too sympathetic or people would walk all over him. At this point, Mirima excused herself from Lady Siobhan's company. She walked to her room. Mirima began to think about some of the activities that were taking place at home. She must stop the deliveries to the witch before it was too late. She wondered if her husband had made other arrangements of which she was unaware. She must guard her fortune before Lintel gave it away.

The festivities prior to the wedding consisted of hunts, jousting, large feasts, musical entertainment and dancing. Lintel could not partake in the hunts but he enjoyed the dinners and the music. He and Aengus sat near each other, conversing and watching the young people dance. Lintel watched Brian and Catherine together. They seemed very much in love. Their conversations were long and serious but every now and again one of them would whisper to the other causing them both to laugh. However, Lintel watched his son very closely. There was a young servant girl with dark curly hair. Brian looked at her from time to time causing a sad look to cross his face. It was a fleeting look. Something else would grab his attention and his smile was radiant. That smile was usually reserved for Catherine. Lintel knew his son was happy but he was unsure from where the melancholy looks came.

Lintel turned his gaze to the dark haired servant girl. She caught him looking at her and smiled. She moved toward him asking if he needed anything. Her curls, her eyes and humble manner reminded him immediately of Maeve. He shook his head and told the girl he was not in need of anything. As she walked away, he looked toward Brian. Brian's head was bent to Catherine. He had nothing but love in his eyes for her. Lintel breathed a sigh of relief but knew deep down that his son felt a loss.

Lintel did begin to feel better since he rested most of the time. Aengus sent his physician to him but the man could not find anything wrong with him. Lintel told him some of his symptoms so the physician could treat them. Knowing what was wrong with his health, Lintel knew there was no cure. He was eager to travel home soon and hoped that he would live long enough to die in his own bed.

On the day of the wedding, the sun shone brightly, the sky was blue and the clouds looked soft. Lintel and Mirima went to the hall together. Mirima was dressed in a beautiful gown of blue. She wore the jewelry she received from Lintel when they married. Lintel felt fairly strong that day and acted as a Lord as he was instructed by his wife before they entered the hall.

They sat in the front row of the seating as Brian escorted his Lady down the aisle. Both their garments were gold brocade. Catherine's hair was woven with flowers. Her gown had a train edged in pearls. Brian could not take his eyes from her. Her brief look to her father sent a tear down her cheek which Brian immediately kissed away. Mirima had brought a garnet necklace with her and gave it to Brian for Catherine. It fell at Catherine's collarbone; the stone caught the candlelight making it shine. There was, however, another stone that caught the candlelight. This belonged to Catherine's mother. It was a diamond hair pin which she wore at the front of her hair.

Once the service was finished the guests went to the great hall for dancing and food. Brian took his beautiful wife by the hand, leading her to the garden. This was their private space and he wanted time alone with her before they went to the hall.

Brian held Catherine to him, kissing her head and then her lips.

"You are the most beautiful woman I have ever seen, love. Thank you for consenting to be my wife. I love you, Catherine."

"Brian, I love you. Thank you for asking me to be your wife. If you had not asked, I am not sure what I would have done."

At this they both laughed. They hugged and kissed more.

Brian finally said, "We had better go. We will have time enough alone later."


The party lasted all night but Lintel excused himself early so that he might rest. They had planned to break fast early and then start for home. He was hoping there would not be any occasion to change their plans.

Lintel fell into a deep sleep but his dreams were filled with disturbing images. He awoke before dawn and he could not go back to sleep. He dressed; leaving his room, he went in search of the kitchen. The cook was about and she graciously fed him. She made him a strong cup of tea, telling him he needed more sleep. He could not have agreed more, so once he was full, he went back to his chamber. Fever consumed him. They were unable to leave as planned.

The physician was deeply concerned as to the illness of Lintel. He treated him as best he could then called for Brian. The physician was more comfortable speaking with Brian than he was with Mirima. She did not seem concerned with her husband's condition; from that time on, the physician called Brian. Brian was very nervous about his father's health. He sat with him when he could to spell the manservant and the physician.

Catherine was worried but she noticed her mother-in-law's ability to occupy herself with trivial things so as not to have to sit with Lintel. Catherine thought this odd. She mentioned to Brian that Mirima had gone for a walk in the gardens.

"Did you want to speak to her about your father?"

"No, love, she will come in when she wants and I will inform her then."

Once Lintel's fever broke, it was decided that he would rest for a few more days and then would start for home. Brian went to visit for a longer period of time so he might speak with his father.

"Son, it is nearing the time for you and Catherine to move to Grashner. I am certain that I will not live much longer so I will need you at home."

"Father, the physician can find nothing wrong with you. Now that the fever has broken and you rest for a few days, he says that you will be fine."

"No, Brian, that is not the case. I am dying; old Melchiarc has confirmed it."

Brian stared at his father shaking his head in disbelief.

"Then you must stay so that I may see to your care."

Lintel smiled at his loving son. He took his hand speaking quietly, "Brian, I must beg your forgiveness for the harm I have done to you. Please remember me in a good light, not when I was unkind."

Brian held tightly to his father's hand, "Father, I can remember nothing that you have done that was unkind. You have always been a good man and loving father. I will remember you as such."

At this Lintel smiled, resting his head against the pillow he fell asleep.

Brian went to make arrangements for his parents' journey to their home. He informed his mother that they would leave in a day's time. Seeking Catherine, they immediately went to visit Aengus.

"Sir, my father informs me that he is indeed dying and I must assume my duties as Lord in Grashner. Catherine and I must travel with my parents in preparation for my father's death."

Aengus' face became sad but he understood the duties of a lord. He smiled, nodding his head then asked quietly, "May I come to visit you?"

Catherine hugged her father, extending an invitation to visit whenever he chose. Handshakes and hugs went around and the young couple made their way to their chamber to pack.

Within the following day, they all left for Grashner. The journey seemed much longer than Brian remembered, but that was due to stopping in order to make Lintel comfortable. Catherine sat with Mirima in a coach so Brian could assist his father.

Mirima chatted about the weather, how much she enjoyed the wedding and the new friends she had made. Catherine asked her, "How is Lord Lintel feeling this morning?"

"He is very fit, dear. He wanted to get out of the coach to ride a horse but they do not have any horses available for him," she smiled, then she giggled as she thought about it.

Catherine was taken aback by this information because she had seen Lintel that morning. He had needed help climbing into the carriage. They had covered him with a quilt because he complained of the cold. At this point Catherine decided she would cease the small talk. She closed her eyes pretending to nap.

# Chapter 21

The family arrived home late in the evening several days later. The servants greeted them in the courtyard. Brian stood in the courtyard giving orders to the servants, "This is my wife, Lady Catherine, please escort her to my chambers. See to her trunks, please. My mother is exhausted. Please see to her as well. We will all need refreshment. If some food can be brought to us, we would appreciate it. My father is not well and will need to be carried to his chambers. I will be up to check on him momentarily. Please ask Melchiarc to meet me there. One final request of all of you. Please do not mention to anyone in the village or the other houses that we have all returned. We need some time to settle ourselves and do not want visitors at this time. Thank you all."

The servants began to bustle about, giving quick looks to each other. It did not take long for the lords and ladies to be escorted to their chambers. The trunks were delivered and food was served.

Brian and Catherine ate quietly together. Brian excused himself shortly thereafter in search of his father and Melchiarc. The old tutor stood near Lintel as the lord sat in a chair in the room. They were quietly discussing his condition when Brian entered.

Brian gave a questioning look in Melchiarc's direction, "How is he, do you think?"

"He has been through much with the journey there and home. I do not believe he has much time left, Lord Brian."

"What is killing him? Can we not find a cure?"

"I have tried. There does not seem to be anything to stop the disease."

Lintel gave his son a tired smile. "Brian, it is as I said. Nothing to be done. I will sleep now if I may."

Both Brian and Melchiarc helped Lintel into his bedclothes and moved him to the bed. The sick man breathed a sigh as he relaxed in his bed. He closed his eyes and immediately slept. Brian and Melchiarc moved to the hall.

"Can you give me no further information than he is dying? What is killing him?"

Melchiarc reached back into his memory. He had come upon something to tell Brian when the boy asked, "Lord Brian, I am afraid it is a disease that ails the stomach. Your father's father died a similar death. There is nothing to be done."

Brian thanked the old man then. He left to find his mother to see how she was feeling.

Brian knocked on his mother's chamber door. She did not answer. After knocking several times, he decided to go to his wife. His mood was dark and sad. Upon entering his chamber, Catherine went to him and hugged him closely.

"Darling, you are so sad, so tired. Come to bed and rest. I understand what you are going through. Come to bed."

Brian and Catherine laid down; hugging each other closely, they fell asleep.

Eventually a certain schedule took over the house. Mirima broke her fast early with her husband in his chamber. A long talk with Brian and Melchiarc had impressed upon her the seriousness of Lintel's condition. She, too, was told it was a stomach ailment. Lintel did not want her to know the real reason for his death and since Brian was in on the discussion with her, Melchiarc could not tell her the truth.

Brian and Catherine took over the management of the manor. Brian asked the servants to keep an eye on things on the grounds for he did not want the neighbors to know of their presence. Brian spent time with his father in the morning and afternoon. Lintel was able to converse about the manor, the management and the servants without too much strain. However, whenever they parted company so Lintel could rest, he would say, "I love you, my son. I am sorry for my past behavior."

Brian would just say, "I love you, father." He would leave mulling over the daily apology.

Since Brian had taken over the running of the manor, Padraig approached him one day. "Sir, I must put a question to you. Your father had instructed me weeks ago now to deliver supplies to the village. I bring a cart every couple of weeks to our wise woman. She distributes the food to the villagers. Sometimes she instructs me to wait three weeks because she has so much. But yesterday, Lady Mirima told me to stop all the deliveries. Although I was to bring supplies today, I have not done so due to her instructions."

Lord Brian listened intently. The expression on his face showed that he was not aware of any of this. "Thank you, Padraig. I will investigate and have an answer for you shortly."

Brian walked away briskly; he headed to his father. When Lintel heard of his wife's orders to Padraig, his eyes filled with tears. "Brian, the supplies must be delivered always….This will save my soul and your mother's."

At that he fell into unconsciousness. Brian attempted to bring him back but he would not awaken. He sent the servant for Melchiarc.

Brian stood my his father's bed when the tutor walked into the room. Brian was looking at his father. Melchiarc approached feeling Lintel's neck, he spoke softly, "He is gone."

Melchiarc began to cry as Brian wrapped an arm around him. They waited until they had composed themselves before bringing the news to Lady Mirima and Lady Catherine.

The funeral was planned but still Brian wanted no one to know. Finally, invitations were sent to a few neighbors, to Lord Aengus and some distant cousins. Everything was conducted discreetly. The morning after the burial, the bell was rung to announce the death of the Lord. By this time all the invited guests had departed. Still Brian, Catherine and Miriam would receive no further visitors. Their grief was all consuming. They lived as recluses for another month.

# Chapter 22

Padraig visited Maeve during the month of mourning for the manor house. He was still a regular visitor but this day, he would pursue his suit. Maeve was working in her garden as he approached. He entered the garden as he said, "Good morning, Miss Maeve."

Maeve looked at him, smiling, "Good morning to you, kind Sir."

Padraig extended his hand to Maeve to help her up, "Please come to sit with me for a short visit."

"I would love a short visit with you," she laughed. She enjoyed his joking demeanor; it made her laugh.

They sat together in the garden as Padraig produced some biscuits. He explained that the kitchen at the manor was overwhelmed with too much food. The funeral guests had left, leaving the servants eating the leftovers.

They remarked on the beautiful day as they ate the delicious biscuits. Padraig then looked at Maeve, as he took her hand, "Maeve, can you not see us doing this as a daily event, eating together as a couple? I would be so happy if you would consider marrying me? I have nothing but love for you. Please promise you will think about it."

Maeve was astonished by this proposal but kept the smile on her face. "Dear Padraig, I have depended on you so much before and since Mum died. You have taken me by surprise today though. I was not expecting a proposal of marriage from you."

She stopped speaking, looked at him to see the surprise on his face. He smiled as he rose to leave. Padraig still held Maeve's hand so he bent to kiss it. "Please, darling Maeve, give my request some thought."

He left her sitting in the garden then. She watched him leave, heading back to the manor. She did not understand why his proposal surprised her. She began to shake and the tears came in fits of sobbing. She ran to the cottage so no one would see her. Maeve laid on her cot continuing to shake and sob. Why was she crying over this?

What made her feel this way? She could not think. Eventually she closed her eyes as she fell asleep.

Padraig had sensed more than she let on to him. He realized that she was upset by his proposal. He could tell by the look that briefly passed over her face. She did manage to keep her smile but she had lost it briefly. Padraig began to think back to the night he had found Lillium on the hill. He had told Maeve about it but not everything. He had given Maeve the remnants of what he found on the ground by Lillium. Maeve did not know what they were. It was something her grandmother had never told her. Lillium did not explain to Maeve why she was on the hill that night. As Padraig helped Lillium to return to her cottage, she muttered many things that Padraig did not understand. However, at one point she turned to him telling him to never discuss this with Maeve. He did not tell Maeve that; he only gave her the items retrieved. Something that night changed Maeve forever. Padraig began to feel it was a lost cause. Maeve would never marry him. She had been educated, tutored as a young Lady. She held herself as a royal; she could ride a horse; she could converse with educated people. Although she lived her life as a peasant, a wise woman, she was meant to be more. Why would the lovely Maeve marry Padraig, a manservant?

Maeve woke from her sleep as her memories came crashing in on her. She looked out at the sun determining that she still had time to visit the village. Gathering her basket she left the cottage to head for her first visit. She managed her smiling countenance the entire time. On her way home she was able to review the marriage proposal from Padraig. If she had been looking for a husband, Padraig would be a kind, caring choice. How did she feel about him? She depended upon him; they had a strong friendship; she enjoyed his visits. She liked him but she did not love him. Should love not be strong? She thought about her parents. Colm would come home, hug her but then he moved to her mother. He would hold her, whisper to her, kiss her. He was heartbroken when she died. Love should be like that.

As she entered the cottage, she had a thought. I might never be able to love. It is not in my desire. I am not looking at young men for one to fall in love with me or me with him. It is not in my ken. I used to think of marriage when I was younger. Mum and I would talk about my marrying, having children. When did that stop? Mum got sick; she crawled up the hill; Padraig helped her down. What happened on the hill?

She went to the herbs she had in her basket removing the items Padraig had brought her. She smelled them but still she could not identify them. She went out to the garden to the forbidden corner. She smelled each plant, eventually finding the herbs her grandmother used that night. She brought a leaf of each into the cottage. Maybe one day she would know what happened on the hill that night. Until then she would try to identify these plants, their usage.

# Part II
## Chapter 23

More than two years after the death of her grandmother, it was still vivid in her mind. Maeve carried out her duties within the village. She thought often of her family; all of them were gone now and she felt love had broken her heart too often. Throughout her days of mending the wounded, attending the sick and holding the dying, she decided never to marry. She felt life was better spent with the villagers, easing their pain as much as she could. Word of Maeve's beauty and caring spirit spread throughout the land. People told her of her beauty and sweetness but she was of a serious nature. She did not find the compliments frivolous; she believed the people were feeling grateful and this was how they showed it. She thanked people quietly but thought nothing more of it as she went about her business.

A young man who had been wounded in battle told his fellow soldiers of her kindness to him. He admitted that he had fallen in love with her and had asked her to marry him. She had declined. This tale was told to a Prince by the name of Ardan one day by the young soldier himself. He thought it was nothing more than a fanciful tale but he listened attentively wishing the soldier his best when he took his leave. He knew he would never himself see this young beauty, promptly forgetting the story.

The prince journeyed closer and closer to Grashner; as he came to the village, more and more of these tales he heard. Curiosity finally got the better of him so he went to the village one afternoon to investigate. He inquired about the maiden. The young livery attendant nodded his head, smiling at the prince.

"Yes, sir, you're not the only one who has asked about her. She is beautiful but refuses to marry anyone."

"Tell me about her."

"She is the granddaughter of our wise woman who recently died. She has become our new wise woman, taking on her grandmother's duties of caring for the poor and sick. She is kind and caring. She passes through here most days."

"Are her parents living?"

"No, she has lived with her grandmother as long as any one can remember. She was educated with the young lord because they were friends. He no longer lives here."

"Why will she not marry?"

"Folks say she is dedicated to the people."

A slight pause occurred in the conversation as the lad looked out of the stable door. He nodded his head in the direction of the road and said, "There is the maid now, Sir."

Ardan turned and looked outside the door. A small gathering of people obstructed the view of the girl so he moved aside in an attempt to catch a glimpse of her. Just as he did a young man bowed moving away from the crowd and Ardan had a clear view of her. Her head was bowed as she listened to an old woman speak. Her black hair was braided into two braids and her eyelashes covered her eyes so he could not see their color. The conversation from a taller man made her turn her head to look at him. He could see now. Her eyes were deep blue and her cheeks held a rose blush to them. Her skin was cream colored and appeared silky. Her rose lips slowly spread into a smile of beautiful white teeth. Her voice was soft and soothing as she spoke to the man who had questioned her. Calmly she removed the contents from her basket, handing items to people who had asked for her help. As she gave her farewells and walked away, Ardan noticed her  comportment. She walked like a Lady of high bearing. Ah, he thought, she had been educated with the young lord.

As he watched her walk away he questioned the young lad, "What is she called?"

"She is called Maeve, Sir."

Once she was out of his sight he realized his heart was pounding. He took a deep breath, thanked the lad and left. He was uncertain of his reaction to this girl. He had seen many beautiful women in his life. He had seen many pretty maids. He had not been prepared for his response to this one. He mulled this over in his mind.

He mounted his horse and turned in the direction of his home. They would be surprised to see him so soon. He was not expected back for a fortnight but he must return now. There was something he needed to discuss with his mother.

# Chapter 24

Prince Ardan was a good man who was much loved by his father's subjects. He was courageous and bold but he possessed a gentle temperament. His twin brother, Prince Dubhlainn, had a dark nature. His selfishness was well-known thus the peasants and nobility alike feared him.

The brothers had been raised by parents who loved them equally and showed no partiality. Their mother, Betha, was a great sorceress who used her powers only for good. Both sons had been taught the art of sorcery by their mother. Ardan was content in his knowledge of white magic. Dubhlainn was a constant source of disappointment to his mother as he searched her books in secret for knowledge of the evil side of his powers.

Dubhlainn had been jealous of his brother since their youth. He believed Ardan to be his mother's favorite. He thought she gave his brother secret lessons in magic that she would not give him. Both men were handsome, but Dubhlainn thought his brother more handsome than he was. Dubhlainn was the younger of the two; his brother would one day be king. All of these thoughts festered in Dubhlainn's mind. He could never be happy as long as Ardan lived.

Upon his return to the castle, Ardan sought his mother's counsel. He told the Queen of the girl's beauty, how she spent her days caring for people and of her vow never to marry. Then he told her how he loved Maeve; although he could not explain his feelings, he would give up all he had to possess her.

Queen Betha listened intently as Ardan revealed his intentions. At first she was surprised by his determination but then she relaxed realizing that she could not stop him once his heart was set. He had met many other women since his young wife had died but he never seemed to be interested or inclined in any way to marry again. There was something in the back of her mind she was trying to remember. This was different; there was more to it than just a young man wanting to marry a maiden.

She and her son talked at great length. He begged her for a solution to the problem. He wanted to marry the girl but he knew she would not accept him.

Betha sent him away so that she could think. There must be a way. In the meantime, she would search her mind to determine what was troubling her.

It was nearing time for bed and she removed her gown. She was still a beautiful woman even though her sons were in their late twenties.

She removed the fasteners from her long auburn hair and began to brush it. As she sat brushing, her mind began to wander over the many years that had passed.

She had been a young maiden on her way to marry a prince. She smiled at the memory of her entourage as they traveled over the countryside. She had only spoken to her betrothed a handful of times but she thought he was handsome. Her father and his father had arranged the marriage to unite two powerful families.

Betha had been afraid to marry. She had not been cautious in her young life finding herself in trouble with an old gypsy woman. Her parents thought the incident silly, telling her not to concern herself with it. She forgot about it for a while but when her marriage was being arranged she began to worry. Nightmares began to plague her.

Her son's plea for her help came back to her. She went to her bed to think how she could aid him. Something came to her that troubled her. As she thought again how she could help him, she fell asleep.

Queen Betha woke in the middle of the night. Her dream had been so real that it jarred her out of sleep. As she began to recall the dream, it came to her. The memory that had been eluding her when she spoke with Ardan. It was the prophecy:

*The prince shall love a lowly virgin enchantress who shall bring forth a son. He will be strong and virtuous; they shall call him peacemaker.*

Betha began to shake. Could this be? It must be. This was why it was so important to Arden. He did not know he was fulfilling a prophecy but it was his destiny, therefore, it seemed right to him. He must proceed with this.

She would have to be sure that this was the correct wording of the prophecy. How? She would speak with the elders. They would know.

Betha conferred with the elders late the following day and spent the evening determining how to go about it. They had confirmed the prophecy; she came away from that meeting attempting to seize on a plan.

She sent for her son holding her breath. She would have to make this sound correct. Her plan was the only one possible, so he must understand.

He entered the chamber and bowed to her.

"Come in, my son." She smiled at him, "Please sit. Please hear me out before you say a word."

He nodded his head and took a seat. She began to pace as she chose her words. He listened to her until she was finished; then the storm erupted. The arguing went on for an hour until he finally agreed to her plan. He listened to her instructions. His heart was aching when he left his mother. This poor innocent girl--would she ever forgive him for what he was about to do?

Betha followed him to the door; she saw Dubhlainn disappear around the corner at the end of the hallway. This troubled her; his jealousy was dangerous. She must add more to the spell to protect Ardan.

Dubhlainn had noticed his brother visiting his mother late at night. He saw that there was something amiss. He suspected they were up to something magical but there was not a rumor about in the castle. No one seemed aware of anything. Try as he would, the conversation between mother and son was soundless. Dubhlainn knew that they were surrounded by enchantment as they conversed. He would find out though; he also had studied at his mother's knee.

# Chapter 25

The day was overcast and cool but Padraig went to the village to see his family early and then went in search of Maeve. He found her at her cottage and told her the news that Brian and his bride were now receiving guests at the manor. Maeve's face broke into a beautiful smile as she learned the news. She thanked Padraig for letting her know, promising to come to the manor to visit as soon as she was finished with her visits.

Later that day a servant announced Maeve's arrival and she was shown into the library. She had been in this room many times before but this was the first time in many years. She and Brian had hidden behind the heavy chairs and drapes. Maeve could almost hear their childish laughter as she stood near the window. She looked out into the yard recalling many happy times in this place. She only hoped that her heart would not break with the sight of Brian. It had been so long since she had last seen him.

The door opened as Maeve turned toward the noise. A man stood in the doorway looking at her. She turned toward him. A few short moments of silence elapsed before either spoke. Brian came toward her with his hands outstretched.

"Maeve? You have grown up. You are not the little girl that I left behind more than two years ago."

A smile broke across her face and Brian stopped. Her face was radiant and the sunlight gleaming from the window captured the blue highlights of her hair making it shimmer. Brian's heart caught in his throat. He had never expected such beauty. Maeve had always been pretty in his eyes but this was different. There was an internal beauty that shone from her, making her outward beauty more intense. He could not speak.

Maeve's eyes rested on the man in front of her. He was taller than when he had left and the muscles of his arms shown through the sleeve of his shirt. His blond hair seemed darker than she remembered it, but the blue of his eyes was still bright and clear.

Maeve came forward then, taking his hands in both of hers. Her voice was gentle and caressing as she welcomed him home, "Dear, dear Brian. I am so happy to see you at last. When you left me you were but a boy, and have come back a man."

Brian's eyes clouded with tears as he placed a gentle kiss on the top of her head. "Maeve, I must tell you about my journey and ...."

"I know, Brian. You married the Lady Catherine two years ago. Your father recently fell ill and died. You are here to help your mother through his passing. I was so sorry to hear of his death. He was always so kind to me."

"Thank you, Maeve; but you too have known loss and grief. I too am sorry to hear of the death of your grandmother. But how do you know so much about what has happened?"

"Thank you, Brian; but you must have forgotten. You have changed, Brian. I have changed. We have both grown up. But some things do not change; gossip in this neighborhood is something that will never change."

Her smile was teasing and Brian nodded his head in remembrance. Then as though time had not passed, they begin to laugh as they used to as children. Their private jokes kept them giggling for quite awhile.

Finally, Maeve wiped the tears from her eyes and questioned him about the details of his life and he answered. Then it was his turn to find out what she had been doing.

"But why haven't you married?"

"I do not intend to marry, Brian. I believe that my life's work is for the welfare of the people here. They need me. I cannot devote myself to them and to a husband and family. There would not be enough time."

"But your grandmother had a husband and a family and she still took care of people."

"Oh, in the beginning, yes-but now I need every moment to devote to it."

"I know you well enough not to argue once you have set your mind on something, but I believe you are selling yourself into a life that will not allow you total happiness."

"Now, now-I am quite content with my life. It is not that I have not had offers of marriage, but I do not feel that I should marry. I really do not feel that I need to marry."

A soft knock came to the door as Lady Catherine entered. She was dressed in an afternoon gown the color of the sky and it brought out the loveliness of her fair complexion. Her blond hair was braided with a ribbon entwined through it and coiled on top of her head. A questioning glance to her husband and a smile brought her to his side.

"Darling, this is Maeve. Maeve, this is my wife, Catherine."

Maeve stood and looked at Catherine as Catherine looked at her. A few seconds of silence fell between the women and confused Brian as he looked from one to the other.

Maeve quietly questioned, "LaLa?"

Catherine questioned, "Tiny One?"

Both nodded and ran into each other's arms, laughing as they did so. Brian stood back and watched as they twirled, hugging each other and began to sing a childish song. Finally, they broke apart and turned to him.

Maeve giggled, "Brian, this is LaLa, my childhood friend from before I came to live with my grandmother. Do you remember? I told you about her. She was my first friend and you were my second."

Brian nodded and looked at the joy in each of their faces. Catherine begged Maeve to dine with them; Maeve accepted the invitation. As they moved to the dining room, Maeve took Catherine by the hand and looked at her.

"LaLa, you are with child," Maeve said softly.

"Yes, I am. It is so wonderful, Tiny One. We are so happy," Catherine smiled as Brian put his arm around his wife.

For the first time in her life, Maeve felt unsure; she believed the feeling was envy. She was happy for LaLa and Brian but she began to second guess the decision she had made. She hugged them both together as they all laughed.

The three young people conversed during their meal explaining what their lives were like. They each listened as they individually explained their duties: Brian and Catherine to the manor, Maeve to the people. Catherine briefly told Maeve of her mother's death which brought back memories of Maeve's mother's death. Both women grew sad and Brian decided Maeve needed an escort home. He went outside calling to Padraig. Catherine and Brian walked Maeve outside, where Padraig waited for her with the small carriage. They left each other promising to talk again soon.

# Chapter 26

In his mother's chamber Ardan knelt before Betha. The Queen's lunar pendant caught the moonlight sending eerie shadows across the walls. The candles flickered as the great Sorceress incanted the spell.

Betha stopped abruptly saying to her son, "You must put all your love into this enchantment for the spell is evil. Only your love can bring good results."

Ardan nodded. He closed his eyes; his mother chanted. They became entranced. Darkness shrouded the room.

Although the morning had been bright and sunny, Maeve began to notice the threatening sky and clutched her heavy cloak about her as she walked to the village. She did not observe the blackbird watching her from the tree near her garden. Just the same, a chill ran through her, making her shiver.

She made her visits quickly this day in the hope of arriving home before the storm. As she walked just outside the village the sky turned black and several people beckoned to her to find shelter in town. Maeve stopped for just a moment to look at the sky. The sun was shining but the sky was black. Villagers were exclaiming about the strangeness of this when a black cloud covered the sun. The wind picked up leaves from the ground slowly at first, and then the speed progressed. The faster it moved it seemed to be seeking a place to settle. The people were frightened. Maeve was unable to move. The wind came closer and closer to her until she was surrounded by dirt, leaves and blackness. People began running in all directions. Children were crying. Maeve seemed to be the target of the wind. Her face turned upward, her eyes closed, her arms extended before her as if to ward off the collision. The sun shone brightly and Maeve could feel its heat on her skin and through her body. It seemed like hours to Maeve. It was only moments. The wind stopped. Maeve was released.

Her face shone radiantly, more beautiful than she had ever been, but only for a moment before a look of terror came over her face. She ran her hands over her face and felt its coolness. Her hands traveled down her body resting on her stomach. Maeve slowly opened her eyes; after a moment her vision focused on the faces of her people. As they stared at her, she knew they were now afraid of her. She smiled to reassure them. It was no use. It was all different. It would never be the same. Even if she could regain their trust, how could she explain what was about to happen? A low keening moan came from the depths of her soul. Maeve fell into a swoon lying motionless on the ground.

Brian stood at the outskirts of the crowd and watched the clouds and the sun. He had never seen such phenomena and was mesmerized. A gasp from a woman in the group and a whispered name caught his attention; he pushed forward through the mass. There he saw her. Her hands extended toward the sun and the expression on her face made Brian's heart lurch. Then suddenly a radiance came upon her face and Brian's attempt to move was prohibited. He found he could not move from the place where he stood. As suddenly as it started, the wind stopped as Maeve fell to the ground. Brian rushed to her side; he moved her hair from her face.

"Maeve, it is over. Quiet, now. I will take you home."

His words found their way to her and she understood. Quickly he lifted her from the ground, carrying her to his horse. The townspeople, frightened by what had happened, moved aside quickly to allow them to pass through. Maeve stopped crying and lost consciousness once they were on their way.

Brian held tightly to the girl and thought about what he had seen. Something had happened, that was clear to him but he did not understand what. He knew that the townspeople had sensed the change and drama of the moment; they were a superstitious lot. Maeve would have a difficult time ahead of her. The people would not go near her.

Although he felt concern about all these things, something else was breaking his heart. Something was causing him deep sadness.

He could not find it. He searched and searched his soul but he did not know what it was.

Brian rode rapidly to the manor. He carried Maeve up to a room in the West wing calling for Tillie as he moved. As he placed her on the bed, her eyes opened and she tried to sit up. Brian leaned over and placed his hands gently but firmly on her shoulders. "Rest, Maeve," he said.

"I cannot stay here, Brian, I must go to my home," Maeve's words were strong but her voice was weak.

"No, you must rest. Tillie is here to care for you and later, once you have slept, Catherine and I will come to you; we will talk."

She shook her head back and forth and her eyes filled with tears. The tears spilled over to her cheeks but she did not have the strength to cry aloud. Brian watched her for a moment with his emotions so confused he could not speak. He leaned forward and lifted her from the bed and held her in his arms. His eyes sought out Tillie who tried to keep her reaction from showing on her face. Once Maeve's tears were spent, she slept. Brian placed her on the bed once more.

"Stay by her side, Tillie, until she wakes. Then, send for me." With that Brian left the room.

# Chapter 27

Tillie was a small young woman who had known Maeve since childhood. Tillie loved Maeve as a close friend because she and her grandmother had cared for Tillie's family for a lifetime. When the young lord gave Tillie the task of caring of Maeve, she accepted without hesitation. She was sorry to see her friend so low. She was afraid for her life and wanted to bring her back as Maeve had done for her family members. Tillie's eyes filled with tears as she looked at the sick woman. The young lord had told Tillie he did not know when she would awaken, if ever. Tillie commenced her work as she had seen Maeve do many times.

She fetched a bowl and pitcher full of water. Then with a wet cloth she wiped Maeve's face to erase the dampness. She loosened her clothing, removed her frock and replaced it with a nightgown which belonged to the chambermaid. Maeve seemed lost to consciousness so Tillie crooned a song softly hoping to give Maeve something to listen to as she slept.

Tillie was amazed that she was able to maneuver Maeve around and change her clothing since she was tiny compared to Maeve. She sat in a chair next to the bed watching for any sign of movement.- Maeve was breathing but did not move or stir in any fashion. Tillie kept the pitcher filled with cool water and hourly wiped the woman down since she seemed to be in a fever state.

Tillie had no idea what had happened to Maeve. She had seen the young lord on horseback return to the manor and one of the footmen had helped him carry Maeve into the manor house. She was in a swoon and had not stirred since he brought her to the manor. When he called for Tillie he did not say what had happened. He seemed upset and very worried. He brought the woman to the guest quarters and Tillie had followed him. His concern was across his face like thunder clouds. Tillie was afraid.

When he had left the chamber, Tillie heard some discussion in the stairwell. The Lady of the manor questioned her son as to why he had brought his friend here to their home. The young lord told his mother that Maeve needed tending and that he knew nowhere else to bring her. The Lady spoke softly about the impropriety of it when the young Lady Catherine came to the scene and said that her husband had acted correctly. Maeve needed care and they could administer it. The Lady left the stairwell quickly after that and the young lord and his lady spoke quietly for a few minutes but Tillie could not hear what more they said.

Lady Catherine came into the chamber quietly to look upon Maeve. There was concern on her face also. She took Maeve's hand, singing to her softly. Maeve appeared to quiet for a time, finally sleeping soundly.

The afternoon passed and the night fell around the house. Tillie bathed Maeve again and covered her with a light blanket. Maeve slept more; Tillie nodded off herself hoping that her patient would wake her if she was needed. The hours passed; Tillie woke and slept fitfully through the night.

Maeve was deep in sleep. She relived the scene in the village many times; she could not see anyone during the episode. Again and again she relived it. She had been covered with darkness and swirling wind but where she was transported, it was bright with light. She had put her hands out to ward off the feelings of dread. She was screaming inside the darkness but she did not know that no one could hear her. At one point she thought she felt arms holding her and trying to soothe her but that only lasted a bit and the dread returned. Maeve had no idea where she was. She thought that she was still experiencing the scene in the village. When the moon came to the window the light woke her from her deep sleep. She looked around the room. No one was nearby and Maeve pulled herself up moving her legs to the side of the bed. She sat and began to shake with cold and loneliness. As she sat she began to cry; the sobs wracked her body as the tears streamed down her face. Her heart was broken but she was unaware of what had happened. She cried and rocked herself. She could feel her heart beating throughout her body but her legs were so weak she knew they would not hold her if she tried to stand. She did not hear Tillie enter the room with a new pitcher of water. Tillie saw Maeve sitting and ran to her side.

"I must go home to Mum. She will wonder where I am and I need her. I need her so much." Maeve said as Tillie came to her.

"No, no, my Maeve, I cannot let you go. You are too weak and the young lord entrusted me with your care. You cannot go." Tillie crooned to Maeve.

"I need Mum…so much, my heart, my heart. She will know how to help me." Maeve whispered.

Tillie spoke urgently, "Your heart, Miss? Do you have pain in your heart?"

"It is breaking."

Tillie knew that Maeve and Mum had a very close relationship and she also knew that Maeve received her strength from Mum's caresses and songs. Tillie tried something she had never tried before. She whispered to Mum to help her with Maeve, to help her give her what her patient needed. Tillie began to hold Maeve in her arms and sang softly to her. She could feel Maeve relax slightly and gradually Maeve held Tillie. But Maeve continued to cry and tell Tillie that her heart was broken and she had no will to live. Tillie hummed and spoke the words that Mum gave her. Gradually, Tillie was able to get Maeve to lie back on the bed, but Maeve's arms held onto Tillie and would not release her. Tillie carefully climbed on the bed and laid down next to Maeve holding her tightly in her arms. Tillie continued to croon and rock Maeve much like Mum had done in her lifetime. The words were sweet, "There is much time to live, much time to cure, much time to love, my girl. The strength will come; your heart will mend." Tillie did not know where the words came from but she knew that they comforted Maeve as she went into a peaceful sleep.

The cock crowed and Tillie woke. She quietly removed herself from the bed and checked Maeve who was sleeping quietly. She no longer seemed feverish but sometimes when she breathed it was more like a deep sob but it did not wake her. Tears streamed down her face. Tillie went to the chamber door and opened it to find the young lord standing there. She moved to give him entrance as he came forward to the bed to see Maeve. His face had not cleared from the worry Tillie saw there the afternoon before. He watched Maeve sleep and then turned to go with a motion to Tillie to follow him.

They walked down the stairs and entered a small sitting room. Lady Catherine was there waiting for them. The young lord turned to Tillie and asked her how the night had passed. Tillie looked at him and then looked away. She was not certain how to answer the question for she was afraid to let on all she felt and probably knew. The lord could sense that and pried a little more.

"I assure you that whatever you say to us will go no further. I just need to know what to do for her."

Tillie smiled and nodded. She knew the young lord and Maeve had been friends since childhood. She trusted him so then quietly Tillie regained her voice and spoke, "My Lord and Lady, Maeve is very sad. I am not certain that she knew where she was or what had happened. I know she believed me to be her mum." Tillie hesitated, swallowing, then continued, "Maeve said her heart was breaking. She wanted to go home to Mum. She said she did not know what to do and that only Mum could help her. I…I held her and rocked her. I sang to her. She held me too. But she cried, a sob so deep within her I believed her heart continued to break." Tillie stood and shook her head.

The young lord nodded as Catherine's eyes filled with tears. He said to Tillie, "Something happened yesterday that I cannot explain but Maeve will need us; we will keep her here as long as she is ill. Continue to be her Mum, Tillie. That was very wise of you. I'm sure that Maeve and her Mum are communicating while she sleeps. Please keep her comfortable. I will check in soon. Thank you."

Tillie nodded, curtsied and left the room. She then went to the kitchen to find some refreshment for herself and her patient.

Maeve woke briefly and ate for a bit while Tillie soothed her with her songs. But Maeve still acted as if she was unsure of the day, time or place where she was located. Early in the afternoon, Maeve was sitting up in the bed with some pillows supporting her back. She was watching as Tillie worked about the room when a knock came to the door. Tillie answered the door and admitted the young lord. He walked toward the bed smiling at Maeve.

Maeve looked confused and said, "Your lordship, I...I, is Brian with you?"

Brian stopped, turning to Tillie who gestured her confusion.

"No, Maeve, Brian is not here at the moment. I wondered how you were feeling."

"Is this your home then? Can you help me to go home to Mum? I'm sure she misses me and is worried where I am."

"Maeve, we have contacted your Mum. We told her you were ill but in good care."

"Oh," Maeve seemed relieved. "Thank you, your lordship, for your kindness."

Maeve then slipped back into oblivion.

The young lord left the chamber with worry deep in his eyes.


Catherine was sitting quietly in the room she shared with Brian when he walked in. She rose, going to him, then beckoned him to sit. He then told her that Maeve did not recognize him and that she thought he was his father.

Catherine thought for a moment and then asked, "Is there not a young woman learning from Maeve we could send for?"

Brain kissed his wife and replied, "Thank you, my love. You have given me an idea." He then left the room. Catherine smiled as she watched him go. Some time later Catherine heard his horse leave the manor grounds.

# Chapter 28

Brian rode until he came to the village where Maeve lived on the outskirts. He went to the livery where Cian was shoeing horses.

"Cian, who helps Maeve with her planting, do you know?"

Cian stood up slowly rubbing his hand over his face. He shook his head; he seemed hesitant to say anything but recovered himself quickly in the presence of the young lord.

"Your lordship, I know that Molly helped her on occasion, but…" Cian lowered his eyes and then his head.

"What ails you, man? Tell me what's on your mind," Lord Brian said impatiently.

Cian made a gesture of apology; he swallowed and then began to speak, "Your lordship, when Maeve had the dark clouds on her the day before, people were scared. They ran and have not come around. I have not seen Molly; some people left …afraid of what it was."

"Cian, I understand. I do. I will see if I can find Molly. Thank you."

Brian left the stable and went in the direction of Molly's cottage. When he got there, the hut was quiet but he knocked on the door and after a while Molly's father opened the door. He was shocked to see the Lord at his door and tried his best to help him. Yes, Molly was there and yes, she could come to talk to him. He left the door and went inside the cottage, calling his daughter.

Molly came to the door and curtsied clumsily. She agreed to accompany Lord Brian to Maeve's home and her father went also. Maeve's cottage was not far from them and Molly went inside to retrieve Maeve's basket of medicines and plants.

"Thank you, Molly. Do you have any notion of what might help Maeve recover? She is feverish and confused. She believes that Mum is still alive and that we are children," Lord Brian said quietly as Molly handed him the basket.

She looked up to her father who nodded his encouragement. "Your Lordship, there is a small bit of tea in the basket, brew some strong, make sure she drinks it. There is a small amount of powder that can be used to wipe her head. She should recover herself in a couple more days if she is suffering from normal fever." Molly hesitated before going further. "Sir, Maeve may be under a spell....What happened to her, Sir. It affrighted me."

Lord Brian looked pained and was unable to answer. Molly's father became alarmed, going to the Lord to give him a steady hand. Lord Brian finally was able to get the words out, "Tell me what you know."

Molly and her father helped the Lord back to their home and Molly ran to fetch Cian from the stable.

"You've got to come, Cian. You must tell the Lord."

"No, Moll, I cannot tell him that."

"You must, Cian. He must know."

So reluctantly, Cian returned to Molly's cottage with her and spoke to the Lord.

"Cian, please do not hesitate to tell me what you saw that day."

Cian cleared his throat, looked briefly at Molly who nodded encouragement and then he began his story, "Sir, I was working when I noticed a change in the weather. I looked about to see people hurrying home. The sky was black, the wind was picking up but the sun was shining. I happened to see Maeve stop in the middle of the road. She seemed to be curious and was just watching the sky. People were calling to her to take shelter but she did not move. The wind picked up the dirt and leaves and they began to blow around Maeve. It was as if she were captured inside the wind. At first she seemed unafraid; suddenly a blackbird flew inside the wind with her. Sir, I have never known a bird to do anything like that. They usually fly away but not this one. It flew directly into the wind. Maeve's face became terrified as if she was witnessing some horror. Her face changed then and the blackbird flew away. Her face shone brightly. Then it was over. The weather was normal again. Maeve was no longer surrounded by wind. She smiled at us as we stared at her. Then she fell into a swoon."

Brian had witnessed the last part of this himself but he had not seen the blackbird. He looked at Cian and Molly asking, "Was it the blackbird that made you think she is under a spell?"

Molly shook her head, "No, Sir, the whole thing was frightening. It was all the pieces together that made us think something had bewitched her."

Brian nodded finally, saying, "Thank you both for your help. I needed to understand what had happened."

With that he walked to his horse, mounted and began his ride home.


Within her dreams, Maeve walked her garden with Mum and brewed tea, made poultices, creams and absorbed all that Mum taught her. Maeve and Brian raced up the hillside and played their games. She studied with him from the big books of their tutor. Mum braided her hair as Maeve told her that she planned to be a wise woman one day just like Mum. Mum laughed and said that Maeve should marry and have children. Then they both laughed. Her dreams only became fretful when Maeve saw herself alone on the hilltop waiting for someone to return to her. When she dreamt this she would cry out, sobbing. Then she would feel the soothing hands of Tillie wiping her brow, holding her hand. Tillie sang quietly and spoke reassuring words to her. Eventually Maeve would quiet down and sleep again.


Brian returned to the manor. He kept reviewing what Cian had told him. As he dismounted his horse, Catherine came to meet him in the courtyard. He noticed unfamiliar horses; before he could ask, Catherine shook her head vigorously, taking him by the hand and leading him into the manor up the stairs to their chamber.

Catherine locked the door behind Brian and they sat to speak.

"Queen Betha has surprised your mother with a visit. She said she was here to give her condolences on your father's death, but there is gossip among the servants that she is here to find her son."

Brian looked at his wife in disbelief. In all the years of his mother's marriage to his father, the Queen had never visited. Brain spoke after a time, "They were girls together, my mother and Betha. My mother has not spoken of her often but there seemed to be a story about it. Mother would never explain what it was."

Catherine spoke then, "Your mother appears to be in a state of shock that she is here. She went bustling into the kitchen to demand a room be prepared and then food needed to be served. She made sure that I was in attendance at the meal. Queen Betha gives me the impression she can read my thoughts. She would look at me and then at your mother and your mother would look away. I became very uncomfortable. I excused myself as soon as I was able."

Brian asked, "How long does she intend to stay?"

Catherine shook her head, "I do not know. I am not sure she has said."

Brian kissed his wife telling her to rest. He left the room to search out their new house guest.

He found the queen in a small sitting room off the staircase. She was alone but had recently been served tea. Brian walked into the room, bending in a bow to greet his guest. Queen Betha smiled at him, inviting him to sit. He did so. Soon their conversation began.

"Your Majesty, I was surprised to hear that you were visiting. How do you feel after your long journey?"

"I am well, Brian, thank you. Congratulations on your nuptials and the coming birth of your child. Your bride is very lovely. I wish you both the best."

It was Brian's turn to thank her. He welcomed her to his home and hoped that her visit would not be a short one.

Betha smiled at him. She gave her condolences on the death of his father.

Brian felt that the preliminary conversation was over. He commenced to inquire as to the reason for her visit, "I know that you were friends with my mother as children but in all this time you have never visited. I am curious as to why you have come now. If I am overstepping my bounds, please forgive me. You may tell me so."

"I have felt guilty for never visiting; I thought with the death of your father, it would be a good time to visit my friend. However, there is another reason I am here. I hope that you may help me because my son has not contacted me for a time now. I am concerned because this is not his manner. If you could allow a servant of yours to guide me in the vicinity of the village, I would be forever grateful."

"Your Majesty, I will help you in any way that I can, but please excuse me for now. I have a friend I must look in on to see how she is feeling. She is quite ill and my wife and I have designated ourselves as her caretakers."

Betha looked at Brian for a long moment. "Can I help in her recovery? I do have some skills that might help her."

Brian hesitated only briefly. He recalled his mother telling him of Betha's skills as a sorceress. She might be able to help.

"Thank you for your offer. Please follow me."

Tillie answered the knock at the door. She left quickly as she saw the Lord with the Queen.

Brian quietly spoke to the Queen, "This is my childhood friend, Maeve. She has been in this state for several days now. She sleeps most of the time. When she awakes, she sometimes believes that we are still children. She thinks her grandmother is still alive and she thought I was my father. We are very worried that she will not recover."

Betha stared at the sleeping girl as she listened to Brian. She walked to the side of the bed, moving the hair away from Maeve's face. "What happened to her?"

Brian resumed his assessment of Maeve's condition, "The people in the village believe she is under a spell. I did not see what happened," he lied as he began to regret that he had brought Betha to Maeve.

Betha placed her hand on the sleeping girl's forehead, quietly chanting words that Brian did not understand. Betha turned to him, speaking softly so only he could hear, "This girl has been placed under a spell, but it is not the first time. She must remain closed off from the world for a week or more. If she becomes the victim of more spells, it will finish her."

Betha seemed shaken as she walked from the room; Brian took her arm helping her down the stairs. Betha did not look at him again. She walked to her chamber.

Inside she lit a candle, chanting for some time. Brian heard her begin the chant; he went to see his wife.

As promised, Brian arranged for Queen Betha to visit the village. She asked the villagers if anyone remembered seeing a young man. No one seemed to recall seeing any strangers about. Disappointed, she returned to the manor. She arranged to leave for home the following day.

She went to visit Mirima that evening. Mirima seemed nervous when Betha walked into the room. Betha spoke to her softly, "I thank you for your hospitality. I am to leave in the morning. Take care of Lady Catherine for she may have trouble in childbirth. Brian and Maeve are not aware of what has been fostered on them. But I am sad to tell you that the dabbling in witchcraft that you have done, killed your husband."

Mirima gasped, flashing her eyes at Betha. "What could you possibly mean? What do you possibly know?"

"Mirima, for years you have denied my abilities. I can see into their hearts. I can see into yours. I know what you did. Did you even realize it killed dear Lintel?"

"No, no, it is not possible," the woman began to cry.

"It is possible. It happened. You must pray for forgiveness, dear friend. Be kind to others. Do not manipulate any more lives that are not yours. I can do nothing to set this right, but neither can you, so do not think on it. Accept your guilt; again pray for forgiveness."

Betha left the room as Mirima cried softly. She felt bad for her friend but there was nothing she could do. Although she did not find her son, she was glad that she would return home. Maybe he was home; she prayed that he was.

# Chapter 29

Maeve's condition improved rapidly after Tillie received the basket from Molly. She stopped sleeping all day; her fever broke and her appetite returned. Catherine would come to see her and they spoke of the new baby Catherine would have in a few months. Brian would visit and although he tried to get Maeve to speak of the day in the village, she would claim she was not sure what had happened and that her memory was slowly disappearing about the matter.

When Maeve was finally strong enough to go home, Brian made her stay a few more days. Then he made sure she got there safely. She had confided in Catherine that she would be leaving her home. She was unsure of her destination but she did not feel she could stay. The people would not let her help them.

Maeve looked about the cottage one last time. The garden was in disarray for lack of attention. The cots were made up as she had left them. There was a thin coating of dust on everything else. Her memories of Mum came to her; she would miss the feeling of being with her but she must leave.

As dusk settled on the village, Maeve picked up the bundles she had prepared, the sword concealed in its case and walked to the woods behind the cottage. She nervously looked around and pretended for a moment to bend and pick some herbs. There was no one in her vicinity so she wrapped her cape around her and began her journey. She called for protection; after a time she felt warm and guarded.

Maeve remembered that she and her father had traveled for days when he brought her to Mum, but she was a child then and not really sure about time. Maybe it wasn't days; she did not know. She also thought she remembered the way, but then decided she was not sure of that either. A deep breath steadied her as she continued to walk.

The only reason she started her journey at this time of day was so she would not be seen. She began to regret that decision almost immediately. Daylight would have been a great help to her. She stopped for a moment, listening. She thought she heard breathing. She closed her eyes to concentrate on the sound. Suddenly a pebble bounced by her feet startling her. She opened her eyes and turned to look around her. She did not see anything so began to move again. A pebble found its way to her. This time she had watched the pebble fall and looked in the direction from which it came.

There was no light to help her to see. The moon had not yet risen and the night was slowly falling all around her. She stopped. She turned in the direction of the pebble's advance. Her voice could not be found. She waited. Her body began to shake and she wrapped her cloak closer to her for warmth. She stepped forward on the path. A low voice, raspy and weak called, "Wait."

She stood still and took a deep breath; her hand found the sword. She turned in the direction of the voice and walked to it. "Who's there?"

"I am no one you know,"

"Who are you?"

"I am a man from Starling who came to your village for your help."

Maeve stepped a bit closer asking, "Are you not frightened by me? Did no one tell you I am to be feared?"

The man began to cough and it took him awhile before he could speak. Maeve's caring instinct told her that she had nothing to fear so she moved to his side. Finally he spoke, "I thought you would be frightened by me."

"Why do you need my help, sir?" She bent down and as if by request the moonlight began to light the woods. She could see the man more clearly; she had never seen him before. He was a hunchback but she could not determine his age. He again began to cough; she knew he had a lung ailment. She untied one of her bundles bringing out a small herb mixture. She told him to chew the mixture and then drink the water. He nodded and did as she said. After a time he rested and his breathing grew peaceful. Maeve repacked her things, quietly rising to again start on her journey. As she reached down to pick up her bundle, his hand reached for her hand.

She stopped and looked at him. The man whispered, "Please do not leave me. Let me rest here tonight and I will accompany you to your destination."

Maeve did not know what to say. Finally she answered him, "I do not want to be seen leaving the village. If I wait till morning, someone will surely see me. Perhaps I can leave before dawn and you can go back to Starling."

"Miss, thank you for your help, but I cannot let you travel alone. Please allow me to accompany you."

Maeve was not sure how to answer this. She looked at the man who was so disfigured she could not see how he could be of help. However, he sounded like a man who thought of himself as a Knight and Protector. Her confusion became evident on her face. The man smiled and said, "I know what you are thinking. However, would you not rather have a companion on the road than go alone?"

Maeve remained silent, thinking for a time. She had asked the spirits for help; maybe this was their answer. She decided to speak to the man some more before making a decision.

Maeve began to sit when the man pulled his cloak from his shoulders and made a place for her beside him. She looked closer and realized he had two cloaks and he was sharing one with her.

"Thank you, Sir. Please tell me why you came to find me for help."

"I was told that you were willing to help the sick and that you might be able to help me."

"No one told you that … I had… changed?"

"I have been trying to get to you for a day or two. I was sick and it took me a week to leave."

Maeve nodded her understanding. This man had not talked to anyone since the incident…he did not know.

"I think you are very sick; you need your rest. We will go back to my cottage. I have a sick room in a small building beside my cottage; you can rest there. No one will know you are there. I will not leave until you are well enough to travel. Is that agreeable to you, Sir?"

The man looked at her while tears filled his eyes, "Thank you, Miss. I will do my best to get well soon."

Maeve stood and helped the man to stand; they retraced her steps to her cottage. She lit a lantern and they walked to the shed where she had a cot ready for her new patient. Before she left him, she gave him more herbs to eat and water to drink. His breathing improved. He laid his head down and slept. Maeve watched him feeling a strange sense of calm. She went to her home and fell asleep as soon as she laid upon her cot.

# Chapter 30

Betha's arrival home made her smile when her husband embraced her. Their love and desire for each other had not diminished since they married. They had long talks in the dark of Betha's bedchamber before Cathal left for the night.

They were concerned since Ardan had not returned home. The rest they left unspoken as they had done for years. Cathal looked at his wife, knowing what she was thinking, "I will leave you to rest, Love. Do not think more on this tonight. We will break fast in the morning together. It will be …"

He pulled her into his arms kissing her deeply. He then left her chamber for the night. Betha then lit more candles so she could see better in the room. She sat down, thinking back a very long time ago.

Betha had been the daughter of a Duke. Her parents doted on her because she was such a pretty child. Being the only daughter of a Duke, the servants tended to pamper her and treat her like their own charmed daughter. She thought the world was wonderful and that everyone would always treat her kindly and love her. She learned the most difficult lesson of her life as a young girl. Not everyone would love her and treat her kindly. But she found out about this at a very young age and the knowledge would change the course of her life.

One day Betha was playing with her brothers out in the garden of their home on a warm afternoon. They were running about creating much mischief when she noticed an old woman walking along the road. The woman was dressed in rags and had a young boy in tow. As they passed, Betha heard the woman berating the child. She could tell the woman was angry because she was shouting, but Betha could not understand the language being used. She thought it was a comical sight to behold and began to laugh as the woman continued down the path. Suddenly the old woman stopped and turned to face the young girl. Betha ceased her laughing then and gaped at the woman. The old woman began to walk toward her staring as she approached; raising a boney finger she cursed the girl with a low voice in a language that Betha understood, the words she would never forget.

"When you marry and marry you will, you will conceive twin sons on your wedding night. The mixture of moon and stars will be upon you and the children of your womb will mix also. One will be your sorrow, the other your joy. Neither will be complete and your motherhood will be shattered."

Betha screamed at the end of the old woman's tirade, running as fast as she could to find her father as the old woman cackled.

Betha's father and mother listened very carefully to all their daughter told them. She was not one to lie and the story was so bizarre that they believed every word she uttered.

Immediately the Duke sent for his magician and relayed the story to him. After much conversing it was decided that Betha would be apprenticed to the magician. He would teach her all he knew about magic and together they would find a way to dispel the curse. In the meantime a search would be conducted to find the old crone.

From that time on fear guided Betha's steps. She feared her teacher, she feared the old woman's curse, and she feared her future. She worked diligently on her spells and potions and gradually became a young friend to the magician. She relaxed in the knowledge that he would not harm her but he was trying to help her. She cried herself to sleep each night. As she grew older she feared that she would be betrothed and her life would begin its spiral turn.

She begged her father not to let anyone have her hand in marriage. The antidote to the curse had not been found and she was frantic. Her father's worried frown became commonplace as the castle buzzed about the poor little girl who cried daily.

When Cathal first saw her they were attending the wedding celebration of her brother. Betha seemed very shy and would not leave her father's side most times. Betha was dressed in a green velvet gown which matched her eyes. Her hair hung in large curls down her back. She did not speak with anyone except the members of her family; Cathal thought this very strange for the daughter of a Duke.

Cathal asked his father about her and whether she was betrothed. The King did make the inquiries but was informed that the girl was too delicate to ever marry; the family would not hear of it. The King, assuming she was feeble-minded, passed the message on to his son. Cathal would not be swayed. He believed there was more to it than that but he decided to quietly bide his time and make certain that no one else won the hand of the beautiful Betha.

Cathal had two very close friends who were his knights. He entrusted the story to them and beseeched them to investigate to find out the truth. Both knights quietly made their way to some of the ladies of the manor house. They were successful in learning the truth of the duke's daughter.

When Cathal heard the truth, he understood the young girl's shyness. She lived with fear all the time so if what the ladies of the manor said was true, she was continually in tears and upset. The fact that her father realized that she could not and would not marry gave credence to the whole story.

Cathal then discreetly inquired of his father's magician for a known antidote to the spell. The magician interviewed countless gypsies in an attempt to find the counter-spell. Most of the gypsies were unable to help. Cathal himself was the one who happened to discover the end of Betha's torment.

It had been two months since his magician had begun his intense search for the cure. Cathal had been away and was on his way home eager to find out the latest circumstance. As he rode through a wood in close proximity to his father's castle, he happened to hear a young gypsy woman cursing a small child.

"You will one day be fit to father hogs and only hogs!" the girl screamed at the boy with her finger pointed at him.

The boy stared at her, not comprehending what she was saying to him.

Cathal immediately realized that the boy was not normal. He seemed lost and was filthy. Cathal called to the gypsy, "Can you not see that the boy is deaf? He does not hear you; let alone understand what you are saying."

The woman looked at him and then at the boy. She stared at the boy for some time before she turned her eyes back to Cathal.

He asked her quietly, "Why do you curse him so?"

The woman's black eyes narrowed and she stated, "My grandmother always taught me to curse someone if they were unkind to me."

"Your grandmother?"

"Yes, she was the one who raised me up. She said I was as good as anyone else and if anyone was unkind to me, they should feel that until they die."

"I see. And where is your grandmother now?"

"Dead."

"Tell me, miss, did your grandmother ever tell you what to do if you wanted to remove a curse."

The girl threw back her head and laughed. Cathal waited until she was finished before he raised his eyebrow at her in anticipation of an answer to his question.

She looked at him very closely, stating, "My grandmother taught me all, but why would I want to remove a curse?"

"Because someone made a mistake."

"Gypsies do not make mistakes."

"I see. Then you would not be willing to help me?"

"I might be. What will you give me?"

"What do you want?"

"What do you have to give?"

Cathal dismounted his horse approaching the young woman. She stood her ground watching him intently.

"I will explain my circumstance. If you can help me, I will pay you; if you cannot help me, I will leave quietly."

"Tell me your story then…I will determine if I can help."

Cathal explained Betha's being cursed, even going so far as to say it was the grandmother of the gypsy. He told the young woman that he wanted to marry Betha but she would not for fear of the curse.

The gypsy's eyes widened as the tale went on. She shook her head finally.

"My grandmother's curses were not meant to be reversed. The only thing I can offer you is a softening of the results. What did the curse say?"

Cathal shook his head then, "I do not know the exact words but I will find out and return to you, if I may."

The gypsy nodded in agreement.

Betha's thoughts returned to the present. It was late, so she got into her bed closing her eyes. She had thought on this enough for tonight. Tomorrow she and Cathal would discuss this again.

# Chapter 31

It took time for the hunchback to heal. After a time he was able to sit outside in the sunshine to warm himself. He did not speak much, but Maeve talked to him about the herbs she made for him and why he was feeling as he did. There was no personal talk between them and Maeve busied herself in her garden most of the day. She prepared him food to eat to increase his strength. He became discouraged after a few days and began to watch Maeve's movements for any signs of her resuming her journey. One day she sat with him in the sunshine and spoke.

"I am beginning to believe, Sir, that you need to go to your own home and not fret about my journey and me. You will need more care and should not exert yourself traveling. Do you have anyone to care for you at home?"

The man's eyes filled with tears and he shook his head slowly. His tears began to fall down his cheeks and Maeve saw that this too was part of his illness. His sadness was palpable and she wished that she had not brought up the subject yet; he was not ready to make this decision.

Maeve smiled, "We will wait a few more days then to see how you are feeling. I am sorry I rushed you, Sir, please forgive me."

The man looked at her and realized that this young girl was more than just a caregiver. She was empathetic to her patients and had a deeper understanding of their ailments than even they did. He reached his hand out to hers and quietly stated, "Thank you, Miss. A few more days will help."

Maeve squeezed his hand lightly, smiled and told him to rest. She stood and went to the garden. His eyes followed her; then he slept.

The next few days held a turn of events. They eventually told each other their names. The hunchback, Cillian, was able to walk around the garden after he rose early and his general attitude was one of hope. He noticed, however, that the girl was not herself. She arose later than usual and her pallor was whiter than usual. She would sit in the sun but would fall asleep easily. He attempted to talk to her but she was lost in her own thoughts and did not hear him.

One evening she came to him and told him they needed to leave. He was surprised because she meant in that very moment. He agreed readily since she had her parcels packed. She retrieved his cloaks and they began their journey. He kept a watchful eye on her and noticed that in the evening she was more herself. They traveled throughout the night but by morning her energy was diminished and they sought shelter in a grove of trees. They both slept; when they awoke she made them a meager meal. Once she had eaten she slept again.

This was the way of their journey for several days. There was very little conversation except to ask each other how the other was feeling. The hunchback felt well enough to travel but his cough returned while he slept. One night he awoke to a fierce coughing fit and once he got it under control, he heard something unusual. He was not sure what it was but after listening for a bit he discovered that the girl was crying softly. He moved toward her and once he reached her, he realized that she was still asleep, but tears were streaming down her face. When she awoke later in the afternoon, he was sitting against a tree watching her. He asked how she had slept and she smiled.

"What is bothering you, Miss? You were crying in your sleep; did you have a bad dream?"

Maeve shook her head, "I do not remember dreaming, Sir. I guess I'm sad to leave my home."

That was the end of the conversation but the hunchback was not convinced this was the reason for her tears.

They traveled at night for several more miles because the girl was feeling better after having slept most of the day. Finally one night they did not travel. They had been packing up their belongings, getting ready to continue their journey when a large blackbird flew above them, cawing. The hunchback tried to hide himself under a tree beneath his cloaks; he began to shake fiercely. The girl went to him to soothe him.

"It's only a bird," she said quietly, "it's already flown away."

"No, Miss, it is still with us," he whispered.

"Maybe it is a bird of luck; it will travel with us to protect us," Maeve said.

"No, it is evil and it will hurt us both. It already has," he stated as his lips quivered.

Maeve looked closely at him and felt his brow to see if he was feverish. His skin was cool but his eyes watered and he grabbed her hand.

"Forgive me, Miss, I have brought sadness and harm to you. Forgive me."

Maeve shook her head and quietly said, "I believe the time has come for us to talk."

She looked toward the sky and then turned her attention to the trees. She heard a rustle of leaves and determined to light a small fire. As she arose to gather some twigs, the hunchback turned his attention to a bird in the tree.

His voice was suddenly strong and fierce, "Go, get you gone, do not stay a moment longer, your evil has permeated the world. Go, be gone."

The bird swooped down toward them then turned toward the sky. They could no longer see it. Maeve turned to the man; she was shaking in terror.

The hunchback had noticed an opening in the rocks earlier in the day as they rested under the trees. It would be a hard walk for him but he felt they would be safer in the cave. He told the girl, it was time to find a new space and they moved up the hill to the cave.

Maeve made the climb without much trouble but she had to help the man most of the way up. They were both breathless when they arrived. She went about helping to make him comfortable.

She tended to a small fire for warmth and to heat water for tea. The man was watching her closely realizing that her tears continually ran down her cheeks. He wanted to say words of comfort but he felt that he had scared her in the first place so his words would mean nothing.

The girl sat across from him on the damp ground and spoke, "While you were ill, you spoke in your sleep. I do not know everything you said but I began to think that we are connected. I did understand that you spoke about the bird, hurting you …I also encountered a bird during my experience. I was at first confused by the wind circling me. I could not move. The sun was warm inside the circle. Then I realized it was over…As it stopped and released me I saw a blackbird fly from inside the circle. I knew I was different…something had changed. The villagers stood staring at me. They were afraid and I fainted."

Cillian looked at her intently and he spoke, "Miss, it is time we spoke. I am not sure what you are saying."

Maeve nodded, beginning her story, "What I am about to tell you, Cillian, I have told no other. I hope you will accept this tale to be the truth since that is the way I think on it. Not long ago I had a dream. In my dream I was with child and my longing for this child was great. I could feel the babe in my belly, loving it with all my heart. I did not know the father of this child because my dream did not reveal this to me. I only know that I was happy to be a mother and when I awoke and found it only a dream, I was sad because I longed to be a mother. I knew that my decision never to marry was a good one and dismissed the dream as best I could. As the days went by when I least expected it, I would find myself thinking of the dream and remembering how I felt. Some time later the strangest event happened. I had gone to visit some people one morning. I had not had time to get home before a storm came up in the sky. The sky became very dark with large, threatening clouds. People were going to their homes as fast as they could; some invited me in to escape the weather. I looked up at the clouds because even though the sky was dark the sun was shining brighter than I had ever seen. This fascinated me; I stopped to watch. Then it happened. The wind began to blow, leaves and dust circled around me. I put my hands up as if to protect myself. That is all I can remember about that. The next thing I knew there were people staring at me and before I fell to the ground I thought that I was with child. I do not know how this would have happened. I had never been with a man. For the longest time after that I could not tell any more of the story because I had no memory of any more than that. After a time I began to remember things that I knew had never happened. I thought about it and wondered if they were pieces of dreams. When the whole memory came back, I knew that it was not a dream; it happened while I stood in the road with my arms extended above," Maeve stood, taking a long breath. She moved to Cillian adjusting his cloak, refilling his cup. Then she sat again resuming her story.

"This is what I remembered. When the sun was bright, I had an overwhelming feeling of evil. This was something that was happening to me and the evil nature of it was frightening. Then, as suddenly as I felt the evil, it changed to a feeling of love, unselfish, pure. It was love in the most beautiful sense of the word. Although I know people could see me standing there in the road, I was not there. I was transported someplace else. I know not where I was or how I got there. The room was full of light and the air was warm. I knew nothing but peace in my heart and I was not afraid. I had never felt more safe. As I stood in the room a man came to me and took my hands. He was tall and strong. He smiled at me and gently put his arms around me and kissed me. I was still not afraid; I wanted to be with him. This all seemed to take a long time but in reality it was only a few moments."

Her eyes began to fill with tears and she took a deep breath before she continued her story, "He told me that he loved me, had loved me from the first moment he saw me; that he would care for me always. He told me that he wanted me to love him as much. I felt that I did love him but I did not tell him so. He lifted me into his arms and took me to a seat where he set me down and knelt next to me. His eyes never left my face and all the while he talked I believed everything he told me. His words were beautiful, filled with love and kindness, but the thing that meant the most to me was his understanding of what I was feeling and how little I knew of the world."

She stood up and began to pace. After a while she said, "I am unable to go on. I thought I could tell you this, but I cannot."

Cillian had been watching the emotions cross her face. He wanted to help her but was not certain what he could say or do. Finally Cillian sighed; feeling inadequate, he softly spoke, "Maeve, I am here to listen, not to condemn; whatever you choose to tell me I accept, whatever you choose not to tell me, I accept. I will do what I can to help you."

Once he had spoken these words, Maeve's shoulders began to shake. Her bent head and closed eyes helped him to understand that she was crying. He got up from the ground and walked over to her. Cillian took her hand and led her to the soft ivy bed where she would sleep this night. He sat beside her as she cried and repeated, "Hush, Hush. Rest yourself, little Maeve."

Her sobs became quiet and she slept. He covered her with his cloak and continued to keep watch over her and the fire. She never saw the tears he shed for her.

In the morning Maeve was quiet and seemed embarrassed to talk. She kept her head bowed as they walked. Cillian allowed the silence to continue. When they stopped to rest and have a small meal of berries and bread, Maeve broke the silence.

"Cillian, I want to thank you for your kindness to me last evening."

"You owe me no thanks, Miss. I have done nothing to deserve it."

"I feel I must tell you the end of my story. It needs to be told so that I may hear the words and think no more about them. Once spoken I might be able to live with the consequences."

Cillian made a gesture which displayed his willingness to hear her story.

"The man in the bright room who spoke to me of all his love, was handsome and I could tell from his clothes that he was high-born. He seemed so gentle and good that I felt I had no need to doubt him. I can see into people's hearts. My grandmother told me it was a gift I had. I know he meant well. He spoke of the time he would come for me. He explained all that would happen so that I would know and would not be afraid. It was not until he told me that I would conceive a child, that I became frightened. He held my hands assuring me that all would be well. Oh, Cillian, he talked to me for hours and hours. But how can that be? It was only a few minutes in the road. People witnessed it. It was only a short time."

She placed her hands on her temples and again began to sob. She rocked herself . She could only say that her head ached. Cillian held her hand in his and waited. Finally she stopped crying and took up her tale again, "My memory does not serve me anymore. It stops there and I cannot remember more. But I knew all he told me about the child was true. I knew I had conceived, I could feel it. Just before I came back to myself in the road, he kissed me again and said, 'It will not be long before I come for you to make you my bride. Wait for me.'"

"Oh," and the pain came up from the depths of her soul and she sobbed. "I waited. He never came. I waited as long as I could and then I had to leave before everyone knew the truth about the babe. This man loved me." She stopped talking then for a while but Cillian could sense that she had more to say. He did not move but waited for her to continue.

"Cillian, I have told you all now. Except that... I am not with child. I believed that I was and that is why I had to leave my home. Everything I can remember I have told you. I thought it would make sense to me if I said the words but it does not. I sometimes think I am insane. To believe that I conceived a child in a dream is insane."

Looking at her with a look of great intensity, Cillian stated clearly and simply, "Maeve, I believe you."

Their eyes met and he saw that his words had meant a great deal to her. For the first time since they had met, she smiled the most beautiful of her smiles. The relief shone in her face and her eyes became bright and luminous. Her smile, one of beauty and gratitude, came up from her soul. Cillian became embarrassed by her openness. He rose from where he sat and busied himself with the provisions for their meal.

The smile lingered on her face. Cillian placed his cloak over her shoulders and moved away from her. His heart ached, his mind raced, he thought of everything she had told him but there was nothing more he could do.

Maeve spoke first and asked, "Shall we travel today or wait until tonight?"

The hunchback gauged her mood before he spoke. She was putting on a brave face but he felt it was not sincere. He finally said, "We will wait until tonight, Miss. I do not feel well enough to travel today. I will sleep some more."

She nodded and moved about disbursing the fire and then sat outside to enjoy the sunshine. As she sat her thoughts began to run. She began to regret leaving her home; she thought of Brian and LaLa. She would miss their friendship but it was time to move to a life of her own. She was happy that her two best friends had found each other and knew they would make each other happy. She knew she could not have stayed there; the people were now afraid of her. She would be useless; no one would ask for her help. The sun lulled her to sleep as the hunchback watched her from the cave until he too fell asleep. Neither saw nor heard the blackbird as it perched on a rock near the sleeping Maeve. It sat and watched the two as they slept. It flew away before either awoke.

They packed up their bundles and set out again on their journey. They had traveled less than an hour before they heard the rumble of thunder. It began to rain very steadily and the wind picked up. The lightning was close and they looked about for a place to shelter. A grove of trees stood about a mile away and they decided to go toward it. Once there, there was no way to burn a fire since the ground was soaked. Maeve kept an eye on the hunchback but he seemed to be alert and unaffected by the storm. They huddled together under the trees and waited out the rain. The night was dark, cold, and wet. By morning they were shivering and each began to feel ill.

Maeve pulled a vial from the bag and each took a sip from it. Their cloaks and clothing were wet so they hung their things in the sunlight. Again the sun seemed to be the solution to their sadness and they sat there for hours. Maeve felt better after a time but the hunchback coughed most of the time. Maeve tended to him and due to his health their travel plans were again interrupted.

As the dark surrounded them, Maeve sat next to him wiping his brow as he slept; she began to do an incantation that her grandmother had taught her. Maeve filled with panic; she was afraid he would not survive. He became delirious and began to speak in his sleep. Some of his words she could not distinguish but she did hear him say, "… wanted you, sorry, …"

Maeve, crying, called to her grandmother to help save this man, "Mum, help me to heal him. He is caring. He is my dear friend. He judges me not. His friendship is pure."

Maeve closed her eyes listening for her grandmother's counsel. She moved to her parcels. She assembled some herbs, washing them with water, chanting her grandmother's words. She administered to Cillian, softly crooning to him.

The delirium continued for several days before his fever broke and he eventually opened his eyes. He was unsure of where they were and what had happened. He looked around and his eyes met Maeve's. She seemed different. She said they would travel again when he was well enough. He nodded and she left him. Maeve assembled their things, brought him some broth and moved away from him. She found some sunlight and sat for a time.

Cillian's voice was not strong. He motioned to Maeve to sit near him so he could speak to her. She moved to him, sitting close by. He took her hand, whispering, "Thank you for your care, Miss. You have been good to me. I want to be good to you as well."

Maeve seemed to frown at this statement but he continued, "I hope that you do not regret telling me your story. You seem to be quieter than usual. I fear you are embarrassed that you told me."

Maeve quietly shook her head, "No I do not wish I had not told you. I wish that it had not happened. I feel confused; I do not understand it. I cannot know what happened."

Cillian held her hand tightly, "I believe you, Maeve. I think that what was meant to happen did not. I think you are fine. It might have been a dream but now it is over."

Maeve accepted his words. She began to think about what he had said.


After a day they began to resume their travels. Maeve explained to Cillian that she had dreamt before she left her village that she should return to the home of her family before her mother had died. She shook her head; she stopped, turning to him she said, "I seem to be living in dreams; for no reason I go about trying to fulfill them. It makes very little sense."

Cillian smiled briefly saying, "It makes all the sense in the world. Maeve, your mother died in childbirth?"

Maeve said, "Yes, she did."

"May I ask what happened to your father and the baby?"

"The baby died with my mother. My father brought me to my grandmother. He said he would return for me but he never did. I believe he is dead. That's the only thing that makes sense to me. I was all he had, but he never came back."

Cillian thought about this for a bit; then he asked, "The cottage where you lived, was it your family's?"

Maeve stopped at this. "Oh..it must belong to the manor. I have never thought…." Maeve began to think that this was a fruitless journey. She seemed to be chasing about with no real idea of what she was doing.

She sat on the ground under a tree. She had a helpless look on her face as she turned to Cillian. "What can I be doing, Cillian? I am lost."

Cillian sat beside her then. He was quiet for a moment but finally spoke. "Maeve, let's continue our journey to where you once lived. It may be that you just want to revisit. If you find that you cannot stay there, I will accompany you home to Grashner."

At this caring, unselfish statement, Maeve's eyes filled with tears. As she took Cillian's hand she said, "My dear friend, thank you. You are so very kind."

They journeyed on but their talk was limited to the scenery, the wildflowers, the green trees. They were content with each other, no longer feeling the need to speak of serious matters.

# Chapter 32

When they arrived at their destination, Cillian sat leaning against a tree in the wood. He thought she should investigate the cottage herself. "Come back for me when you can; I will wait for you here."

Maeve left the bundles with Cillian but she took the sword with her. She had managed to keep it concealed so Cillian had no idea that she possessed it.

The cottage looked much smaller to her than it had in her memory. She knew though that she was in the right place; she quietly walked to the door. There was smoke coming from the chimney and that stopped her. She did not recall having a fireplace in her home but maybe they did. Someone was inside. She had hoped that the cottage would be empty and she could live there without anyone knowing she had come back. Coming back to the cottage of her parents had been her idea all along when she left her home. She remembered her plan: she would return here, be the wise woman and care for people. They would not be afraid of her. They would trust her; she could stay forever. Maybe this was not the right cottage. She backed away going to the path.

She leaned against the tree where Cillian rested. He had fallen asleep but his breathing was harsh and he coughed without waking. Maeve shook him gently and fed him the remaining. He muttered his thanks and closed his eyes. She stood and walked back to the cottage. As she came to the corner of the entrance, her eyes fell to a stone lying near the door. She bent to look at it realizing it was not loose but embedded into the ground. She ran her hand along the top and felt scratch marks. She traced them slowly and then again and again. The tears began to slide down her cheeks. This was the cottage and her name was scratched into this stone. This was her home.

Knocking on the door, she entered. The light from the fire illuminated the room and she could distinguish two people sitting near it. There was a man and a boy. The dog lying beside them growled on the hearth as she entered but soon the growl turned to a soft whine.

The boy turned to see this girl in the home and he stood quickly. As the boy stood, so did the man. They walked to her and stood before her. The boy stared, vaguely shaking his head to indicate he did not know her.

The man's serious aspect eventually calmed and a smile creased his face. His voice was deep and loving, "Tiny One?"

Maeve stared at the man. Then recognition came and she began to cry. The questions flooded her mind but at the moment the answers didn't matter. Her father stood in front of her; she ran to his arms. They hugged and cried. She thought he was dead; she thought she would never see him again. She stepped back; just looked at his face which had aged since she last saw him. He shook his head and pulled her back into his arms. "I will tell you all later."

After a time, her father led her to the hearth; she sat next to him in silence. Finally, the boy sat as well and said, "I am Rylan." Maeve's eyes shot to the boy and looked long and hard at him. She recognized the large green eyes of her mother, the light brown hair of her father. Her intake of breath registered shock and her father's arms went around her quickly. "This is your brother, Maeve. I am sorry for the secrecy. I never meant to let it go this long."

Maeve reached out her hand to Rylan. He grasped her hand and held to her tightly. The three sat for a while as each took in the ideas of how their lives would change.

Suddenly Maeve jumped up, "My friend is outside. He's been sick; I need to make a place for him to rest."

Rylan said, "I will come with you. We'll bring him in, give him food. Come."

The two of them left the cottage walking down the path where Maeve had left her friend.

There were voices of men talking. Rylan took Maeve by the arm, pulling her behind a tree. They quietly moved about to where they could see who was speaking.

A tall dark haired man stood above a sitting man who Maeve realized was Cillian. He was saying something about the other man being selfish and he needed to go away.

Maeve ran to Cillian. She bent to him to assess his health. The other man moved away when she entered the clearing. She stood then, and turned to the stranger, her voice strong with authority. "My friend has asked you to leave. He has not been well. You should not disturb him."

The stranger began to laugh. He looked at Cillian and spoke, "Your little maid is brave. She does not recognize danger when she sees it."

At that comment, Maeve pulled her sword, lifting it toward the dark haired man. Cillian started at Maeve with a sword drawn, standing in a fighting position.

The other man jumped back quickly as she advanced on him. He then spoke some words sending a spell which illuminated Cillian. The man stood and looked at the dark haired man.

"You have made the past few weeks very difficult but I have done my best to continue."

"The Queen is searching for you, blaming me for your disappearance. You'd best go home; forget this lovely maiden."

Maeve realized that Cillian was no longer hunched. He stood tall and straight. His voice was not as it was but strong and steady. The dark haired man looked in the direction of Maeve. He began a low laugh and turned back to Cillian.

"You must leave; I will take my rightful place here with the maid."

Maeve's voice was strong, "You are the one who must leave. This place has nothing to do with you. We have nothing to do with you."

The man looked sharply at the girl, "You do not give me orders."

Cillian quickly moved to protect Maeve; but she advanced on the other man. Her sword caught the moonlight as she swung it. She advanced more, speaking quietly and threateningly to her enemy. Her voice was clear but her words were an enchantment.

Cillian sent a spell at the stranger, "Get ye gone, blackbird. May you enjoy your flight."

The man laughed but dodged the spell Cillian sent to him.

Maeve jumped in front of Cillian. She lunged at the stranger sending a slice up his arm with her sword. He reacted to the blow with an intake of breath. She swung the sword again sending the tip into the man's side.

The stranger turned his full gaze on her. He raised his uninjured hand sending a spell in her direction. With great agility Maeve moved the sword deflecting the spell. The spell recoiled, hitting him; at the same time Cillian sent a spell to the stranger. All the enchantments met their mark.

The man crumbled to the ground, as a blood curdling cry pierced the darkness and the man disappeared. At the same time a lightning flash struck Maeve; she screamed, falling to the ground. Cillian ran to her and lifted her into his arms. He noticed that her shoulder had been burned as her gown was singed. He quickly placed a healing enchantment on her but within a few seconds a clap of thunder sounded; with a cry Cillian vanished. Rylan ran to the place where the men had stood; Maeve was lying on the ground. Her brother went to her. There was blood all around her. Rylan assessed that she was alive but shaking. He helped her to stand. He looked her over for injury, finding that the skin of her shoulder was red with a burn but that seemed to be her only wound.

Cillian's cloak laid on the ground; Maeve stooped to pick it up. She quickly hid the sword in the cape. She held it to her. Her friend was gone, leaving her with many questions. Rylan urged her back to the cottage.

Maeve sat in the cottage drinking broth, trying to regain her strength. Her father had dressed her burn so at the moment she felt very little pain. The questions mounted as she looked at the fire, her brother and father thought dead, both alive; her friend the hunchback, not a hunchback, vanished; the blackbird, not a blackbird but a man who seemed dangerous, gone. The warmth of the broth helped her to regain the warmth in her body. Rylan told his father what he knew about the two men in the woods; he had not seen much for he had been hiding. He did not know that his sister held a sword battling the stranger with it.

They made a bed for her in her old room; she fell fast asleep. Her father paced, concerned about his daughter and the story his son told. Who were these men? What did they want with Maeve? How could he protect her? His guilt began to mount as he thought how he left her years ago never traveling to see her. How he wanted to protect her now but had not then? He was ashamed of himself.

# Chapter 33

Suddenly Ardan was lying in front of his mother the Queen. He looked shocked as he saw her standing over him. Her smile was beautiful with relief. Ardan looked at her, sheepishly grinning.

"Mother, I apologize. I meant not to have you worry."

"I am so glad to see you, my son. Now tell me of your adventures."

"Did you bring me back here?"

"Yes."

"How? Why?"

"I managed to find you and Dubhlainn. So I brought you both back."

"Dubhlainn is here? Is he wounded?"

"Yes, he will be fine but it was serious at first. His wound is infected. The physician needed to stitch him. Did you wound him?"

"I may have added to it but I did not inflict the original wounds."

At this Betha looked at Ardan for further explanation. He said nothing more. Betha cleared her throat; she offered him some wine. Then they sat together to converse. Betha gave a brief review of her visit to Grashner; how she looked for him in the village but was unsuccessful in her search. Then she spoke of seeing Maeve at the home of her friend. She had accompanied the young Lord Brian to the sick room to see if she could help with Maeve's health.

"I discovered that she had a physical reaction to the spell we put on her. She might have died if we had been successful in our quest. She has had another spell placed on her. It was a very powerful spell; I was shocked to see her condition. Then I realized I should have listened to you and not pursued the path we took. I am grateful that it worked out the way it did. You might thank Dubhlainn for that."

"Mother, he thwarted my plans so I should thank him?"

"Ardan, his interference saved her. We did not finish. It was a blessing."

"I see. Now I am at a loss as to how to continue. I need to speak with her to explain what happened. I am where I was at the beginning. How do I persuade her to marry me now? I almost killed her."

Betha smiled at her son with loving eyes, "Ardan, I think you must court her. Persuade her to marry you through charm, love and sweetness. I believe you will be able to sway her. You are after all handsome, kind and brave."

Ardan laughed at his mother's flattery. Then he became serious again, "Mother, you said she was the victim of another spell. Do you know what that was?"

Betha shook her head lying to him, "No. I was unable to discern it. I only know it was very powerful. She is still under the incantation. It is meant to last her lifetime."

This explanation, although lacking in detail, troubled Ardan. He felt his mother knew more than she was willing to disclose. He accepted that for the present but would press her later.

"Mother, I need to freshen up but I want to return to where I left Maeve. Might you help me to return?"

Betha nodded, "Of course, my son. I would like to know your plans before you leave."

"I will give that some thought before I return to you. I will also visit Dubhlainn."

Ardan retired to his chamber to clean himself, shedding the garb and whiskers of Cillian. He deliberated briefly choosing garments that were not too fine. He did not want to face Maeve in his princely clothing. He then left his chamber to visit his brother.

As he entered Dubhlainn's chamber, his brother looked to the door managing a smile.

"Ah brother, you too have returned to the home of our childhood."

"Brother, how are you feeling?"

"I have felt worse but I have felt so much better than I do at the moment," he attempted to laugh but it was too difficult.

"Mother tells me I must thank you for interfering in my plans because you have saved the girl."

"How fortunate!"

"So thank you."

"What do you intend with this maid…a brief encounter or something more permanent?"

"Nothing has been confirmed as yet. When I know, I will tell you, but I must ask you to remain neutral in this; please, stay away. Allow me to follow this path."

"I will do as you request. At this time, I am unable to move let alone interfere."

"I must go now. Rest, brother."

Outside the chamber door, Ardan whispered a spell to bind his brother to his bed. He then moved to his mother's chamber where he knocked softly on her door.

"Mother, I have visited Dubhlainn, thanked him, asked him for no further interference and wished him well in his recuperation."

Betha nodded, "What have you decided to do, Ardan?"

"I want to return to Maeve. I will explain myself as best I can. Hope that she will accept me eventually. I do not know when I will return."

"Did your brother promise to leave you be?"

"Yes, he said he would."

"Fine, then you are ready?"

"Yes, mother, I am."

With that, Ardan was gone from her room.

The night went on as Colm sat in the cottage thinking. Suddenly a loud clap of thunder made him start. He went to the door; opening it he saw a tall, finely dressed man. The gentlemen approached and said, "My name is Ardan. I apologize for the late hour but I would like to speak with Maeve. Is she here?"

Maeve's father only stared, not answering the man. Quietly, Maeve came to the door, standing next to her father. She looked at the man for a very long time without speaking. Finally some recognition came to her face; Ardan's eyes implored her.

"Father, please stoke the fire. This gentleman and I must speak to each other."

Her father was hesitant to leave her alone with a stranger. Rylan also came to the door. He spoke to his father, "I will stoke the fire, Da." He went inside to tend the fire.

Maeve realized what her father was feeling; she turned to him taking his hand. "Please stay."

She turned to the man, "What is your name, Sir?"

"My name is Ardan. You know me as Cillian but as you can see I am not a hunchback. I was under a spell when I came to find you. I remember everything about our journey together, how you cared for my illness, and..." He stopped speaking then, afraid he might say too much.

Maeve patiently waited for him to resume his discourse; finally he spoke again,

"I want to explain myself to you. Please say you will listen to me?"

Maeve looked at the man with compassion; she looked at her father with much the same compassion. Maeve closed her eyes, drawing in a deep breath she stated, "There are many things I must have explained to me, Sir. However, I would ask that you give me a few days here with my family. My father has much to tell me also. I would like to start with him. I need some time to think."

Ardan frowned asking, "Your father? Are you certain this man is your father?"

Maeve nodded, "Yes. This is my father." She briefly thought that if this was indeed Cillian, he was making sure she did not need his protection.

Colm looked at this man and then at his daughter. He wondered how much this man knew.

The gentleman bowed as he began to leave.

"But first, Sir, before you leave, I must ask you...am I safe?"

Ardan slowly nodded his head, "Yes, Miss. I have made sure that you are safe."

"Thank you, Sir. We will meet again," with that Maeve led her father into the cottage, closing the door behind her.

The man stood waiting, hoping that the door would again open. When it did not, he turned to leave. He would not go home just yet; he would wait for her no matter how long it took.

Maeve kissed her father as she went to her cot; lying down she thought about the last few hours. Nothing was as it seemed. Her father and brother both very much alive. People making decisions about her life without consulting her. Maeve did not realize that there was more to that than she knew. She laid awake for hours. When the sun rose, she slept; her dreams as always filled with sorrow but she would not remember them upon awakening.

# Chapter 34

Maeve did not sleep very long, a couple hours at best. She rose, walking through the cottage which was too quiet. Neither her father nor Rylan were about. Suddenly she was a little girl again alone in the house where her mother died. She stood perfectly still, closing her eyes.

"I remember this feeling, this quiet. Where is my Mama? Where is my Da? Where is the baby?" Maeve did not move; the memory so vivid she felt the fear of that day. With a deep breath she went to dress.

Maeve walked to the garden, moving about the plants as old friends. The garden was in very good condition. Someone here was tending to it with meticulous care. Now to follow her next endeavor. She thought about this quite a bit as she laid awake. She moved away from the cottage, beginning to walk to her destination.

The little cottage stood before her as if lost in time. It had not changed much except for a wooden stool placed on the front stoop. Maeve walked to the door, knocking softly.

The woman came to the door, greeting her visitor. They looked at each other but the older woman did not show recognition; then in an instant a smile creased her face. Maura said,

"Child, you look so much like your mother I thought you were her ghost."

Maeve embraced Maura, holding her tightly for a long time.

"I did not know if you would remember me."

" I not remember Maeve? I have missed you dearly all these years. I am so happy to see you. But come in, come in. Let me feed you, child."

Maeve went into the familiar cottage sitting near the fire to warm herself. They chatted about easy matters before they delved into the more serious topics.

Finally, Maeve approached her subject. "Maura, I would ask you a favor if I may?"

"Of course, ask whatever you need."

"I have been thinking long about this because although I have experience with herbs and daily care of the sick, I would like to learn midwifery. I wondered if you could teach me?"

"This is a most opportune time for that; I have several ladies about to deliver. I could use the help. I would love to have you work with me."

"Oh, thank you, Maura. Tell me what to do; I will help you prepare."

Maura patted Maeve on the hand, "Let's finish eating; then we will get to work."


Maeve and Maura spent the day gathering herbs, folding cloths, all while Maura instructed Maeve in all aspects of childbirth. They were tired by the time everything had been prepared. They sat down to drink tea when Maeve finally asked the question Maura expected all day, "Please tell me about my mother's delivery and death."

Maura nodded. She began to describe all the aspects of her mother's delivery. The baby was turned and try as they might, they could not turn him. It began to look like they would both die.

Finola begged the physician to cut the baby out of her to save the child at least. He tried to save both but in the end it was impossible. Finola had lost too much blood; they stitched her up and sedated her so she would go peacefully, which she did.

Maeve looked closely at Maura, asking quietly, "Did you poison her so she would die?"

Maura's eyes widened, "What? No, no, no. Finola was my friend; we gave her a poppy mix to relax her. She was not going to live. We just helped her sleep. She was exhausted but she was in pain. She wanted to be able to speak with your Da. She needed to help him."

Maeve listened intently, "If a woman were to have a delivery like my Mama, would you be able to save her now?"

Maura said, "I hope so. Both the physician and I learned that night. We have spoken several times about it. I am not certain but I think it would be a better delivery."

Maeve cried then; she hugged Maura saying, "I am so sorry, Maura. I never should have said that."

Maura held her speaking softly, "Do not cry, Maeve. Your mother loved you so much but she would not want you to feel sad about what happened. She is still with you. You know that? She is still with you."

After a time, Maeve left with a promise to return the following day. She was very tired. She went back to the cottage but still her father and brother had not returned. Maeve started a fire. She prepared a meal for all of them for they should be home soon. She sat on the hearth, falling asleep.

Colm and Rylan found Maeve asleep in front of the fire when they arrived home. They found the meal she had made them so they woke her so they could all eat. They enjoyed the meal while speaking of their day. Rylan accompanied his father to the stable to learn his trade of farrier. Colm was grateful for his son's company and help at work because he was finding the job was becoming more and more difficult for him. His hands hurt; they would swell on hot days. His bones ached on rainy days. Maeve took note, promising that she would make him a potion to alleviate his pain.

Maeve asked about the garden to find that her brother was the gardener in question. She complemented on well he cared for it, asking permission to assist him. He accepted the offer of help grinning at her. She asked if she might plant some new herbs that were not in his garden but that she needed for medicine. He readily agreed. They walked out to the garden so they might determine where she should plant. Colm followed them to the garden standing by the fence so he could enjoy their interaction. They were very gracious with each other, possibly treading lightly until they got to know each other. Maeve marveled at the beauty of some of Rylan's plants, how large they had grown and how well cared for they were. Maeve ran to fetch a parcel to bring out for Rylan to see the herbs she wanted to plant. He remarked about them asking their purposes, the methods used to mix them. Maeve began to discern an intense interest in her brother that she recognized. He too wanted to know the ways of a healer. She began to smile at him realizing that time spent with Rylan would be learning and teaching. He looked up at her in that moment having the same thought. They began to laugh as they continued their discussion.

After a time Colm went into the cottage to check the fire. He sat resting by the fire waiting for his children to join him. Maeve came in first to sit near her father. As Rylan entered he sensed his father and sister needed to speak to each other so he excused himself, leaving the room.

Maeve was the first to speak, "Da, I wonder if you want me to stay or if I am intruding here?"

Colm looked at her with the saddened look that often crossed his face. "Maeve, I want you to stay. I want to know you."

There was a long pause as Colm sat staring at his hands. How could he say, this is your home please stay? How could he say, you are my daughter I love you? How could he say, I want to protect you from the world? He could not say these things to her without feeling the hypocrite.

Maeve saw his dilemma; she understood what he was feeling. She took his hands.

"Which hand bothers you the most, Father?"

He indicated it was his left hand so she began to gently massage it along the bones. She spoke softly to him explaining what she was doing, how he could exercise his hands to help his pain. She then spoke, "I know life sometimes is difficult. I wanted you to come for me but you never did. I thought you were dead. I thought Rylan did not even exist. Mum helped me. She loved me as she loved my Mama. She sang to me, taught me so much about healing. Then there was Brian. He was my friend. He helped me the most. We played every day on the top of the hill. He told me you were on a quest…all brave knights go on quests. I knew then that you would be gone for a long time. When it came time for him to be tutored, he insisted that I be tutored with him."

Colm was surprised by this, asking, "He was tutored? You were tutored? Who was this boy?"

"Brian is the Lord of Grashner now. He married LaLa, Father."

"Lord Grashner was your friend?"

"Yes, we rode horses together. I learned so many things from our tutor. He even secretly instructed me in the art of healing. He knew so much. I used to love talking to him about the world. Once Brian was old enough, he would go with his father to learn about the business of the manor. That is when Melchiarc would instruct me. Brian never knew. I could not tell him because Melchiarc made me promise. That was the only secret I ever kept from Brian."

"I met Brian when he would come here on business; then when he was betrothed to Lady Catherine. I had no idea he knew you. He was always kind to me; not like some of the lords who come to visit. I was happy for him and Catherine; they seemed to love each other very much."

"Yes, they do. I am happy they found each other."

"Maeve, I am not making excuses; I apologize to you for what I have done. I do not expect you to forgive me. But I do want to know you. I…," he began to cry so Maeve hugged him.

"Da, do not cry. Tell me….I will try to understand."

"When we first lost your mother, I was deep in grief. While she was dying, she told me to take you to her mother. She wanted you to be instructed in the ways of the healer because she felt you had an intuition toward it. One of the nights as we travelled to Lillium's, I dreamt of your mother. She came to me telling me not to worry about bringing you to her mother's. She said it was the best thing for you. I wonder now if she saw your future…being tutored, horses, friendship. I did not lie to you…not intentionally that is, when I said I would be back for you soon."

"When I arrived home here, Rylan was very sick. He was a large baby which was why your Mama could not deliver him, but he was sickly. He had a wet nurse but her milk caused him to be sick. I did not feel I could leave him. I walked the floor nightly with him. With the help of Maura and the physician at the manor, we developed food we could give to him that he was able to eat. He began to grow. His disposition changed as he began to act as you did at his age. He began to laugh, crawl and eventually walk. I realized then that it had been two years since I left you. I thought I should come for you but I kept putting it off. I wanted to see you but …I was afraid of the effect you would have on me. You look so like your mother."

"I know. Maura said that to me today. It made me realize that looking at me might be difficult for you."

Colm nodded, whispered, "That was no reason for me to ignore you. I am a coward."

Maeve spoke after a bit, "I had many opportunities living with Mum. I often wonder though how my life would have been different living here with you. I wonder if Mama had lived what my life would have been like living here with both of you. Now we are together. We should just get to know each other."

"Maeve, you are right. So may I ask you some questions?"

Maeve laughed at the way he said this and nodded.

"If you thought I was dead, why did you come here?"

"Oh…I had to leave Grashner. I did not think it through. I thought this cottage might be empty and I could live here."


This conversation went on for a while longer. Some of Maeve's answers did not satisfy her father. She was not forthcoming with all the details. Finally Colm asked her, "Why are you not married yet?"

"I do not intend to marry, Da. I want to be a healer. I am going to learn midwifery from Maura."

"You can be a healer and marry. You should have a family."

"Father, why does a woman have to belong to a man in her life?"

"Belong?"

"I do not want to marry. I have had proposals but I have refused the offers."

"I see. We can discuss this more at another time but I need to sleep now. Work in the morning."

"May you have a good night, Da."

"A good night to you as well, Maeve."

# Chapter 35

Ardan tried to be patient waiting for Maeve to speak with him. He let two days pass before arriving at the cottage where he had left her. It was mid-morning but no one was around. He wandered around looking at the garden where some work had been done recently. He took a path which led to the stables of the manor house. He thought better of conversing with anyone working there. He walked back to the cottage. He waited there for an hour or more before heading back to the nearby tavern where he was staying.

The following day he went back to the cottage. It was earlier this time but still no one seemed to be home. This began to concern him. Where was Maeve? Had she left the area to travel somewhere else? He felt responsible for the girl's confusion. He sat near the garden to think about what might have happened when Maeve spoke with her father. She thought her father was dead but he was here. What did he tell her about returning for her? Did she feel abandoned more now than she had as a child? Then an additional thought came to him. What about me? How did she feel about me? Deciding that she should bear my child before I married her must have felt like an imprisonment. If she comes back, how will I convince her that I meant no harm when that was all I did to her? How will she look at me? I know how she felt while it was happening in the windy mist. She told me she believed the man loved her. I cannot tell her what happened except that my brother interfered. The Queen said I should be grateful to him for disrupting the spell. How will she ever believe my feelings for her? It might be better if I leave, never to return. I have harmed her enough. She will never want to marry me.

Ardan decided then to leave. He would go to the tavern, pay the fees, leave for home. It would not be so difficult a life to live alone. He would be King someday. Some maiden would be happy to marry him. He might not love her but it might work. As he stood, he heard movement on the pathway. Looking in that direction, he saw her then. She was disheveled, covered in blood and moving slowly. He ran to help her.

"Maeve, you are injured?"

She was startled to see him before her.

"No, Sir, I am not injured; just very exhausted. We have been awake for two nights delivering a woman of her child. It was a difficult birth but both the mother and child are healthy and resting. I am home now to rest as well."

"Oh, I saw the blood. I thought you might be hurt."

"Thank you for your concern, Sir," at this Maeve took a deep breath before continuing. "I know you are here to speak with me. I would ask that you give me some time to sleep. We might be able to speak tomorrow as long as all remains quiet. You see, there are other mothers here about to give birth at any time. If I do not have any to help deliver, I will be here tomorrow."

"I will return then, Miss. Thank you for agreeing to speak with me."

Maeve smiled at him, then moved toward the door.

Ardan watched until she was inside the cottage before moving away. He thought about continuing with the idea he had before Maeve appeared. Should he wait until tomorrow or should he go back to the castle? He thought about this on his way back to the tavern. He decided that he would stay another night. In the morning, he would make his decision.


Ardan woke before dawn; he tried to think things through. Would it be better for Maeve if he left never to see her again or did he owe her an explanation? He came to the conclusion that she deserved to know what had happened to her. He dressed, went to down to eat and started on his way to Maeve's cottage.

He arrived at the cottage earlier than he had the other two days. He looked about to see a young boy come out of the cottage.

"Can I help you?"

"Is Maeve about?"

"Who are you please?"

"I am Ardan. Maeve agreed to speak with me."

"Maeve is at the river washing. Just down the road there," he pointed.

Ardan thanked the boy, heading down the road. He came upon the river but saw no sign of Maeve. The information that she was washing was curious. He was looking for someone in the water but he was also trying to be discreet. He came upon an eddy then where he found Maeve scrubbing the dress she had been wearing the day before. She had not seen him coming so when he spoke she started.

"There you are, Miss. I hope I am not disturbing you."

"No, Sir, but you are very early."

"Yes, I did not want to miss you."

"I think I will be home most of the day. There are no women ready to birth. The next two are a few weeks away."

"I see. How long have you been a midwife?"

"I am just learning. Maura is teaching me."

"Maura is the midwife here?"

"Yes, she was the midwife when my mother died."

Maeve began to scrub the dress again as Ardan watched her intently. He was not certain how to proceed.

Maeve broke the silence. "Sir, perhaps we could walk back to the cottage. We can talk on the way."

So they started down the road to begin their conversation.

"Tell me, Sir, do you remember the dream I told you about? Do you remember everything I told you?"

"Yes, Miss, I remember everything we talked about while we traveled."

"You were involved in this dream?"

"Yes, I was. So may I tell you what happened?"

Maeve nodded, so Ardan began his story, "I heard about you from a young soldier. He told me of your beauty, how he had fallen in love with you. He proposed to you but you refused him. I thought the story was interesting. One day I found myself near Grashner so I stopped. I asked about you; then you happened along in the village. The young man I spoke to pointed you out to me. You were surrounded by people; you were giving them things from your basket but I could not see your face. Finally the person blocking you moved away; I saw you then. I held my breath. My heart began to pound in my chest. I felt such a longing for you; I had not known a feeling like that since …"

Maeve turned to him then, "Since?"

Ardan replied, "I married several years ago, but she died. She was dying when I married her. We both knew it but I loved her. I wanted to make her a princess. We were not married very long before she became so ill she could not leave her bed."

"That is very sad, but how could you make her a princess?"

"Hmmm, I will explain that later if I may. I had been told that you would not marry. So I went to see someone who might be able to help me. I explained about you; I explained how I felt. She tried to help me. We came up with a plan."

"Whom did you ask for help?"

"Hmmm, her name is Betha; she is a sorceress."

Maeve stared, "Betha? Queen Betha?"

Ardan swallowed, nodding confirmation, "Do you know her?"

"She was visiting the home of the Lord of Grashner while I was there. I was not well. I was told she came to see me. I was not conscious. She was upset when she saw me."

Ardan said nothing more but continued to walk. Maeve did not speak again until they reached the cottage.

"Let us sit in the garden; I will bring water out for you to drink."

Ardan moved to the garden; he sat waiting for her return. How should he continue? The truth was the best.

Maeve handed him water when she returned. She sat near him encouraging him to continue.

"The plan was to transport you to me while you stood in the town. This was a very powerful spell. My instructions were to put all my love into my discourse with you. I did that while talking to you. The rest of the plan was to bed you so you would conceive a child."

At this there was a strong intake of breath from Maeve; her eyes searched Ardan's face as her face blushed crimson. She could not speak for a time. He looked at her as tears sprang to his eyes, "I am so sorry. My intention was never to hurt you but I did."

Maeve thought for a bit before speaking. "Ardan, did you never think to speak to me before attempting this plan?"

Ardan shook his head, "I never thought you would listen to me."

"You never tried. You went immediately to sorcery. Do you remember our conversation in the bright room? Do you remember that I told Cillian how I felt about you?"

"I remember everything, Miss."

"I am struggling to reconcile my feelings for the man in the bright room, for the hunchback, Cillian, for Ardan the man before me. Do you understand how confused I am?"

"I think I can understand that. Can I help you to reconcile these feelings, Miss?"

"I have people making decisions about my life without consulting me. You and Queen Betha use sorcery and impregnate me. My father leaves me with my grandmother but never tells me he is alive nor that I have a brother. Once my grandmother died I thought I was alone, but I had planned my life. You changed all that. I could not stay. They were so afraid of me no one wanted my help." She sighed then, in silence she thought for a moment, then said, "Tell me why you came to me as Cillian, please?"

"As I told you in the bright room, I would come to you. I did not know what had transpired. I thought we completed the spell although I had no memory of it. My brother met me, casting a spell on me, turning me hunchback. I was sick then; I tried to get to you sooner but I was unable. When we finally met, I did not feel I could pursue my suit. I could only be a supportive friend."

"It took us some time to warm to each other. You were sick but you thought yourself a knight. I finally learned to trust you; by that time my memory was coming back."

"Aye, your memory confused me. I did not know what happened. I began to feel ill at ease with you. My brother hovering did not help. I was afraid what he would do to you."

"Your brother?"

"The blackbird, the man in the grove is my brother."

"I wounded him. Is he alive?"

"Yes, he is confined to bed but very much alive."

"This is all too much to take in. May I think on this?"

"Of course, Miss. May I ask about your father?"

"As I said, my father and brother are alive. When I went into the cottage that night, they were both there. My father recognized me… after a bit. We were both in shock, I think. We waited to talk on what had transpired. I have accepted it; that is all I can do..accept it."

"The family you thought lost to you is still with you."

"Yes, I have a brother. We are getting to know each other. He is the gardener of my mother's garden. Look how well he keeps it."

Ardan looked about noticing the beautiful plants, but Maeve's pride in her brother was evident. He smiled at her before questioning, "Is your brother the baby you thought died with your mother or has your father remarried?"

Maeve looked at him then. He could tell by the look that the thought had never occurred to her. "He is my mother's son. His eyes are green like hers. Maura, the midwife, took him to a wet nurse the night he was born. I did not see her leave the cottage. I thought he had died with Mama; no one told me differently."

Ardan nodded thoughtfully but did not intend to pursue this conversation. He rose then looking at Maeve intently. "Miss, I will leave you now; I am going home for a time but if you will allow me to return to you, I would much appreciate it."

Maeve closed her eyes briefly, sighing. "May you travel safely, Sir. I will see you when you choose to return."

Ardan took her hand; bowing, he kissed it. He took his leave then with much in his mind.

Maeve did not watch him go; she began to think about all he had told her. She moved to the cottage then. Her decision was to visit Maura.

# Chapter 36

Although she spent most of her days with Maura, Maeve was quiet in thought. She paid attention to the instruction from Maura, always asked good questions but daily conversation was lacking. Maura said to her after about a week, "What is troubling you, Maeve? You are always deep in thought. I know you are learning because I can ask you anything; you have the correct answer right there, but then you go back into a reverie from which I cannot shake you. Please tell me what troubles you."

Maeve smiled after this nodding her head, "I know how I have been acting. I am sorry for my behavior. Da and Rylan are upset with me also. I have much on my mind that I am trying to work through but I do have one question I know you can answer."

"What is it, child?"

"Is Rylan my mother's son?"

Maura's eyes grew large as she stared at Maeve, "Why would you ask that, girl? Can you not see her face in his? Those green eyes are her eyes. Yes, he is your brother, completely. Why?"

Maeve relaxed then smiling, "I thought he was; I just had to ask. Someone asked me that question; it confused me. I had to ask."

Maura shook her head as she went back to what she was doing before she spoke, "All right, Maeve, continue, what else is bothering you?"

Maeve cleared her throat, "Did Da want to marry again?"

At this Maura began to laugh, "Heavens, child, if he wanted to marry, he certainly could have. All the single women and widowed women here tried to get him to notice them. He was always wanted by the women here on the manor. Your Da loved Finola so much that I was afraid he would not survive her death. It was a blessing that Rylan was unwell in the beginning. His health gave Colm a reason to live. He walked the floor with that little boy nightly. He did everything possible to save Rylan. Finally with the doctor, the wet nurse and me, we solved the problem. Rylan began to thrive. By looking at him now you would never think he was a sickly child."

Maeve smiled, reaching for Maura she hugged her, "Thank you for my family, Maura."

"Is there anything else?"

"Yes, there is something else. I had decided a few years ago that I would not marry. I wanted to give my life to the people in Grashner. I wanted to be their wise woman; it was going fine until something happened to make them afraid of me. I left then so my reason for not marrying no longer exists but I still do not feel the need to marry."

"Maeve, why would you decide this? Do you love someone you cannot marry?"

Maeve stopped to think, her face doubtful but she finally answered, "No, I do not love anyone except my family and in friendship but not the marrying type of love. I do not think I could love that way."

"You have never met a man who wants to marry you?"

"Yes, I have had marriage proposals but I cannot accept them because I do not think I can love them..not like I should."

"I see. My best advice here is that you have not met the right man. When you do, you will know it. You will want to marry him."

"I do not know. I feel like a child not a young woman who should know her own mind. Thank you, Maura, for talking about this with me. You are someone I love."

Maeve hugged Maura as she left for home.


Maeve's heart was lighter after speaking with Maura so she went to Rylan's garden to sit among the plants. It was pleasant there; it helped her to think. She was working with some herbs when a voice made her look up.


"Miss, we should walk to the river to get water. Some of the plants look thirsty."

Maeve looked about, then she answered, "You are right, Sir. Let me get the bucket."

Ardan took the bucket from her as they began to walk toward the river. Without further discussion, Ardan looked intently at Maeve asking, "Did you never want to marry?"

This question took Maeve by surprise. She stopped in her steps to turn facing him, "I really do not know the answer to that question. My grandmother would talk about when I would married. She told me what it was like to have children. I do not recall ever wanting that but maybe I did."

"What happened to change your mind?"

Maeve thought about this for a long moment. She shook her head, "Why must something have happened?" The look in her eyes only confirmed for Ardan that something had indeed happened, but she looked as if she were searching for the answer.

"I do not know. It seems most women want a husband and family. I was thinking that something must have changed your mind."

"I will now ask you the same question I recently asked my father. Why must a woman belong to a man in her life?"

This question took Ardan aback. A smile crossed his face as he looked at her. The look on his face had a reaction on Maeve that she did not expect. She turned quickly so he would not notice her blush.

He did notice so he approached his next remark very cautiously, "I do not see it as a woman belonging to a man. I see it as a couple... a man and woman who love each other, who feel that life is better together than apart, who want children together to leave something of themselves on the earth."

Maeve looked at him then, a long steady look. She did not say anything right away so Ardan stood quietly not wanting to move, in fear that she would say nothing.

She turned to begin walking again. Ardan still had not moved so she turned back, waiting for him to join her. He moved quickly then to join her. Finally Maeve began to speak, "I have not witnessed marriage closely. Mum was a widow when I went to live with her. I do not really remember my parents' marriage. My memories of them are each of them with me, separate from each other. I remember the day my Mama died. I remember my father crying; the sadness never seemed to leave his face. I believe it is still there but I have added to it."

Ardan moved to her then taking her hand in his. He bent to kiss her fingers. When he stood, her eyes were filled with tears.

Neither spoke again. They continued to walk to the brook where Maeve took the bucket. She began to place it into the water. Ardan bent beside her, removing the bucket from her hands. He grinned at her as she questioned with her eyes what he was doing. "Marriage is a partnership. Husband and wife help each other." He then winked at her, which made her laugh.

Ardan only stayed for the afternoon. He was coming to visit every few weeks but then would return to his home. He just wanted to get to know Maeve. Maeve, on the other hand, was confused by these visits. It seemed to her that he had nothing better to do. This, of course, was wrong; he had much to do. He traveled for his father as an ambassador for the kingdom. His visits home included discussions with his mother about Maeve, plus discussions with his father on how he had finally persuaded Betha to marry him.

One evening his mother suggested he bring Maeve to visit. He thought about this for quite some time before he answered. "Mother, she does not know I am a prince. She knows about you but she does not know I am your son. This is another complication. If she does not want to marry, how can I persuade her to become a princess with the possibility of becoming a queen in the future?"

"I see. So you are still not being completely truthful with her. You must change your approach, Ardan. Tell her the truth; bring her here to meet us. There might be a chance that we can help you."

"Not through spells, Mother, not again. You said it would kill her."

"Not through spells, for spells might kill her. I want to meet her; I can tell what her hesitations are. Let us try."

Ardan agreed, for his longing for Maeve was becoming difficult to navigate.

Ardan was unable to visit Maeve for a fortnight but when he did, he found her in a glen near her home. She was alone but he could hear her voice. It was past twilight so he was afraid to approach her without frightening her. He stood by himself to watch her. He realized she was singing a song of worship to the moon. She was also dancing. He discovered he could watch her forever. She was beautiful with the moonlight turning her hair to a color of blue. When she finished, she sat for a moment breathing deeply. Then, without warning, she pulled her sword from her parcels to practice wielding it. She suddenly changed into a magnificent warrior. Her practice lasted for some time before she bowed to her invisible opponent. Ardan waited longer until she placed the sword so he could not see it. She sat again for a bit. He moved then, making some rustling noises.

Maeve turned her head to look at her visitor. When she was able to see his face, she stood, "Good evening, Sir. I did not expect you so soon."

"It has been some time since I last saw you, Miss. Is it too soon for me to visit you?"

"No, it is not. Oh, Sir, I did not realize it was you."

"Were you expecting someone?"

"Yes, I was. I was expecting a messenger from a young woman with child. I thought she was in labor."

"Ahh, no it is only me. Do people know you visit this glen?"

"My father and brother know. They would have sent him here."

"Maeve, can we speak for a time? There is much I must share with you."

"Sir, of course we may. Our conversations are not usually very long. They consist of you questioning me with me answering your questions."

"Yes, I guess you are right, but tonight I would like to speak with you seriously."

Maeve nodded, indicating the place beside her on the ground. Ardan sat next to her then, beginning his conversation as he took her hand in his. "I visit you as often as I can; as often as I dare. I do not want you to become tired of my suit, but I must be completely honest with you. My name is Ardan, that is true, but it is really Prince Ardan. I have mentioned Queen Betha to you but you do not know that she is my mother. My father is King Cathal. They know my desire is to marry you; they are not against it. I do not understand your unwillingness to marry at all. I cannot explain it to them. They want me to bring you home. They want to meet you. You want to be a healer to take care of the people, but now you have left that village. Miss, please explain to me; tell me your heart so I may understand."

Maeve was looking down as she listened to his words; she looked at him then speaking, "Sir, I must start at the beginning when we met. You were very ill, Cillian, and I was afraid for your life. I did all I could to make you well. We then began traveling together; as we did, we became friends, I think. I must have thought you a friend because I told you what happened to me. You were very kind to me; you said you believed me. Once we arrived here, you were no longer Cillian."

"I have tried to reconcile that my friend, Cillian, does not exist. You have continued your kindness to me as Ardan. Now I learn you are Prince Ardan. Your mother is Queen Betha, the sorceress. You want to marry me, but I am a peasant. I have no idea how a high born lady comports herself. I would bring shame on you. I have thought overmuch about why I do not want to marry; I do not know. I like my freedom but I must admit that something is missing in my life. I do not know what it is though. Is it the love of a man? Is it the love of my own children?"

Ardan was taken aback by this honesty from her. He smiled at her, brought her hand to his lips; then on impulse he moved toward her, kissing her lips. She pulled back; looking at him her eyes growing wide. He whispered softly, "Hush, Maeve," as he kissed her again, this time holding her close.

Her eyes filled with tears; she stood, taking her sword. She began to move out of the glen as Ardan followed her.

"What is it, Miss?"

"I do not know; a memory I do not......," she shook her head. She turned to him then , stopping all movement. He moved to her, took her sword from her hand placing it on the ground. This time, his arms went around her as he pulled her close to him. His lips bent to hers; he kissed her again, this time allowing his passion for her to move through her. She was breathless but neither spoke. He continued to hold her as she moved her arms around him. He whispered to her again, "Please travel with me; I do not think I can leave you here another time."

They stood there in a sense of longing for each other; he took her hands, moving back from her, "Maeve, you said you would shame me since you are a peasant but I must tell you since you are unaware.

You comport yourself as a high born lady, you have been raised and educated as a princess. The way you move, speak, sit shows you are educated in the ways of the nobility. You would never bring shame on me. I would be proud to have you as my wife."

His words to her showed on her face. It was astonishment there as he laughed gently at her reaction. "I knew you did not know; you are fit to be my wife."

He walked her home then. At the cottage he introduced himself to her father once again. He explained his suit; asking for her father's permission to bring Maeve to his home. Colm was surprised by this; he looked at Maeve whose face shone with the moonlight. He then asked her if this was her wish. Her eyes were bright but she nodded slowly. He gave his permission.

Ardan then said he would arrive in the morning to begin their journey. He left then after kissing Maeve's hand.


In the morning Colm was standing outside of the cottage with a horse. He had instructed his son to get ready for this journey.

Ardan road to the cottage as Maeve, Rylan and Colm were discussing the arrangements. Colm turned to Ardan, explaining, "I am sending my son, Rylan, to accompany you and Maeve. I feel she needs a chaperone. I hope that is agreeable to you."

Ardan smiled, "That is agreeable, Sir." Turning to Rylan he asked, "Do you ride?"

Rylan looked ashamed as he shook his head, "No, Sir, I do not."

"I do, Sir. Rylan will ride with me."

Ardan's surprise crossed his face quickly, "Miss, you ride as well?"

"Yes, Sir, I learned to ride here as a young girl; I then continued my lessons in Grashner."

"I see. Sir, we will be on our way. I will take good care of your daughter and son."

Colm smiled as he watched them leave. He quietly whispered, "Excellent idea, Fi."

# Chapter 37

The journey was pleasant as the weather was crisp. It was necessary to wear capes but they also helped to keep them warm in the evening. Ardan spoke frequently to Rylan so he could learn as much as possible about him. Ardan watched Maeve ride; he shook his head as he realized that there seemed to be no end to what this woman could do.

They had traveled two days when they heard pipes and drums playing in the distance. Ardan realized that they were coming upon the inn where he intended to stay that night. He only wanted Maeve's comfort and he was deeply absorbed making the correct decisions.

Since they had begun traveling Maeve had reverted to thinking about Cillian. She was still having difficulty comprehending that her friend Cillian did not exist; he was a man named Ardan who wanted to marry her. When possible she would steal glances at him to memorize his features. He was a large man with auburn hair and brown eyes. His smile warmed her heart as his features softened. She decided he was very handsome and his manner was kind and friendly. Then she would think of Ardan's visits to her; the last time when he kissed her came to her mind. She realized that traveling now was far different from traveling with Cillian. Her brother now accompanied them; they were not walking. When they stopped for the night, the conversation was usually about the travel. Darkness had settled as they looked for a place to rest for the night when they noticed firelight ahead. As they neared the light, they became aware that the pipes and drums were now right ahead of them. Maeve looked quickly at Ardan. She was unsure if they should continue on their present path. Ardan smiled down at her and said, "I believe we have come upon a celebration."

As they approached the village, they could see people milling about while much laughter and merriment could be heard. After they dismounted, Rylan saw the stable so he took the horses to tend to them.

"Good even," an old man came forward bowing slightly to them as they advanced, "my wife has rooms to let for ye and your wife, sir, if ye looking for a place to sleep."

"Aye, that we are, my good man," Ardan replied.

"Just up ahead then. She's called Damatha. Tell her I sent ye."

As they continued up the path Ardan noticed Maeve stiffen. He looked down at her saying, "I promise you, Maeve, you will enjoy the quiet of a room alone. You need not fear me."

The celebration was a wedding but before they reached the cottage, they noticed the bride and groom had just begun their wedding dance. The music of the pipes and drum was so enticing, they stopped to watch as Maeve found her feet tapping to the delightful tune. As she watched the couple twirl to the reel, Ardan moved to accept a tankard of ale someone had offered him. He turned in time to catch the look on Maeve's face. She was radiant as she watched. Her mind had moved her ahead in time as she became the bride dancing to the piper's wedding reel.

She was caught in the spell of the moment, with people cheering the couple, laughter all around. When the dance ended, Maeve sought Ardan. She found him a couple of feet from her and travelled quickly to where he stood. She stood on her toes kissing his cheek. He was so surprised by her sudden boldness that he almost choked on a mouthful of ale. His surprise embarrassed her, so he quickly regained himself, leading her to the innkeepers' cottage. The wife of the old man bustled about as she showed them to two rooms upstairs, one for Rylan, one for Maeve. She told them about the newly married couple inviting them to partake in the celebration for as long as it lasted. She then left the room to get some water for the basin.

Ardan waited till she left and then turned to Maeve, "You rest here for the night. I will see you in the morning." He left then before she could thank him.

The old woman came back quickly with the water, "To wash the dust of the road from ye. Your husband's a handsome man; he said ye need resting so I will bring ye some food to eat."

Maeve removed her garments and poured the cool liquid into the basin. As she began to wash, she thought of the day. Now she was a guest of an inn with a warm bed to sleep in and food to eat. Once her body was clean she poured the remaining water through her hair. It felt so good to her. Maeve pulled a fresh dress from her sack and put it on. As she began to brush her hair, the music began to filter up to her window. She pushed the shutter open to look down into the garden. He was not hard to find as he leaned against a tree with a tankard of ale in his hand. He was conversing with the bride and groom but was so at ease in the situation Maeve felt a bit envious.

He felt her gaze and looked up to see her in the window. She became embarrassed then, quickly closing the shutter. The bride and groom left him shortly to speak with their other guests. This gave him a chance to think more about Maeve

He began to realize that although she had carried much responsibility on her shoulders, Maeve was very young. She was used to being with a crippled man who needed her. Now she was with the same man, but this one was strong. She could be protected now. She knew he loved her but she did not love him. He realized then that he would need to be very patient with his beauty Maeve.

The old woman brought some food to Maeve; once she had eaten her full, she climbed into the bed. Her body relaxed as soon as she laid down. She thought about Ardan; what he wanted from her. He said that he wanted her to be his wife. She did not understand any of this. It scared her. He said she was beautiful and he had wanted her from the first day he saw her. None of this made sense to her but what was that other thing he had said. She was tired now so she was not keeping up her with her thoughts. She closed her eyes as his voice came to her memory, "I saw you in the village one day; I have loved you ever since." He has loved me ever since. Yes, that was it, he loves me. Sleep took over her thoughts.

Maeve woke early in the morning; she immediately dressed, leaving her room to find some refreshment. The innkeeper's wife was in the kitchen so she served Maeve as they carried on a friendly conversation. Once she had eaten, Maeve went in search of the horses. She found them in the stable; she saddled them, bringing them around to the front of the inn. Ardan came out from the inn shaking his head, "You have saddled the horses? You have eaten? Rylan is just getting dressed. Does this happen most mornings?"

"No, Rylan is up before I am on most days but he is out of his routine. I imagine his body aches from traveling."

"Come back into the inn. I will tie the horses."

She went into the inn where she found Rylan eating his breakfast. He smiled at her saying he felt better after sleeping in a bed. She nodded to him as she drank some milk. Ardan came in then joining them at the table. He had not eaten so the innkeeper's wife served him. The woman chatted about the wedding, how lovely the couple was, how happy everyone was for them. Ardan and Maeve smiled as she kept up her conversation not needing anyone else to join. Once they had finished, they went to mount the horses to begin their final leg of the journey. Ardan said they would be to their destination by early evening. The ride was easy since they were well rested. As they came upon the castle, Maeve had a sense of foreboding as she looked at it. Ardan smiled broadly as they rode into the courtyard. Rylan seemed quite impressed with Ardan's home as he asked questions about growing up within the castle grounds.

When they made their way into the castle, a servant came to greet them. A maid bowed to Maeve, picked up her parcel as she guided her to a bedroom on the second floor. Ardan instructed the servant to install Rylan in the bedroom next to Maeve's; the man immediately picked up Rylan's parcel conducting him to his accommodations.

Ardan went to find his parents who were in a downstairs sitting room. The fireplace was blazing as Ardan bent to kiss his mother. He sat then to explain the presence of Rylan; his parents loved the story of Rylan as chaperone. Plans were made for a quiet dinner so as not to intimidate Maeve. Ardan then went to the servants to ask that they tell the guests what time dinner would be served. Ardan went to his chambers. He removed his clothing, then he lay upon his bed. He was glad to be home but the only thing that would make it better would be to have Maeve in his bed as his wife.

Maeve pulled her best dress out from her satchel. She could not imagine it would be adequate for a dinner with a King and Queen. Maeve stood in the room staring at the dress when a knock came to the door. The maid was there with a message that dinner would be served in an hour; then she produced a dress for Maeve to wear. The maid entered the room quietly saying, "Prince Ardan sends this with his compliments, my lady."

Maeve was confused by this; the young maid saw her confusion. She smiled as she said, "Prince Ardan is a very thoughtful man, my lady. I was told he ordered this for you some time ago."

This seemed to perplex Maeve even more; she smiled at the maid as a means of encouragement asking, "More than a fortnight ago?"

"Yes, my lady, it was at least two months."

Maeve shook her head but the smile did not leave her face. She thanked the maid as she left. Maeve began to dress for dinner. Once she was ready, she looked at herself in the mirror. She did not believe her eyes. Was this really her? She moved about checking to be sure that it was her. Then she laughed out loud. Yes, it was her. The dress was beautiful in a subtle way. It was not lavish. The color matched her eyes, bringing a glow to her cheeks. The dress had a modest neckline with pearl accents, a full skirt with accents of pearls at the sleeves. She felt beautiful. She had never dressed as a high born lady.

A knock came to the door. She answered it to find her brother and Ardan waiting outside. Ardan had made sure that Rylan had been dressed fashionably also. He looked very handsome. Ardan stood to the side. He could not take his eyes from Maeve. She was more beautiful than he had ever seen her. She looked at him, smiling, "Thank you for my dress, Sir. It is the most beautiful dress I have ever seen."

He bowed to her then, extending his arm for her to take. As they walked down the stairs to the dining room, Ardan whispered to her, "Truly no woman in the world is more beautiful than you."

The three young people walked into the dining room to be greeted by the King and Queen. Ardan presented Maeve to his parents; she curtsied to them. Young Rylan bowed to his hosts. They were all seated then; dinner commenced. Maeve spoke eloquently during the meal; her education had not been neglected. She was complete in all ways. Ardan observed his parents' reactions to her. He knew they were impressed but there was something more. His father looked at her as a cultured guest. His mother was drawn to her; Betha wanted to know Maeve. After dinner, they retired to the sitting room where the fire continued to burn. Maeve was relaxed now; she felt the dinner had gone well. She and Betha sat near each other as Cathal, Ardan and Rylan sat by the fire.

Betha said softy, "How are you feeling, Maeve? I saw you when you were ill and worried for your life."
Maeve smiled, "I am well, Your Majesty, thank you. It did take some time but I finally feel like myself with much energy."
"I am glad. I do hope you and I can get to know each other while you are here."
"I do look forward to that. I have heard much about you."
Betha smiled, "Really?"
"Oh yes, Ardan has told me about you as did LaLa, Lady Catherine, while I was ill."Their conversation was filled with

pleasantries until Cathal rose from his chair. He looked to his wife as her eyes met his. She stood also excusing herself from Maeve. Maeve caught the nuance in their silent communication. Cathal extended his hand to Betha as she moved toward him. They bid the young people good night leaving the room.

Maeve sat watching the doorway where they had just departed. She rose then to join Ardan and Rylan closer to the fire. The three conversed for some time before Rylan excused himself to retire. This was the first time Maeve and Ardan had been alone since the night of their kiss. He held her hand as they sat in silence. Both of them were marveling at how comforting it was to just sit together. They began to talk again. This time the conversation was more personal.

Ardan escorted Maeve to her chamber. He wished her pleasant dreams, kissing her hand as he made his departure. She closed the door, leaning against it. Maeve began to think about her feelings for Ardan. He had said he loved her some time ago; he had stated more recently that he wanted her for his wife. How did she feel about him?

She removed her dress, put on a nightdress, got into the bed. She laid awake for a bit asking herself, "How do you feel about him?"

# Chapter 38

The morning arrived as the maid entered Maeve's chamber, opened the drapes, served some food. She informed her that the Queen would like to meet with her in her special chamber.

"Will you direct me to her special chamber?"

"Yes, once you are ready, my lady."

"Thank you, Miss."

The maid departed as Maeve got up to dress. She decided to wear the dress that was her best. This was the one she had almost worn to dinner the night before. She looked presentable she thought as she brushed her hair and she decided to braid it. She finished the food on the tray. She had some tea as she waited for the maid to return. The maid returned shortly to bring Maeve to the Queen.

Maeve entered the room thinking it might be a sitting room but it was not. She curtsied to the Queen; the Queen began to give her a tour of the room. It was filled with plants sitting near the windows. There was a long work table with several jars on the shelves above. A cabinet stood in the corner with glass jars containing dried herbs. Flasks stood on the table. Betha told Maeve about potions she made. Maeve was fascinated by this; she absorbed everything the Queen told her. The Queen noticed she was a fast study. They discussed Maeve's ambitions to become a midwife. Maeve explained her mother's death; how she did not want that to happen to anyone else ever again.

Betha was impressed by Maeve's empathy; she brought her to another space to show her some herbal mixtures for childbirth. Betha prepared some vials for her to take with her when she left.

Betha taught Maeve much that first morning. They enjoyed each other's company while Ardan took Rylan to the stable to check the horses. Then he put Rylan on a horse to begin to teach him to ride. Both Maeve and Rylan were enjoying their stay.

During the weeks that followed Rylan excelled in riding. Maeve had not seen him ride as she usually spent the mornings with the

Queen in her special chamber. They conversed about the spell that they had been placed on Maeve. Betha explained that it was a dark spell that she found. She told Ardan that he had to pour his love into it for it to bring the results he wanted. Ardan was unhappy about the idea. They argued long over it but he finally accepted because he wanted Maeve. Betha saw the results of that spell on Maeve in Grashner. She prayed for Maeve's recovery. She had been ashamed because she did not know about Maeve's history.

Evenings were spent as was the first evening with quiet dinners, conversations in the sitting room. Maeve observed the Queen's relationship with her husband. There was a closeness that could only be explained by their years together. A look here, a gesture there, eye contact so subtle that when they rose at the same time to retire for the night, it seemed as if Maeve had missed part of the conversation. When she and Ardan were alone, she asked him about it.

"Your parents are very connected to each other. They do not seem to communicate but they know what the other is thinking. It is something I have never witnessed."

"My parents are very much in love with each other. They communicate very often. We have not seen it because it is private. They are available to us but they are available to each other first. It is what I explained to you; it is a partnership. My father fought for my mother to marry him; he wanted her but she was afraid to marry. It worked out in the end. Neither have taken their union for granted; they remember where it all started."

"I have so enjoyed being here, Ardan. I have learned so much from your mother. I just wonder why they have welcomed me. I am, after all, just a peasant girl."

"Maeve, the peasant girl, it is time to retire for the night," Ardan laughed when he said this.
Maeve smiled shaking her head, "Yes, it is. I am very tired."

"I knew that since you were beginning to talk nonsense. Come, I will escort you to your chamber."

Ardan was pleased that it was going so well until Dubhlainn came home. Dubhlainn had recovered from his injury after a few weeks. He was eager to leave the castle grounds so he left for a time.

Dubhlainn came to the stable as Ardan and Rylan were tending the horses. The brothers looked at each other.

"Ardan, you are here. Who might this young one be?"

"This is my friend, Rylan. I am teaching him to ride."

"Ah, it is a worthy pursuit, brother. How do you do, young Rylan?"

Rylan bowed slightly saying, "Fine, thank you, Sir."

Dubhlainn left his horse for the groom as he headed for the castle. Ardan stood watching him wondering if he should follow him. He then remembered that Maeve was with Betha so she should be fine.

Betha and Maeve were in the sitting room when Dubhlainn entered. He bent to kiss his mother, then turning to Maeve, he said, "The Sword Maiden, how are you this day?"

Maeve looked at him, remembering him vividly. She said courteously, "I am fine, Sir. I see you have recovered from your injuries."

Betha looked between the two of them before saying, "Maeve, you were the one who injured Dubhlainn?"

Maeve looked embarrassed as Dubhlainn looked amused. "Yes, I must admit that I did injure him, Your Majesty."

Betha smiled broadly, then said to Dubhlainn, "Dinner will be at the usual hour. I would suggest you clean up from the road."

Dubhlainn bowed to his mother before leaving the room.

Maeve sheepishly looked at Betha who spoke, "To be bettered by a woman is a good lesson for him. He is not always courteous or kind."

This was all she said but Maeve felt there was much more to this. They both retired to their chambers to prepare for dinner.

The dinner this night was not as relaxed as the others had been. The conversation was more formal. Maeve chose to speak only when spoken to and Ardan was extremely quiet. Betha, Cathal and Dubhlainn did most of the talking. Rylan sat observing the behavior of everyone at the table. When they retired to the sitting room, Dubhlainn excused himself to retire to his chamber. Both Cathal and Betha watched him go. They sat together this evening. It took a few moments for relaxation to come upon them but soon they began having a pleasant conversation with the young people.

Ardan told everyone how well Rylan was doing with his riding lessons. Betha remarked how astute Maeve was with herbs and healing. Both Rylan and Maeve blushed as they were praised. Everyone was laughing; enjoying themselves. There was a crash from upstairs; a woman's voice could be heard shouting, "No." The two men looked at each other as they rose to leave the room. Maeve, Rylan, and Betha sat not moving or speaking.

The men went upstairs. After a time, there was shouting. Footsteps could be heard dashing down the stairs as a girl was sobbing. The girl was running toward the kitchen as the crying subsided. Betha rose then, running from the room. Maeve looked at Rylan as he looked back. He spoke, "I would like to go to my chamber but I am afraid what I would find upstairs." Maeve nodded.

They sat together not talking. Finally Ardan came into the room. He suggested they go for a walk. They left the castle.

As they walked, they did not speak until Ardan broke the tension. "My brother can be difficult. He enjoys causing harm to people. My parents were not aware for a long time what he did here. Now they know and have tried to put a stop to it. It is troublesome to them because he is their son; they love him but they do not love his behavior."

Maeve did not know what to say; she did not feel it would be appropriate to ask questions but the questions were coming to her one after the other. They moved to a wooded area where they could sit for a time. As they watched, they saw Dubhlainn mount his horse, leaving the castle grounds. Ardan waited, then moved everyone back inside. He accompanied Rylan and Maeve to their rooms telling them both to bolt their doors.


This next morning was different. It was not the usual maid who came to Maeve's chamber. There was a knock so Maeve had to unbolt the door to let the maid into the room. It was an older woman this time. She did everything the younger maid did leaving after a few minutes. Maeve dressed quickly so she could go to Betha's special chamber. She found Betha crying softly when she arrived. She had spent several weeks with the Queen but she was not sure of protocol. She quickly made up her mind as she put her arms around the Queen.

Maeve spoke softly, "I am sorry you are so sad, Your Majesty. Is there anything I can do?"

Betha changed the subject asking, "Do you love Ardan?"

Maeve continued to hold the Queen; softly she answered, "I ask myself every night if I love him."

Betha pulled away from her then, holding on to her shoulders. The Queen looked into her eyes, "I do not see any love for a man in your eyes other than my son. You have been witched. This is why you are confused. You did not want to marry because of this spell but now you are not certain. I see the spell has been softened; it was changed from its original intent some time ago. This adjustment has allowed you to find love. You must accept it if you want it, for it is now in front of you."

Maeve stared at Betha, "I am under a spell that did not allow me to love?"

"That was the original spell; it was changed so you could love."

"Oh, who? Who would do such a thing? Who hated me that much?"

"It was not hate but love; that was why it was changed…guilt because of love."

Maeve quietly said, "Please stop, Your Majesty. I do not want to know any more. My heart is already broken."

Betha hugged the girl. "We all have broken hearts, Maeve. My son, Dubhlainn has broken my heart many times. Cathal and I do not think it was the way he was brought up. He should be more like his brother but he is far different."

Betha moved to the window bringing Maeve by the hand. She pointed to a tree outside. "Do you see that tree? We had that planted on the day the boys were born. See how one side is beautiful with leaves turning colors, but the other side is dead; there are no leaves. We have had the tree cut back several times but the one side is dead. This tree represents my sons. One side is beautiful, alive; the other side is ugly, dead."

Maeve looked outside in time to see Rylan and Ardan ride across the meadow. She then said to Betha, "Your Majesty, may I ask, was your marriage arranged?"

Betha laughed saying, "My husband arranged it. I did not want to marry. I asked my father to refuse all suits. He did refuse all suits. Cathal saw me at the wedding of my brother. He inquired about me but he was told that I would not marry. He sent some friends to investigate the reason. I was afraid to marry. When I was a child, I laughed one day at an old gypsy woman because I found the way she spoke funny. She cursed me for laughing at her; she said, 'When you marry and marry you will, you will conceive twin sons on your wedding night. The mixture of moon and stars will be upon you and the children of your womb will mix also. One will be your sorrow, the other your joy. Neither will be complete and your motherhood will be shattered.' I decided never to marry. Cathal found out why I did not want to marry. He began a search for the old gypsy woman."

The Queen continued, "My parents had me learn at the hands of my father's magician. Together, he and I tried to reverse the damage. My father also looked for the gypsy woman. She was never found but Cathal did find a younger gypsy woman who was cursing a boy one day. He asked the woman about curses. He truly believed that she was the granddaughter of the woman who cursed me. We went to visit her; she said she could lessen the curse but not reverse it. We put our trust in her. She said the curse was lessened. So I married him."

Before Betha resumed her story, she poured each of them some wine, "Now we are not so sure if she lessened the curse at all except the part about being complete. We believe our sons are complete. Ardan is completely good but Dubhlainn is completely bad. It is so hard to escape. We talk about this overly much. Last evening Cathal told Dubhlainn to leave the castle for good. I do not know what will happen but for now all is quiet."

After a time Betha said, "Your curse was against your loving, but it was changed so you would love."

Maeve nodded, "I will go to my room, if I may."

Betha smiled, hugged her again to let her leave.

Maeve went to her chamber where she got on the bed; she realized that there had been another betrayal. This time so she would not love. Why? Betha said it was for love of her.

"I cannot think of this. This hurts so much; it is another loss," The tears were a steady stream down her cheeks; finally she cried herself to sleep.

Later there was a knock on her door; as Rylan came into the room she awoke.

"Maeve," he said, "Ardan would like to see you if possible."

Maeve sat up, "Where is he, Rylan?"

"He is downstairs in the sitting room. He is alone."

"Thank you, Ry. I saw you ride today. You look very accomplished."

"I love riding, Maeve; I am so grateful to Ardan for teaching me."

She nodded to him, giving him a hug as he left the room.

Maeve straightened her dress, checked her hair in the mirror and left the room in search of Ardan.

He was sitting near the fire when she came into the room. He stood immediately; moving to her, he took her into his arms, "My darling, Mother said you were upset when you left her. Are you feeling any better?"

"I believe I am feeling better. I cried myself to sleep but I seem to have a better outlook now."

She put her arms around him, holding him close. He bent to kiss her; her heart was full. "Oh, Ardan, could we feel this way for the rest of our lives?"

Ardan looked at her face; he looked into her eyes. He began to kiss her again but she pushed him away. "Please stop. I cannot keep kissing you. My heart is bursting, Ardan."

Ardan was confused until she moved to kiss him. He then began to laugh. "I know, Maeve, my heart is bursting also."

They sat down then opposite each other in front of the fire. Ardan spoke first, "Maeve, you have moved my heart. For a time I did not believe I would love again but you have shown me that I have never loved till now. I want to live my life with you. Please say you will become my wife. I do not think I can live without you."

Maeve's eyes blurred with tears, "Ardan, I do love you; I will be your wife if you will be my husband, my partner. I do not want to belong to you unless you will belong to me."

Ardan pulled her off her chair then as they landed on the floor, "I will belong to you, Maeve, all of my life."

He kissed her then, again and again. She struggled to breathe as he said her name over and over. They were still on the floor when Betha and Cathal entered the room.

"Mother and Father, Maeve has consented to be my wife."

Suddenly there was much laughter; Ardan and Maeve stood up to hug the King and Queen.

Betha stopped and said, "When shall we make the wedding?" The laughter continued.

# Chapter 39

Melchiarc approached Lord Brian with respect but intent on making his point. "My Lord, I believe it is paramount that Lady Catherine travel to Parrisal before she is much further along. She will need an experienced midwife but there is no one here who can help her."

Brian looked at his old tutor with intensity. "I see. Do you believe that my wife is in jeopardy or possibly the child?"

"Yes, I believe they both are. Queen Betha informed your mother before she left that the Lady might have difficulty delivering the child."

"Why is this the first I have heard about this?"

"I am sorry, My Lord, I just found out myself."

"Thank you, Melchiarc. I will see to the arrangements."


Brian went to visit Catherine in her chamber. Catherine had been having trouble sleeping for a time during her pregnancy. She was unable to get comfortable so Brian chose a lovely room for her to stay. He did not want to disturb what sleep she was able to enjoy. They spent the evenings together in their sitting room but then he would walk her to her new chamber before going to the room they used to share.

Catherine was reclining on her bed when he came into the room. She was awake but did not sit up. Brian sat in a chair next to the bed after kissing her.

"How are you, my love?"

"I am fine, Brian. I was feeling fatigued as I sat reading so I laid down to see if I could sleep. Of course, as soon as I did, our child began to kick," she laughed, "I was enjoying the movement."

Brian placed his hand on her stomach and the baby kicked, his eyes grew very large. "He is in great form today." They continued to sit together without speaking.

Catherine broke the silence after a few moments, "Brian, did you want to discuss something?"

Brian came back from his reverie saying, "Yes, I did come to speak with you. Do you feel up to traveling? We thought it might be wise to move to your father's home for the birth of the child."

"Yes, I can travel now. In a few weeks I might not be able. But, my darling, who is we?"

"Oh, Melchiarc is concerned since there are no midwives here. My mother is also concerned."

"I see," was all Catherine said. Brian sat looking out the window at the leaves turning colors in the trees.

Again Catherine broke the silence, "Tell me, Brian, will you come to stay with me or will you return here to come again later?"

"I have not given it much thought," he said honestly, "I will probably come with you to stay unless I receive word that my presence is needed here. I do not see that happening, to be honest." His eyes went back to the leaves being blown from the trees by a strong wind.

"When shall we leave?"

"I will send word to your father, give some directions to the necessary servants, make arrangements here. Hopefully in two days time."

"I will be ready then."

Brian rose from his chair, kissed Catherine, left the room to begin the arrangements. Catherine closed her eyes hoping she could sleep for some time.

Brian went first to speak to Melchiarc. The old man was seated at his old desk reading a manuscript. He look up to see a very troubled young Lord standing before him.

Brian spoke, "Melchiarc, what is the problem with Catherine's pregnancy? Will she survive the birth? Will the child survive the birth?"

"My Lady is a small woman, but from the way she looks, I believe she is carrying a large child. No one in Grashner is a midwife. I fear the birth will be difficult for her. I can give you what potions I have to alleviate pain but someone with skills should be in attendance at the birth."

"Please give me whatever you can for her. I must make arrangements for the journey."

In two days time Brian and Catherine were ready to leave. They made their farewells, setting off early in the morning. Catherine sat in the carriage as Brian held her hand. They enjoyed the scenery but Catherine had something on her mind, "Brian, why could we not have sent for Maeve?"

"I asked Padraig to bring her to the manor. He informed me that Maeve left some weeks ago."

"Left? Where did she go?"

"I do not know. Padraig was not certain either. He said the garden had not been tended for some time. Molly, from the village, distributes herbs to the people now but she has let the garden go to seed."

"Maeve might have gone to Parrisal. She may have gone home to her father and brother."

Brian looked at Catherine, "Her father and brother? Her father never came back for her. Maeve believed he must be dead. She thought her brother died with her mother."

"She did? If she believes they are dead, then would she go home?"

"Why go home if you do not think your family is alive?"

"You know her father, Brian."

"I do?"

"Yes, Colm, the farrier at the stables, is Maeve's father."

"Colm, I liked him; what about her brother? Do I know him too?"

"His name is Rylan. I have only seen him a few times when he was young."

"No, I have not met him."

After two days' travel, they arrived at Lord Aengus' manor. He came out to greet them; he gave instructions to the servants to get their parcels to the rooms.

Aengus looked at his daughter, then gave her a hug, "You are a beauty, Catherine. You look so much like your mother standing there with child." Brian and Catherine laughed at this. They all walked into the manor to see a small dining table set with refreshment.

Catherine smiled as she said, "I am so hungry, Father. Thank you for this."

Brian grinned saying, "We ate but an hour ago, my love. Please do not let your father believe that I starve you."

Aengus replied, "I remember it well, Brian. I told you, Catherine, that you look like your mother; she was always hungry too."

They all sat at the table enjoying the food. Once they were finished, Brian accompanied Catherine to their room. They found two beds which was not the way it was once they were married. A servant came in telling them that the Lord told them to replace the large bed with two smaller ones so the Lady could toss and turn to her heart's content. Brian helped Catherine settle on her bed for some rest. He left the room heading for the stables.

When Brian arrived, he found Colm immediately. Colm looked at him, smiling, "Lord Brian, it is good to see you. We heard you would be visiting."

"We are here for more than a visit. Colm, I just found out that you are Maeve's father. Have you seen her recently?"

"Yes, she came back a few weeks ago. She is not here now though."

"Do you expect her back any time soon?"

"I am not certain when she will be home."

"When she does come home, could you let her know that Catherine and I are eager to see her?"

"Yes, I will send her directly to you, Sir."

~

Maeve and Ardan began discussing their return to Parrisal but both were reluctant to leave their present accommodations. They were close in proximity to each other; they were enjoying their interactions with Ardan's parents.

However, one morning Betha went to Maeve's chamber accompanied by Ardan. Maeve opened the door.

"Is something wrong?" she asked.

Ardan spoke first, "We are not certain but Mother believes that Lady Catherine has gone to her father's home to have her baby. There was no one in Grashner to help deliver the child."

Betha stated, "Melchiarc told Lady Mirima to get Catherine to her father's home where there are midwives."

"Is Catherine in trouble with her pregnancy?"

Betha answered, "I believe she is. I told Mirima to take care of her before I left."

"Then we must leave as soon as possible, Ardan."

"Yes, we must."

Betha added, "We can send you in the small carriage."

Maeve looked at Ardan shaking her head, "No we can ride; it will be quicker."

Betha turned to Ardan, as he said, "No, Mother, my love is a wonderful horsewoman."

So they packed with the plan to begin the journey early in the morning. They were up before dawn, broke fast but heard rushing footsteps as they started out the door. Betha came running to Maeve with a small vial in her hand, "You remembered the herbs and potions I gave you? This is especially for Catherine. Use it for her labor, it will give her strength."

"Thank you, Your Majesty; it may save Catherine."

Shortly after this they started for Maeve and Rylan's home. They traveled past the inn where they had stayed the night before they arrived at the castle. Maeve wanted to travel as far as possible the first day; Ardan and Rylan agreed with her. The day was cold but they went quite a distance before they decided the horses were in need of watering and rest.

Rylan built a fire as Ardan tethered the horses nearby. Maeve brought water from the brook for them before laying out the meal for her travel companions and herself. Rylan seemed to be exhausted so he ate quickly before making his bed to sleep. He fell asleep as soon as his head rested on the ground. Maeve smiled at him then grabbed her sword as she held up a finger to Ardan. She leaned in for a kiss, "I will be right back."

Ardan watched her go knowing full well what she was about. He smiled remembering the night he had watched her in the moonlight. He would watch again some other night. Tonight it was best to keep an eye on the fire, Rylan and the horses.

Time seemed to pass slowly for Ardan but then he heard the horses whinny; he looked about to see if Maeve had caused this. Soon he saw the man creep from the woods, moving slowly toward the horses. He clucked at them as he untied the first horse. Rylan woke suddenly, dashing toward the man but he was grabbed by the robber around the throat. Ardan moved to the man with his sword drawn.

Ardan spoke softly, "Now what do you think you are doing, good Sir?"

The robber turned to Ardan holding the reins on the first horse but he still held Rylan with his other arm. "I'll be takin' your horses. If this young man doesn't quit his jumping about, I'll break his neck with a twist of my arm."

Rylan stopped moving with this warning as Ardan glanced up to see Maeve coming softly behind the robber. She pressed the point of her sword into the man's back.

"Let go of my brother."

The robber felt the sword being pushed toward his left side. He slowly moved to turn but the point of Maeve's sword pressed harder, drawing a pin prick of blood. The man released Rylan as Ardan grabbed the boy's arm pulling him around to the back.

Maeve then commanded, "Release the horse."

The man did so as he turned to face his attacker. Maeve caught Ardan's eyes then; she moved her head to let him know there were more men in the woods behind her. She mouthed, "Two."

Ardan moved swiftly up the bank to the wooded area. A grunt or two could be heard before the two men came down the bank with their hands in the air and Ardan behind them with his sword. Rylan grabbed a rope from a horse; he then aided Ardan in tying the men to a tree.

Maeve looked at the man she was holding, "So I saved your life so you could aspire to the grand occupation of horse thief."

"Oh, Miss, it is you?"

Ardan walked up to the two looking at the man who tried to rob them. "Aye, he is the one who told me about you."

"Yes, I know him. This is Liam, once soldier, now horse thief."

"Please, Miss, do not look harshly at me. We are desperate to get to the soldiers' camp. We have not been able to catch them on foot. We must get there quickly. Your horses seemed our best chance."

"Without a thought for the people who own these horses, you decide this is your opportunity."

"Miss, surely you can travel on foot. You are not in a hurry as we are."

"Ahh, again you have made presumptions that are untrue. We are in a hurry, Liam. I am trying to get to my friend who may die in childbirth if I cannot get to her. Two of these horses belong to the King and Queen, one belongs to Lord Aengus. These are not mine to give you." Maeve was furious.

Ardan stepped to the young man, moving him to the fire to sit.

Ardan then began to question him. "Why are you not with the soldiers? Are you deserters?"

"No, Sir, we are not deserters. We were separated from them. I was wounded, as were my companions, but they did tell us to get to them as soon as we could travel. We went the wrong way, finding another camp of soldiers but they were not ours."

"Ahh, in what direction should you now travel?"

"We are going south of the castle where our companions will be waiting."

"What is the hurry?"

"We have heard there is a battle coming. We must join them before it begins."

"What battle? Who is fighting this battle?"

"I dunno, I only know gossip."

"What gossip?"

"The Prince is gathering an army to fight for the throne."

Ardan stood then. He looked down at Liam before walking to Maeve who had not moved since she came down the hill.

"Did you hear what he said?"

"Yes, I heard. Of what Prince does he speak?"

"My instinct tells me it is my brother. He is angry with my father, jealous of me."

"Should you go back to the castle then?"

"No, I will see you safely to Parrisal before heading back."
Ardan then moved back to the fire where Liam sat staring at his friends. Ardan's glance to the others was just in time to see one of them pull the rope from himself as he ran to the trees. Rylan was lying near the other, unconscious.
Maeve ran to her brother; she found a wound on his head which was bleeding. He had been struck by a rock. Ardan ran to the other prisoner, untied him, and dragged him to the fire where he tied him and Liam to a tree nearby. He warned them to sit still.

Ardan retrieved Maeve's bag, and bringing it to her, he knelt beside Rylan. Maeve tended to the wound as Rylan woke. He gasped in pain, apologizing. Ardan whispered to Maeve that he would see if the third robber was up in the woods. He left then as Maeve stood with her sword in hand. She walked slowly to the two prisoners.

"What army is this you are joining?" she asked.

Liam answered, "The King's army, Miss."

"King?"

"Yes, Miss, King Cathal's son is raising an army to fight for the throne. It seems there is a usurper attempting to steal the throne."

"Usurper? What is the name of the usurper?"

"I do not know, Miss. This is all I know."

Maeve heard Ardan behind her with the third man. He tied him to the other two. Maeve moved toward Rylan as Ardan came up to them.

Maeve whispered, "This army they talk of is for your father to fight off a nameless usurper. The army is being raised by your father's son."

"I see. Rylan, do you think you can travel now?"

Rylan looked at Ardan, "Yes, I believe so. My vision has cleared."

"You will ride with me, Rylan. You can rest as best as possible. We will stop later to see how you are feeling."

Ardan moved to the horses. He checked their saddles and reins. He helped Maeve onto her saddle and lifted Rylan behind her. He mounted his own horse as he turned to the prisoners.

"Do not believe these rumors you are hearing. Sit here by the fire until you can untie yourselves. To join an army the prince is raising would be treason."

The three left the prisoners by the fire. They traveled quickly, Ardan held the reins of Rylan's horse. Rylan leaned his head on his sister's back closing his eyes. After traveling for a small amount of time, Maeve felt Rylan slip to the side but Ardan grabbed him before he could fall. Maeve looked at Ardan with tears in her eyes. They found another place to stop. Ardan lifted Rylan from the horse, as Maeve made him a bed. They covered him as he slept.

Ardan took Maeve by the hand as he led her away from the sleeping boy. He pulled her to him; as he kissed her hair beside her ear he spoke, "Do not worry, Maeve. Rylan will be fine. Do not worry, Maeve, Catherine will be fine."

Maeve put her arms around him saying, "I am worried about you and your family."

Ardan chuckled then whispered, "Do not worry, Maeve, we will be fine."

He kissed her deeply then.

They went back to Rylan where they laid on either side of him to create warmth. They managed a few hours of sleep without disturbance. Rylan woke as the sun arose in his eyes. He found himself in the middle of Ardan and Maeve. He laid still until they woke themselves.

Maeve looked at his wound as they readied themselves for the road. Rylan seemed fine; he mounted his horse as they mounted theirs. Ardan knew of a small inn on the way where they would stop to eat.

When they came to the inn, the proprietor brought them food, hot tea and news. He told them of the soldiers going off to what might be a civil war. He was not certain what man was raising the army but the soldiers passed through some days ago.

"How many soldiers, Sir?" Ardan inquired.

"Dozens but then three passed through alone a few days later. They were on foot."

"News travels quickly, does it not?"

When they had finished their meal, they again mounted their horses heading for Parrisal. Two more days of travel brought them to the manor.

Colm was at the stable when they arrived. He rushed to see his daughter and son. He shook Ardan's hand thanking him for the safe return of his children. He imparted to Maeve that Brian and Catherine had asked for her. She was to see them as soon as she returned. Rylan stayed with his father to care for the horses. Ardan and Maeve went on to the cottage. Maeve cleaned herself up, changed her clothing, running out the door just in time to see Ardan coming back from the river. He had cleaned up as well.

They then went directly to Maura's cottage. Maura was not at home so they headed to the manor. A servant answered the door; holding them in the foyer, he went to find Lord Aengus. The Lord came from his study. He looked at his servant then, "This is Miss Maeve, bring her immediately to my daughter."

The servant scurried up the stairs with Maeve running behind him.

Lord Aengus turned to Ardan, introducing himself, "I am Lord Aengus of Parrisal, Sir."

"I am Prince Ardan, son of King Cathal and Queen Betha."

Lord Aengus' eyes grew large as he bowed to the Prince, "How good to meet you, Your Highness. Please come to my study. I will send for refreshments."

# Chapter 40

The servant knocked at the door of Catherine's chamber, announcing Maeve's arrival. Catherine had been asleep so Maeve stood quietly by the door waiting for her to realize she was there. Catherine looked at Maeve. She sat up in bed as Maeve went to hug her.

"Oh, LaLa, it is so good to see you with rosy cheeks. You are a beautiful mother-to-be."

"Tiny One, I am so glad you are here. We heard you had left Grashner but no one knew where you went. I thought you had come here to see your father and brother, but Brian told me that you believed them to be dead. I am so sorry you believed this. I could have told you they were alive."

"It is all right. We have spoken about my mother's death, what has come to pass. My father is not over her death; he feels ashamed of his treatment toward me. I understand his longing for her; he looks at me only seeing her. His face wears the mask of grief always; even when he smiles it is melancholy."

Tears came to Catherine's eyes as she hugged Maeve again. They did not break their embrace immediately. Maeve began to ask Catherine questions about her health. Catherine said that she could not sleep very well because she could not get comfortable. The baby was not due for a few weeks. She stood so Maeve could see how she was carrying the baby; Maeve confirmed that she was not ready to deliver yet.

"Tomorrow, Catherine, I will bring Maura here. She is the midwife. I want her to confirm what I have told you. I think you should walk daily. I will walk with you because you must gain strength to deliver the child."

"I will do what you tell me to do. It will be wonderful spending time with you again. When you were at Grashner you were so ill, it was difficult to spend time with you."

"Yes, I know. You and Brian took such care of me. I will always be grateful. So now it is my turn to care for you and I am up to the task."

"Maeve, when you left Grashner, how did you travel here? Were you alone?"

A sadness came over Maeve's face but then she smiled, "No I was not alone. I was accompanied by a hunchback who became a friend. He made sure that I arrived here safely. He was ill but I was able to help him in his illness."

"A hunchback, Maeve, were you not afraid of a stranger?"

"No, I knew he meant well."

A servant knocked at the door then, "Lady Catherine, your father inquires as to whether you can come down for dinner this evening."

"Yes, I will be down. Thank you."

The servant curtsied leaving the room.

Catherine turned to Maeve, "Father has made accommodations for you down the hall. He wants you close by if I need you. Will you stay?"

Maeve smiled, "I will do as requested but I do need to see my father sometime this evening."

Lord Aengus and Ardan were having refreshments in the study when Brian came into the room.

Both men stood as Brian entered. Lord Aengus presented Prince Ardan to Lord Brian of Grashner. Both men bowed to each other, taking their seats.

Brian seemed surprised to find the Prince visiting, "I believe, your grace, that our mothers are acquainted. Your mother visited us a few months ago in Grashner. Was it for you she was searching?"

"Yes, I am afraid I caused her much worry then, but she has forgiven me," Ardan smiled.

Lord Aengus answered the question for Brian, "Prince Ardan accompanied Maeve here."

Brian's eyebrows lifted then, "Oh?"

Ardan found all of this amusing, but he kept a straight face as he stated, "Maeve and Rylan were guests of the King and Queen. We heard your Lady would be here to deliver her child. Maeve was extremely eager to come here."

With that Lord Aengus asked the Prince where he was staying while he was visiting.

Ardan answered, "There is a tavern a few miles away where I stay. The innkeeper has become a friend."

Aengus shook his head, "May I extend an invitation to you to reside with us? There is plenty of room."

"That is very kind of you, thank you, Sir."

Brian inquired, "Will you be here for a time, your Grace?"

"No, Sir, I will be leaving almost immediately. I have heard rumors that trouble me so I must visit my father."

Brian and Lord Aengus both nodded.


A servant knocked politely on the door, "Your Lordship, Lady Catherine says that she will be down to dinner." Aengus thanked the servant, requesting that he escort Prince Ardan to the guest quarters as soon as it was ready for him. The servant bowed; as he turned to leave Maeve stood behind him. The servant announced Maeve's presence.

Maeve walked in smiling, as she curtseyed to the men. All the men stood as she entered; she turned to see Brian who immediately hugged her wishing her welcome.

"I have news," she said, continuing to smile, "Catherine is not in any danger at this time. The child will not be delivered for a few more weeks. Tomorrow I will bring our midwife, Maura, to meet her and you, of course. I believe that Catherine needs exercise so we will walk together in the mornings. It will help her gain strength for labor."

Brian and Lord Aengus both smiled broadly, thanking her at the same time.

A servant again entered the study to announce that dinner would be served immediately. Brian left the room to escort his wife into the dining room. Maeve looked slightly perplexed as she seemed to be ready to leave the manor entirely.

Lord Aengus noticed this so he spoke, "Miss, please join us for the evening meal. You are most welcome. Catherine told you, did she not, that a room has been prepared for you?"

"Yes, my Lord, Catherine told me. Thank you for your kind invitation."

Ardan smiled as all this took place. He then extended his arm to Maeve as they proceeded to the dining room. As they walked he whispered, "We are in a slight dilemma, Maeve. I have not yet formally asked your father for your hand in marriage. Therefore, we cannot tell these kind people our relationship. I have been invited to stay the night also."

Maeve whispered back, "Yes, I saw this would an interesting state of affairs. But after the meal, I must see my father. Will you accompany me, kind Sir?"

Ardan laughed, "Yes, of course, I will be honored to escort you, my Lady."

As they all gathered around the dinner table, Ardan noticed how attentive Brian was to Catherine. He also noticed that Brian seemed baffled by Ardan and Maeve. Lord Aengus kept the conversation flowing but it did eventually come around to Ardan having to leave in the morning.

"Your Grace, I do not mean to pry but you talk of rumors and your father. Might it be these rumors we have heard about an army being raised for a battle to come?"

"Yes, Sir, I heard of these tales on our travels to Parrisal. I know that when we left the castle, my father had not heard any such rumors. I must get to him immediately."

"Your Grace, the roads are full of soldiers, would you permit me to send some of my men with you during your journey?"

"I had not expected such a kind offer, Sir. That would be most appreciated."

Brian whispered to Catherine briefly. She gave him a nod of her head before he spoke, "Your Grace, since my wife is not near her time, would you accept me accompanying you on your travels?"

"Sir, you are certain you want to do this?"

"Yes, your Grace, I would be most honored to travel with you."

"Very well then, we leave at dawn."

The men who would also travel with Ardan and Brian were sent for so they could meet to discuss the arrangements. The meeting did not last very long. Brian came to escort Catherine to their chamber. Maeve was waiting for Ardan as well. She bid farewell to all explaining that she must visit her father. Ardan announced that he would accompany her to the cottage. They left then as the three others stood watching and questioning.

On the walk to the cottage, Ardan held Maeve's hand as they spoke of the beautiful evening. When they arrived at the cottage, Ardan knocked on the door. Colm came out looking between Ardan and Maeve. Ardan spoke softly, "Sir, may I have a word with you?"

Colm accompanied Ardan down the road a bit.

Maeve went into the cottage to pack a few things that might be useful to have at the manor house. Rylan came in, "Is Ardan asking for your hand in marriage, Sister?"

Maeve turned, "Do you know?"

"It was hard not to hear the gossip in the castle."

"Gossip? What was said, Rylan?"

"The servants seemed excited that Ardan was to be married. They like you very much because you are kind and thoughtful. They do wonder who you are. They never heard of you, but they think you are beautiful."

Maeve nodded but did not say anything. This was something she thought would happen.

After quite some time, Colm and Ardan returned to the cottage. They invited Ardan in for the first time. Colm looked at Maeve, drawing her into his arms, "Your mother once said that you would be perfect for a prince. We did not believe that it was ever possible."

"Father, do you approve?"

"How can I say no to a prince who loves you? How can I say no to my daughter who is radiant like I have never seen her? I approve; I wish you years of happiness together."

Maeve hugged her father close. Ardan smiled as Rylan shook his hand. Then Rylan hugged Maeve.

"I will not be leaving until after Catherine delivers her child. There is some time before that happens. I will bring Maura to her tomorrow. Ardan is leaving tomorrow though."

"How long will you be gone?"

"I am not certain, Sir. It will depend on the state of affairs at the castle. I do not intend to be away for very long."

"Da, I forgot to mention that Lord Aengus requested me to stay in the manor to be close to LaLa. So I will be staying there at night. I will come to visit you during the day."

"My daughter staying in the manor is not anything I ever thought would happen," Colm chuckled, shaking his head.

"Sir, I will be leaving at dawn with Lord Brian, Barry and Breccan. They will travel with me."

"I know their horses so I will make sure all is well with them. Are you returning with both of the horses from the castle?"

"No, Sir, I will leave Maeve's horse for her."


Ardan and Maeve bid goodnight to Colm and Rylan. They walked back to the manor to find the house very quiet. There was a servant there who brought them to their rooms. Maeve looked about her room as she realized that she and Ardan had not said farewell. She placed her herbs and potions on a small table. As she walked to the wardrobe, she heard a soft knock at her door. She opened the door cautiously. Ardan stood in the hallway.

"My love, I came to wish you a peaceful night. I hope to be back soon," he kissed her lightly on the lips as he checked to be sure no one was in the hallway.

"Please be safe in your travels; I will miss you."

At this Ardan looked at Maeve realizing that they had been together for weeks but now they would be separated. He pushed her into her room lightly pulling the door closed. Then he turned to her; his hand pushed some curls from her face. "I will miss you. Even if I am gone but a day, it will feel like an eternity until I see you again." He kissed her passionately then. When he stopped, he looked at her sheepishly. "Maeve, I am sorry. I should not be here in your room. I think you should check the hallway to be sure no one is in the vicinity."

Maeve smiled opening the door. She did not see anyone in the corridor so she motioned for Ardan to leave. He did so. He headed to his chamber further down the hallway. He stood outside his room for a time just to be sure no one was hiding. It was very quiet so he moved inside.


Maeve was awake before dawn. She heard movement in the hallway so she investigated. The servants were scurrying about lighting fires in the bed chambers. Brian emerged from his room as did Ardan. Catherine even came into the hallway. The four young people said goodbye to each other as the men went downstairs. Catherine said she was going back to sleep longer. Maeve went downstairs. She helped herself to a biscuit as she headed for Maura's cottage.


The cottage was quiet but Maeve knew that Maura was an early riser. She knocked on the door. There was no answer. Maeve knocked again. She peeked in the window but all was undisturbed. The kettle was not on the fireplace. She knocked again. Still there was no answer.

She sat on the stoop noticing that the wooden stool was not there. She then became more observant. The garden was in disarray. An old woman walked down the road from her cottage; she looked at Maeve, frowning. Maeve recognized the woman so she moved toward her as she came along side Maura's cottage.

"Good wife, please tell me if you have seen the midwife about."

"Not for days have I seen her, Miss."

"Do you know where she was going when she left?"

"Did she leave then?"

Maeve was confused by this. "Maura does not seem to be here at her cottage. Is she somewhere delivering a babe perhaps?"

"No babies here. All women have delivered or died."

"Died? Who has died, Good wife?"

"May, flowers on the corner died. Her baby died with her."

Maeve did not know May; she was not one of the women she had met with Maura. Maeve thanked the woman; she ran to her father's cottage.

Colm was not at home nor was Rylan. Maeve remembered that he was going to check the horses before Ardan left with his party. Out of breath though she was, Maeve ran to the stables.

Colm was standing by the fence speaking with Rylan when he saw Maeve running toward them.

"Hold, my girl, what troubles you?"

"Da, where is Maura?"

"I do not know. I have not seen her recently."

"Did someone called May die in childbirth with her baby?"

"May? I know no one by that name."

"I saw the old good wife. She told me May, flowers on the corner, died."

"Your mother had flowers on the corner of the garden."

"But her name was Finola not May. That was years ago."

"The good wife, you said? The old woman gets confused; she probably thinks your mother died yesterday. She used to call Fi, May. 'Flowers come in May', she used to say."

"But my mother's baby did not die with her."

"No, he did not; but at first, people thought he did die."

"But, Da, where is Maura?"

"Maeve, go back to the manor, have something to eat and I will ask here."

"Thank you, Da." She hugged her father as she headed back to the manor.

She went back to her bedchamber to rest for a bit. Her heart was pounding. She entered the room to find a maid stoking the fire. "Miss, I have brought you some breakfast. I did not know if you were coming back to your room."

"Thank you so much. The room feels good, so warm. I was outside; I am chilled I think."

"Your tea may have gone cold since I brought it in. I will bring you more."

The maid left the room. Maeve looked to see what was on the tray. She ate some fruit until the maid returned with hot tea.

Maeve looked at the girl, asking, "Miss, do you live here on the manor?"

"I live here in the servants' quarters."

"Do you know Maura the midwife?"

"I know of her. She has not returned I hear."

"Where did she go?"

"She left to deliver a child in Lavandor some two weeks ago."

"Oh dear, did anyone accompany her?"

"I know not, Miss. That is the rumor on the manor grounds."

"Thank you."

The maid left then leaving Maeve to pace the floor. She drank her tea as she finished the food on the tray.

Maeve could ride to Lavandor to ask about Maura. It was a small village. It should not be hard to find the woman who had the child. However, she could not leave Catherine. She was in her care. She must stay here with LaLa. These were rumors, that may be all or Maura may need help. She had to go. Why did Maura travel to Lavandor to deliver a child?

Maeve went to Catherine's room to find her dressed, sitting in her chair. Maeve asked her if she was ready to go for their walk. Catherine stood and the two women began their exercise. Maeve thought they should visit the horses so they walked to the stables. Maeve walked to her horse to speak to him. Catherine came up to her saying how she remembered Maeve talking to the horses. Colm came up to Maeve then, "I have asked around. One of the men here say that she went to Lavandor to deliver a child."

"I heard that too. I cannot imagine why she would go to Lavandor."

"No one here knows any more than that."

"I was told she left two weeks ago."

Maeve then said to her father, "Can you saddle my horse for me, Da? I am riding to Lavandor."

Colm stared at his daughter, "Alone? You cannot go alone."

Maeve said, "I am going, Da, alone, if necessary. I am terrified for Maura. She may be in trouble."

Catherine heard this debate. She came up behind Maeve placing her arm around her waist. "What is the trouble, Maeve?"

"Maura is gone from her home. She is said to have left two weeks ago to deliver a child in Lavandor. I am worried for her safety."

Colm shook his head, "Maeve, how can you risk your own safety? Ardan does not want you to leave the security here. You cannot go."

Catherine said, "We will ask my father to send someone to find her. I do not want you to risk your safety to find Maura."

Colm breathed a sigh of relief, "Thank you, my Lady, that is a wonderful solution."

Catherine smiled as she took Maeve by the arm directing her back to the manor house. They found Lord Aengus in his study. He looked up when the two young women walked into the room.

"Father," Catherine started, "Maeve's friend, Maura, the midwife, is said to have left to deliver a child in Lavandor. She has been gone for two weeks. Maeve is so concerned that she wants to ride herself to find her. I thought that we might be able to send a messenger to investigate Maura's whereabouts."

"Maeve, I will send someone to investigate. I cannot allow you to leave by yourself."

Maeve smiled, "Thank you, my Lord, I appreciate your willingness to help. I also think we need Maura here for Catherine's delivery."

"Done. We will send someone immediately."

Maeve curtseyed as she and Catherine left Lord Aengus.

Catherine took Maeve's arm saying, "Do you feel a little better, Maeve?"

"Yes, my dear friend, I feel I can relax a bit, but who knows how long it will take for word to come back to us."

They went to Catherine's room after asking for some food to be delivered. They sat conversing for some time until Catherine finally asked, "Maeve, who is Prince Ardan to you?"

Maeve smiled warmly, "He is my betrothed. We will be married after your child is delivered. We could not tell you last evening because Ardan wanted to ask my father for my hand in marriage before we told anyone our plans."

Catherine was unable to say anything at first. Finally she hugged Maeve congratulating her, calling her Princess Maeve. They both laughed at this.

Maeve stood then, telling Catherine it was time for her afternoon walk. The women left the manor house to walk the grounds.

Colm saw the women on their walk so he met them on the way.

"Lord Aengus has sent a man to search for Maura. He has just left the grounds."

"Thank you, Da."

"Thank you, Lady Catherine, I could not face my daughter going off looking for this woman."

"You are most welcome, both of you. I could not stand by to let Maeve leave."

Colm walked back to the stables breathing easier.

After dinner that evening, Maeve accompanied Catherine to her chamber. She helped her to get ready for bed, adjusting pillows for her to ease her pain.

Maeve instructed Catherine, "If you wake and cannot sleep, come to get me or send someone for me. I do have some medicines that might allow you to sleep but it is better that you sleep naturally if you can."

"I understand. I was able to sleep last night; but for Brian leaving I might have slept longer."

Maeve smiled at her friend, "I know. I laid awake myself thinking of Ardan leaving. I will see you in the morning unless you need me sooner."

With that Maeve kissed her friend on the cheek, leaving the room.

# Chapter 41

Ardan and his party travelled very well the first day. They had no contact with anyone on the road. They decided to camp that night for they had been given food provisions. Barry started a fire as Breccan watered the horses. Brian made up a bed for himself as Ardan did the same. When the other men joined them, they too made up beds. The firelight was bright and warm. They spoke quietly as Ardan told them about the last time he had camped on the road. He spoke of the three soldiers who decided to steal their horses. Ardan was a wonderful story teller as he described everything in detail including Maeve coming down the hill with her sword. Brian smiled at this saying that Maeve was excellent with a sword. Ardan's smile was warm, full of love for Maeve. Brian wondered about this. He still did not know the truth of their relationship.

In the morning the men were up just before dawn to begin their day of travel. Again they were not seeing any travelers on the road. Ardan hoped this was a good omen. He and Brian were able to converse for a time as they rode. Brian asked if he knew the man who was attempting to raise an army. Ardan acknowledged that he believed it was his brother. Brian thought about this so he did not ask the question in his mind. He did ask about Ardan's relationship with Maeve.

Ardan smiled at this question, "Maeve is my betrothed. We will marry after your child is born."

Brian smiled, "Congratulations, your Grace. Maeve is a lovely, kind woman. May you have a long life together."

"Thank you, Sir. We are looking forward to just that."

The day wore on as they made good time. They arrived at the inn a day near to the castle so they stayed the night. The wife of the innkeeper remembered Ardan as she asked for his wife. He smiled saying that she was in very good health. Brian raised an eyebrow not saying anything. Ardan made a remark that it was a way of protecting Maeve's virtue.

The following afternoon they arrived at the castle. Betha and Cathal welcomed them graciously. Ardan mentioned quietly that he needed to speak to them privately. The servants bustled about preparing rooms, dinner arrangements and conducting the guests to their chambers. As soon as the guests were delivered to their rooms, Ardan told his parents why they were there.

Cathal's frown was one of trying to come to terms of what he was hearing. "He is raising an army?"

"That's what is being said in the country. We heard it from three soldiers who attempted to steal our horses on the way to Parrisal."

"How did you manage to keep the horses? How did you defeat three soldiers? Three to one…"

Ardan laughed at this, "Did I tell you that Maeve is very accomplished with a sword?"

Cathal chuckled, "You have found yourself a wonderful woman, Son. I commend your choice."

Betha laughed too, "She is a remarkable young woman. But I see Brian has traveled with you; he was not hesitant to leave Catherine?"

"We had it from Maeve that Catherine is a few weeks from delivery. Brian and Catherine made the decision that he could travel with me."

"It will be good to speak with Brian. He is a nice young man. I should like to inquire as to his mother."

"Father, what are we to do about Dubhlainn? He is lying to the soldiers, telling them that your throne is in jeopardy, that there is a usurper coming to steal it. He is your son, why should they not believe him?"

"I will speak with my commander on the morrow. We must handle this wisely. Dubhlainn can be difficult but this is beyond anything I ever thought him capable."

"Yes, it is. Since he has been gone, has everything been quiet?"

"It is quiet, maybe too quiet now that I think of it."

Cathal arose then; he walked to the servant standing near, "Summon the commander, please. Send him to my study immediately."

Ardan rose then. They went to Cathal's study; Betha went to her special chamber.

Betha took a deep breath in her chamber but in a concentrated effort began gathering bottles, surgical tools, threads, needles, alcohol, and bandages to assemble saddle bags for the field surgeons. If war was coming, they needed to be ready in all aspects of the fight.

Cathal, Ardan and the Commander of the King's troops stood looking at the maps of the kingdom. The commander assured King Cathal that he was unaware of the rumors but suggested a scouting mission first to determine the accuracy of the situation. He thought he should send out his most talented scouts. They would report to him their findings.

Cathal cleared his throat, "What then, Commander, if the rumors are accurate?"

"Then, I go to the men assembled with my army and command that all soldiers report to the castle. Thank them for their loyalty. See what transpires next."

"I should be the one to command them to the castle. If they see me and they are loyal, they will come."

"I will accompany both of you then," Ardan stated in a finality of tone.

The men agreed upon this plan of action. The Commander would summon his scouts upon his return to the fortress.

Cathal and Ardan went next to the sitting room to find their guests had been served some ale before dinner. Cathal noticed Betha was not among them; he excused himself going in search of her.

Betha was not in her bedchamber so he moved to her special chamber. There he found her in battle staging planning.

He took her by the arm, turning her around, he said, "I hope your preparations are premature, my heart." He kissed her then.

"It is best to be prepared, my king. Do you have a plan, Sire?"

Cathal raised his eyebrow, "My king, sire? We are in battle staging, are we not, my queen. Yes, we have a plan. I will explain it to you after dinner when we are once again alone. But let us go down now, our guests are assembled in the sitting room with only Ardan to entertain them."

Dinner was a pleasant affair; Betha noticed that both Cathal and Ardan seemed very at ease. It appeared that Ardan and Brian had a budding friendship which made her smile. It was determined that the three men would stay until Ardan felt it safe to leave the castle to return to Parrisal.

After dinner they adjourned to the sitting room where Brian sought a chair near Betha. The conversation started with the usual banter but then Brian was more to the point.

"Your Highness, Melchiarc tells me that you warned my mother about Catherine's pregnancy; I wonder if you can tell me what it is that concerns you."

"Melchiarc told you?"

"Yes, he did."

"It is something that I cannot explain very well. It has to do with my intuition. I felt that Catherine was in danger with her delivery. Her pregnancy will be very healthy; there will be no jeopardy in that time period. It is when she goes into labor she needs to have expert help. Tell me, Brian, your mother did not convey this information to you?"

"No, Melchiarc came to me saying Catherine needed to be moved to her father's house because she needed a midwife. He said that he spoke to my mother; it was then she mentioned to him that you had cautioned her. He found out the same day he told me."

"She is safe now. Maeve will do all she can for her including bringing in the more experienced midwife. I have sent some medicinals with Maeve for Catherine that I thought might help."

"Thank you so much, Your Highness."

"You are welcome, Son. Now may I ask how your mother is faring since the death of Lintel?"

"She is different, your Highness. Some days she is quite the same; pleasant, social but other days, she does not emerge from her chamber. She cries but you can hear her talking to an invisible personage. The servants knock on her door to bring her food but she will not open. They do not like to go to her room on those days. I am not certain what to do for her. One other thing I might mention but please do not convey this to anyone. On some days she appears to be jealous of Catherine. We have talked about it but do not know how to handle this either."

"I am so sorry to hear this. If I may think on this I might come up with something to soothe her."

Brian nodded but then resumed the conversation. "My parents were never the type of people to tell me about their youth. I do not know how they met or fell in love. Or why they married. I know you knew my mother as a girl; can you tell me anything about them?"

Betha nodded but wondered where to start; she finally began to speak."My father and your grandsire were friends. Your grandfather came to visit us during the summer almost every year.

When Lintel was old enough to enjoy the summer with us, he would come with his father. He grew up with my two brothers and me. Now your mother was the daughter of my father's top advisor; she had her own friends but there were times on special occasions when we would all play together. As we got older we would be thrown together more and more. I tried to stay out of the limelight. I did not want to marry. I persuaded my parents to keep me single. I was afraid to marry. With many of the parties that were conducted to celebrate this and that, there came a group of young women who set their cap for my brother, the future duke; your mother was one of them. My brother was a handsome man, Ardan resembles him at times. He was not terribly interested in marrying; he was only 18 at the time. He enjoyed hunting most of all, but he was a good dancer. The girls flocked about to dance with him; he accommodated them. He danced with them all. There was one particular girl who danced as well as he did. Her name was Mary; she was a pretty little thing. He liked dancing with her because she could anticipate his moves. One evening he and Mary had been dancing for a long time; Lorcan, my brother, had neglected to dance with all the girls. The music stopped for a bit so all the girls and boys were milling about the room. Suddenly there was a loud commotion; Mary was found on the ground with a twisted ankle. Lorcan went over to Mary, picked her up and brought her to a room so our physician could look at her injury. Lorcan came back to the party to dance with the other girls. Your mother was the one he danced with mostly. He found her to be fun; she was also a good dancer."

Brian interrupted the story, "Your Highness, tell me, was my mother the reason Mary twisted her ankle?"

Betha looked at Brian rather stunned, "There was gossip that it was Mirima's fault but it was never confirmed."

Brian continued, "I am sorry for the interruption, Your Highness, please continue."

Betha resumed, "In another year or two it came time for Lorcan to choose a wife. It was then he came to me. My intuition had been tested within my family; they would ask me my opinion on things mostly concerning people. Even my father would ask me what I thought of gentlemen who visited. So Lorcan asked for my opinion of the girls he liked. There were five of them that he thought he might like to wed. I thought that was rather a strange way to think of marriage but I accepted his challenge. I began to socialize more with the girls my brother danced with at the parties. My other brother began to dance with the same girls plus a few more who thought he might make a good husband. I had conversations with all of the girls. There was one I thought was perfect for Lorcan. Her name was Brigid. She was the daughter of a lord."

"You did not like my mother?"

"I liked your mother but not for my brother. I had the feeling that she would always have to come first in their marriage. He was very giving; he needed a giving woman. I talked to both my parents about marriage suggesting to my father that he should have a conversation with my brother about falling in love and marriage. My father did speak with him. Lorcan decided that none of these women were right for him. He waited two more years until he met the love of his life, Aoife. She was a true godsend to him."

"So, had my mother met my father yet?"

"Oh yes, she met him years before this but her eyes were on the moon not a star. The girls who were fighting for Lorcan moved to my other brother, including your mother. Now my second brother would not be a duke but he would be well off; the problem is that the girls are getting older too. Lorcan married at 23. My brother, Nollaig, started to look for a wife. He was 21 at the time. He was easier than Lorcan. Nollaig fell in love very fast with a girl called Katerina. The other girls began to scramble to find husbands. Lintel, dear sweet man that he was, looked at Mirima thinking she would be a good match for him. I know that they tried to dissuade him. Melchiarc told him she was not the girl for him. Lintel did not wait to fall in love; he proposed. Mirima put him through a long waiting time before she accepted. She looked for a better option but no one else was interested. Lintel and Mirima were married at the Grashner manor. Now the rest of the story, I do not know."

"I know some of it. I am sorry that I know it. I found journals of my father after he died."

Betha was concerned with this information. How much did Brian know of what his parents did to him and Maeve?

"Father wrote in his last journals that the marriage had been a mistake. He did for her but she was not inclined to do for him. He said he never fell in love with her; some people advised him that love came later. He said it did not."

"I am sorry, Brian. I probably told you too much."

"No, Your Highness, you told me what I surmised. It was just more accurate detail than my assumptions," Brian laughed as he said that.

"Brian, your marriage to Catherine is happy, is it not?"

"Oh yes, I have not been an observer of marriages; but I knew that I did not want a marriage like my parents'. Catherine is wonderful; we want what is best for each other."

"You are friends, Brian."

"Yes, we are friends."

Brian noticed that Cathal had stood, made eye contact with Betha. She stood then, excusing herself from Brian, wishing everyone a good night. Cathal took her hand as they left the room. Brian watched thinking to himself; they are friends.

Cathal and Betha went to her bedchamber. She poured them each a goblet of wine as they sat near the fire. Betha shook her head, stating, "Brian asked me about his parents tonight. I feel guilty for telling him the story of his mother chasing my brothers."

Cathal laughed, "Did you tell him about his mother chasing after me?"

Betha laughed then, "No, I will save that story for another time."

Cathal then changed the subject to the plan for the armies being raised. He explained everything to Betha; she asked questions but agreed that it was a sound plan.

Betha said, "It is a beginning. I just hope it is the end as well."

"Yes, my love, I agree."

Cathal looked intently at Betha saying, "Darling, would you mind if I stay here with you tonight?"

Betha smiled, "Cathal, of course, you can stay. May I ask why you are still leaving every night to sleep alone?"

Cathal frowned, "I do not know. We started it when you were pregnant with the boys. You could not sleep so I left so you could sleep alone. Then it continued as I walked the floor with the boys at night so you could rest. Then I could not sleep so I walked the floor myself at night. I did not want to wake you so I have stayed in my room."

"May I say what I have been thinking? We are getting older, I want you by my side at night; I want to be able to touch you. Can we please go back to the way it was when we were first married; when you used to hold me as we fell asleep? I want you, Cathal, for the rest of my life."

Cathal stood, pulled Betha into his arms, "I want you, Betha, for the rest of my life."

Cathal removed her clothing as she removed his; their passion for each other had never wavered during the years. He lifted her, placing her on the bed. As he moved in next to her, he began to kiss her lips; his kisses moved down her neck.The bed became a paradise for them as their rhythm created a frenzy of passion. They released together. They held each other closely, falling asleep beside each other.

# Chapter 42

The weather was getting cooler as the leaves turned colors falling to the ground. Maeve began her day early as she went to the stables to bid her father good morning. She also went to find out if the messenger had returned home. Maeve then traveled to Maura's cottage to see if her friend was home. This continued each morning; she then went to Catherine's room so they could walk. They spoke of everything possible. Catherine was intent on keeping Maeve's mind off her friend, but she could tell that Maeve became more nervous by the day.

Maeve met with the Parrisal physician to discuss Catherine's condition. He felt Catherine was doing well; the walking helped her to become stronger. The exercise helped her to sleep at night.

Maeve was ill at ease. She found it hard to sit still. She would leave the house to walk on her own retracing her steps from the morning. Her father saw this; his concern was palpable. Rylan noticed how tense Maeve was and it was causing his father's worry. He ran to catch up with Maeve to walk beside her.

"Maeve, you must calm yourself. Do you see you are causing father worry?"

Maeve glanced as they passed their father. She noticed the tense set of his jaw.

"I see what you mean, Ry. I must keep myself away from him while I struggle with worries."

"He does like that you come in the morning but when you start walking for something to do, he begins the worrying."

"Rylan, can you say something of comfort to me? Something to help me to feel my heart beat normally."

Rylan stopped walking; he held Maeve by her shoulders, looking directly into her face he softly spoke, "Maeve, what can be done has been done. Someone has been sent to investigate. You think it is a messenger, but it was not a messenger. Tierney was sent by Lord

Aengus. Tierney is a warrior. Tierney is in love with Maura; he wants her back so he can marry her."

Maeve stared at Ryland, "Is this true, Ry? I never knew Maura had a suitor. He must have been worried like me."

"He was; when Lord Aengus said he was sending a messenger, Tierney volunteered. Lord Aengus was hesitant at first but when Tierney told him his relationship with Maura, he let him go."

"He's been gone two days now? How long does it take to get to Lavandor?"

"He should have been there early afternoon yesterday."

"Oh please, Tierney, find Maura for both of us." Maeve began to cry. Rylan hugged her. They began their walk again. Rylan walked her back to the manor house suggesting she lay down for a time; he promised he would come to tell her any news. Maeve went to her room; she laid down. Her heart settled into a steady beat. She began to picture Maura coming home. It made her happy as she fell asleep.

Maeve awoke realizing she and Catherine had missed the afternoon walk. She got up running down the hall to Catherine's room. She knocked on the door but there was no answer. She turned the doorknob going into the room. Catherine was on the bed. Maeve shook her but she did not respond. Maeve shook her again but there was still no response.

Maeve ran into the hall calling for a servant. The young maid appeared; Maeve directed her to get the physician. He came into the room a few minutes later to find Maeve shaking Catherine. He began an examination of Catherine. She was not breathing so he checked her throat. He found a piece of apple in her airway. Once he removed it, he began to push her chest. They sat her up as Catherine began to cough. Maeve's eyes filled with tears. She silently vowed never to sleep again in the afternoon.

The maid brought tea to Catherine's room. Catherine and Maeve sat together speaking of ordinary things. Maeve kept watching

Catherine, afraid she would vanish before her eyes. Maeve asked Catherine if she knew whom her father sent for Maura.

Catherine smiled, "He sent Tierney."

"Do you have faith in this Tierney?"

"Yes, Tierney is a very large man. He is strong and they have whispered that he loves Maura."

"In other words, if anyone can find her, Tierney is the one."

"Yes, Maeve, Tierney is the one."

In the morning Maeve checked on Catherine before she did anything else. Catherine was up but not dressed. Her throat was sore so Maeve sent to the kitchen for tea along with her breakfast. Maeve told Catherine she would be back for her soon but first she was going to check Maura's cottage. Maeve left the manor then heading straight for Maura's cottage. There was some reason for her intensity this morning. Was it intuition? Maeve did not know but it was urgent that she get to Maura's cottage.

When she arrived there was a horse tethered to a tree in the front of the cottage. Maeve paced up and down for a minute until she decided to knock on the door. She tapped on the door, calling Maura's name. She waited. She waited. She paced. The door opened and there like a miracle stood Maura. Maeve grabbed her, crying.

A man came to the door next speaking softly, "Maura, do I need to rescue you again?"

Maeve stopped hugging Maura, asking, "Are you Tierney?"

"I am, Miss." Maeve grabbed him, hugging him, crying, "Thank you."

Maura said to Tierney, "Do I need to rescue you?"

Maeve stopped and they all began laughing as Maeve wiped her face of the tears. Maura took Maeve by the hand, pulled her into the cottage, "Let us have tea. There is much to tell you, darling girl."

As Maura put the kettle on, Maeve and Tierney sat at the table.

Tierney spoke, "Thank you, Maeve, for your worry for Maura. If you had not requested someone look for her, she might not be here now. I was worried that she had not returned but the Lord would not have sent me to look for her. It was your request plus your insistence that Lady Catherine would need her as midwife that got the Lord to find someone to go. I told the Lord that I wanted to so he let me."

"I have been so worried; I have been pacing, crying and just worrying. But tell me, what happened to you?"

Maura smiled, "Maeve, I was very frightened. The woman whom I was meant to help went into labor before I arrived. There was no one there to help her. She died with her baby. I arrived before she died, but I could do nothing to help her. Her husband was distraught but he decided that I would stay to be his wife. He would not let me leave. He told me we would marry once his wife and child were buried. He would not listen to reason. He then decided that we did not need to marry. He wanted to know if I could bear children before he married me. Thankfully, Tierney, got there during the funeral. He asked about and found me. We left immediately, but not before Tierney told the bereaved husband that I was not available to marry him. Tierney and I were married last night."

Maeve sat there staring at both of them. "I am so happy for so many reasons. I am happy for your marriage, for your safe return and because you are home in time to help with Catherine's labor. Oh, yes, I am to be married."

"You are to be married, Maeve? To whom?"

"To Prince Ardan, son of King Cathal and Queen Betha; we will marry after the birth of Catherine's child."

Now it was Maura and Tierney's turn to sit and stare.

"I will leave both of you, for this is your wedding morning. When you can, please come to the manor to meet Lady Catherine." With that Maeve left the cottage; she went then to the stables to visit her father.

Colm saw the smile on Maeve's face; he surmised that Maura and Tierney were back but Tierney had yet to bring the horse.

He whispered to Maeve, "Are they back?"

"Yes, but say nothing. They were married last night; Tierney will bring the horse back." Colm winked at his daughter. She hugged him before leaving, heading back to the manor.

At the manor she found Catherine dressed, drinking tea. Catherine was waiting for Maeve to walk with her.

"LaLa, how is your throat? Do you feel better yet?"

"Yes, the tea was a good idea; it is soothing the soreness."

"Can you tell me how you came to choke on an apple slice yesterday?"

"I was tired, but as I was reading I took a piece of apple. I must have fallen asleep with the apple in my mouth. I think my sleep was deep because I was unaware of anything."

"We need to be careful, Lala, Brian would not appreciate it to find you were brought down by an apple slice."

Catherine and Maeve both laughed at this but Maeve was very conscious that she almost lost Catherine. They walked then; it got colder every day so Maeve made sure that Catherine wore a warm cape, bonnet and gloves. Catherine made Maeve do the same saying that she needed to be well when she married.

That was the second time Maeve's upcoming marriage had been mentioned, although it was Maeve who brought it up first with Maura. Maeve had not thought very much about it but now she went deep in thought. Catherine noticed the concentration on Maeve's face.

"Tiny One, what is it? Are you afraid to marry?"

"No, I am not afraid but I do have concerns. Ardan scoffs at my worrying about our different positions in society. Rylan told me that the servants at the castle like me but they wonder who I am and from where I came. I do not understand the willingness of the King and Queen to accept me."

"Queen Betha seemed very nice when I met her in Grashner but I got the feeling she was reading my mind."

"She is very astute. She has the ability to see people, to see into their hearts."

"I see; did she say anything about me?"

"No, but she was worried about your delivery. She told me you came to Parrisal to use the midwife since there are not midwives in Grashner. I came back as soon as I could."

"Maeve, I am so happy you will be with me when I have this child. You will make certain that I survive and my baby with me."

"Catherine, I will do whatever is necessary to get you through this." Catherine hugged Maeve. They continued walking.

When the walk was complete, Maeve retired with Catherine to her room; they had some more tea with biscuits. Maeve noticed Catherine was attempting to get comfortable on her bed. They adjusted pillows around her body to help her to rest. Maeve covered her, telling her to sleep; she picked up the remains of their meal leaving the room. The maid was about so she took the tray from Maeve; Maeve instructed her to not feed Catherine again until the midday meal when Maeve would be with her.

Maeve walked out of the manor again to look about the gardens. As she moved about the herbs, she saw Maura heading toward her. The two women hugged when they came together but Maeve took Maura by the hand, drawing her to a quiet seat away from all activity.

Maeve looked at her closely, "Maura, was the story you told me this morning complete? Is that all that happened?"

Maura nodded knowingly, "Tierney does not know all. I cannot tell him all."

"Were you raped?"

"I …no, I was not raped, but the man was crazed. He stripped me of my clothing. He locked me in the room, naked. He would come to see me. He talked about how we would have children together. The only reason I was dressed when Tierney found me was because the man's neighbors were coming to the cottage after the funeral. He made me dress, clean and prepare food."

"Maura, this is a dreadful tale. Tierney would have killed him if he knew."

"He almost did. He held the man at the point of his sword; he told him that I was his, his betrothed. The man was nervous but crazed, as I said. He told Tierney that he had already impregnated me. I had the feeling he wanted Tierney to kill him. I whispered to Tierney that the man was insane; that he hoped Tierney would kill him. Tierney got on the horse. We rode away but he did ask me if I had slept with the man. I told him that I had not; we married in a small village with a church. He found out that I was still a virgin on our wedding night."

Maeve smiled, hugging Maura, "I am so happy you are home. Do not let these memories trouble you. Put them behind you."

"Thank you, Maeve. I will try. I walked over to meet Catherine. Are you concerned with her pregnancy?"

"Catherine is tiny. She is carrying the baby quite high right now but she is large with child. She had not been able to get comfortable so she was not sleeping. I have mixes I could give her to help her sleep but I have waited before doing that. Yesterday she fell asleep with a piece of apple in her mouth. It choked her. I happened to find her unconscious. The physician determined she was choking so he managed to save her. I sat with her then; the baby was moving normally."

"I would like to meet her if now is a good time."

"Yes, it is almost time for the midday meal so we can wake her if she is still sleeping. We have been walking twice every day. Her strength seems to be increasing but it also helps her to sleep."

"That is good news, Maeve, you are doing good work. So as we walk to the manor, please tell me about this prince you are marrying."

Maeve laughed; she held Maura's arm as they walked to the manor.

# Chapter 43

The Commander of the King's army presented himself to the King two mornings after sending the scouts to investigate the rumors of the Prince raising an army. Ardan joined them as they sat down to discuss the results.

"Sire, there is indeed an army being raised but it is your army. The scouts recognized the men who are training. They are your soldiers. The Prince was not seen. They saw tents that might be the Prince's headquarters but he never showed his face."

"Then we continue with our plan. We ride to command the men to assemble here at the fortress. We do not tell them until they have gathered here that they have been duped."

All three were in agreement; they would leave at dawn the following day.

Cathal went to Betha who was still in their bedchamber. She was sitting at her dressing table brushing through her hair. Cathal came to her, moving his hand through her hair.

"Betha, the rumors are true. Our soldiers have been gathered; they are training for war but Dubhlainn was not seen."

"You believe it is him?"

"I can think of no other prince who would do this, using our men."

"I have loved him. I did not play favorites; I loved them both the same. Why did he turn away from us?"

"May be because I forbade him to return here."

"That was the last straw. All of those young women being taken and raped. He is not a good man but I do not know who in our families he resembles."

"He is the one to cause us sorrow. That gypsy girl had no means to lessen her grandmother's curse. I wanted to believe her because I wanted you."

"I wanted you, so I believed her."

"We can only hope that we are able to thwart this plan of his that will bring death to our soldiers, chaos to our land."

Betha thought for a moment before she spoke. "Cathal, should you be dressed for battle in case something goes awry? Should the field surgeons be equipped for battle?"

"I believe you are right, Betha. I will speak to Ardan and the Commander. We must be prepared for all eventualities."

Cathal went to see Ardan; Betha went to her special chamber to finish packing the bags in case of wounds or injuries.

After dinner that evening Ardan and Cathal adjourned to discuss the plans for the morning. A knock at the door caused a pause in the discussion. Brian came into the room, "Your Grace, Ardan, might I offer our services in the morning?"

"Brian, this is no fight of yours. Why would you want to place yourself in jeopardy?"

Brian backed up to the chamber door, opening it to admit Barry and Braccan.

"Your Grace, we came here with Ardan to make sure he arrived safely. If we do not assist you in completing this plan, then we came for naught."
Ardan and his father looked at each other, shaking their heads and smiling.

Ardan spoke, "Gentlemen, we accept your kind offer but let us work out a strategy that allows us to use your expertise to its maximum."

It was decided that the three visitors would accompany some of Cathal's soldiers into the hills above the campground to keep watch. They would leave first with a scout to guide their way. Cathal, Ardan and the Commander would follow. They adjourned for the night then.

Ardan asked his father, "Why do you think Dubhlainn, would try to defeat you in your own castle? Do you think he really wants the throne?"

"No, he has not been trained for the throne as you have been. I think he was jealous of you because you were the older brother and would one day be king. He always accused us of playing favorites but we were very careful that we did not. I think he was furious with me when I told him to leave forever. I think he is retaliating for that."

"Father, those poor maids he raped, impregnated; that poor girl who threw herself off the balcony. You have grandchildren all about the country. How do you forgive a son for that? I cannot forgive him."

"I cannot forgive him. His last attempt to hurt that new maid was the end of it. That's why I told him to leave. I am sad; your mother cries over it. She blames herself."

"Poor mother."

Ardan left for his bedchamber but stopped by his mother's work chamber first. He knocked on the door. When he entered the room, his mother had piles of herbs, bandages, and operating tools all the way down her work table. He helped her finish up; then he hugged her long and hard. "I love you, Mother, sleep well."

Betha smiled as he left; a feeling of warmth encouraged her to think of the lovely Maeve who would soon be Ardan's wife. "She will brighten this castle; she will brighten my son."


The men left early the next morning as planned. Betha arose in time to bid Cathal goodbye. She dressed, ate a small breakfast; then she paced the floor. She sat for a time where she could look out the window. She dressed warmly to go out into the garden. Betha walked up and down the garden path, listening for the sound of horses. One of the maids came out, begging her to come in for a small meal. Queen Betha thanked her, said she would be there shortly; she continued to walk the garden path.

The maid waited a time before returning to the Queen. She watched the Queen pace but as she started toward her, the Queen stopped. She turned her head, listening. There it was, the sound of horses. The maid heard it too. In their places they watched and waited.

The first soldiers could be seen heading to the fortress; some officers were at the head. Betha watched. There were more soldiers coming than had left that morning. As long as Cathal, Ardan, Brian, and the Commander came soon, it might have been a success.

Finally at the end of the battalion, she could see Cathal. He was strong in his saddle; she knew then he was unharmed. Ardan rode next to him with Brian next to him. They were safe. She went inside.

Cathal did not come into the castle for a time. He had ridden to the fortress. Betha guessed that the third part of the plan was taking place while she waited. She paced but this time she was just eager to learn the details of what had happened. Finally, Cathal walked into the bedchamber. She flew to him; they embraced.

"Darling, can you tell me?"

Cathal chuckled, "I think I should take you with me the next I almost go to battle. It went well. Dubhlainn was not visible to anyone. I rode into the training ground; I called the men together. I told them that they were to assemble at the fortress for further training. I explained that they were needed to guard the castle. They packed their weapons, gear, and mounted their horses; they lined up and rode off. Once the campground was empty, Ardan and I looked for Dubhlainn. He was not any where about. One of his officers told us once we came there that he had not been seen in two days. Once the soldiers came here, I told them that they had been duped. I instructed them to remain at the fortress. I said that my son, Prince Dubhlainn, was causing mischief. If they followed him in the future, it would be considered treason."

"How did they react to that?"

"They were astonished, I think. There was brief speaking to each other, shaking heads. Once I was finished speaking, the commander shouted, 'All Hail King Cathal.' They did. We left; I came here."

Betha poured them each a goblet of wine as they relaxed for a little bit. Cathal went to change for dinner; he came back to escort her to dinner. Ardan, Brian, Barry and Braccan were seated in the sitting room. They all rose as Betha and Cathal entered the room. There was thanking and toasting for a time before they went to dinner.

It was decided that Ardan and the others should stay a few more days to scout for Dubhlainn., to secure the castle. Betha looked at her son; she could tell he was torn between his duty to King and country and his eagerness to get back to his betrothed. The marriage was still on hold until after Catherine had delivered her child. Betha had an idea; she would discuss it with Cathal before she said anything to Ardan.

Cathal and Betha retired earlier than usual since Cathal had a long day. When they arrived at their chamber, they sat near the fire to drink some wine. Betha approached her subject carefully.

"Cathal, you are in agreement that Ardan marry Maeve, are you not?"

"Yes, I believe as you do that together they will fulfill prophecy. Please quote it to me once more."

Betha smiled, "The prince shall love a lowly virgin enchantress who shall bring forth a son. He will be strong and virtuous; they shall call him peacemaker."

"Yes, Maeve is an extraordinary young woman. Ardan is all I could ask for in a son. Together they will rule this kingdom. Their son will be a peacemaker! How could I refused this marriage?"

"Good, Sire, but if you watch Ardan closely you will see that he longs for Maeve to be his wife. He is in agreement that Catherine have her child so Maeve can be there for the birth. Then they will come here to marry; but…."

Cathal looked at Betha questioningly, "But?"

"But what if they marry quietly at Parrisal? Once Catherine has her child, they can come home as planned to have a more formal wedding."

214

"But….what if she conceives on their wedding night; what if she is with child for the second wedding?"

"We can handle that when the time comes; there are many ways to handle that situation."

"Now, do you not want to be there for their nuptials?"

"I do, but I will see the formal wedding here. We will make it a grand celebration. I just think their longing for each other is becoming difficult to manage. We should encourage Ardan to marry her now."

Cathal nodded, "I remember waiting for you, my love. It was difficult. Ardan has been courting this girl for weeks now; yes, let us encourage him to marry her as soon as he returns to Parrisal."

Betha sent a servant to summon Ardan. He arrived in their chamber with a confused look on his face. He had never been invited to this room while they were both here. He sat as his mother poured him some wine. They both began to speak but Betha gave way to Cathal.

"Son, we think that upon your return to Parrisal you and Maeve should quietly marry. Once you return here we will have a formal wedding."

Ardan sat with his mouth open, saying nothing.

Betha continued, "We think it is for the best. Maeve has given her word to be with Catherine, thus putting her marriage off. Maeve and your happiness are paramount here. You should marry."

Ardan replied, "But will you come to this wedding?"

"No, we will wait for the formal wedding here."

"I want you at my wedding whether it be small or formal."

"We can come if you want. We will make an excuse or reason for being there. The wedding should be quiet though. No one should know."

"People will know, mother. Parrisal is very small."

Betha sighed looking at Cathal. Cathal spoke then, "All right. We have the wedding at Parrisal. It is not a secret but it is small. We will invite many people here to celebrate the marriage after the fact."

The King and Queen looked at Ardan then for his reaction to this. He thought, he smiled. "I think it might work."

It was arranged that the king and queen would leave a few days after Ardan who would make the arrangements for the wedding. When Betha and Cathal arrived, the wedding would take place.

Cathal and Ardan had meetings with members of the army who had been preparing for war. There were speculations of Dubhlainn's whereabouts. Ardan and Brian roamed the grounds where the army trained. They rode into the hills, looked on the shores of the lakes. There was no indication of anyone having returned here to find the army gone.

Brian spoke at length with Ardan about his brother, where they went as children, what they played. Nothing that Ardan recalled helped. Ardan said that Dubhlainn had left the castle once he recovered his injuries. He had been gone for a few weeks but Ardan did not know where he went.

Then it was Ardan's turn, "Brian, did you hear any rumors at Grashner about a dark haired man or a black bird visiting the village?"

"He might have discovered that Mum's cottage is empty. He could be there. The villagers spoke about a black bird flying around the village. If he were watching Maeve, he would know the cottage was empty."

"You are right. I think he may have been there."

"You are not planning to travel there now, are you?"

"No, Brian, the only thing I am planning is a wedding."

Brian laughed saying, "I am planning to be a father. Let's head back to Parrisal."

In the morning the four men set out for the journey back to Parrisal. The roads were quiet, with no wandering soldiers. They rode as fast and hard as the horses allowed. When they arrived at the stables, Ardan found Colm. He explained the plan for the wedding.

He insisted that Maeve did not know as yet but he would tell her soon. Colm smiled, shaking Ardan's hand.

# Chapter 44

Ardan and Brian found Lord Aengus to let him know they had returned. Both men then went in search of their ladies. They found both of them in Catherine's room enjoying tea. Catherine beckoned Brian into the room as Ardan beckoned Maeve out.

Ardan took Maeve by the hand leading her outside to the garden where they could speak privately. He explained that Betha and Cathal were coming here for their wedding. It would be a small wedding so they no longer had to wait for Catherine to deliver. Maeve sat for a bit just looking at him.

Ardan then decided he had done this all wrong, "I am sorry. I have not asked you if it is agreeable to you. Would you rather wait? Did you want a large wedding? We will still celebrate at the castle. Are you angry with me for this?"

Maeve was just looking at him. She stood, then sat again. She adjusted her shoulders. She looked at him. "Sir, I am confused. Do you still want to marry me?"

"Do I still want to marry you? What are you asking me? I am here talking about getting married here as soon as my parents arrive. What can you possibly mean?"

Maeve said, "Sir, I have been missing you since you left. I have been worried about the state of affairs at the castle. I have been eager for your return. But I wonder now if you still want me."

"Still want you? I am longing for you, my love. That is why I think we should move the marriage date to three days from now not weeks from now."

"I have missed you, Ardan, I have missed your embraces; I have missed your kisses. We have been together since your return for some moments. Do you still want me?"

Confused, Ardan looked at her, then he caught on to what she wanted. He pulled her into his arms holding her close to him. He bent to kiss her, long, deep, passionate.

When they pulled away, Ardan said, "Yes, my love, I still want you. Will you marry me?"

Maeve smiled, "Yes, my love. I will marry you in three days."

Ardan spoke to Lord Aengus. Since Aengus was a romantic at heart, he was excited by the idea of a wedding at his manor with the King and Queen in attendance. The rooms were prepared for the guests. Ardan chose a lovely room for the wedding itself. He spoke to the friar. He provided clothing for Colm and Rylan. Then he remembered, his bride. He ran to his room, grabbed the package. He ran to Maeve's room. He knocked on the door; he was nervous. Maeve answered the door. They stood looking at each other.

Ardan cleared his throat, "Miss, I believe everything has been arranged for our wedding. I almost forgot to give you this. I hope you like it."

Maeve took the package he handed her. "Thank you, Sir." She closed the door moving to her bed. She pulled the packaging off. She found the most beautiful wedding dress. It was a champagne color with pink embroidered flowers as trim. She held it up to herself looking in the mirror. "How lovely it is," she said aloud.

She put the dress down, moving to the door where Ardan still stood on the other side waiting. "Oh love," she cried as she hugged him, "it is beautiful, thank you, thank you so much."

"It is not as beautiful as it will be once you put it on."

They hugged, then Ardan said, "I brought the blue dress also so you can wear it the night before the wedding when my parents arrive."

"Thank you, Ardan, you are so good to me."

"Wait until you are mine. I will lavish you with riches."

"Lavish me with your love. That is all I require."

The King and Queen arrived the following day as expected. Maeve and Ardan went to meet them as soon as they arrived. Maeve found herself very busy but she kept up with her walks with Catherine and her meetings with Maura. She told Brian about

Catherine almost choking so he could watch her as Maeve had been doing since the incident. She and Ardan had not had many chances to talk privately. They tried to meet here and there but it was only for moments. Both of them agreed once they were married, things would calm down. They talked about adopting the type of life Betha and Cathal had. Meetings together in the morning, before bed, and sometimes at the midday meal. It sounded easy but Maeve had her doubts that it was easy at all.

The night before the wedding, dinner was served in the great hall with pipes and drums. Many people were in attendance, including Maura and Tierney, the Commander and his wife, Barry and Braccan, Catherine and Brian, Colm and Rylan, plus other soldiers, friends of Colm's, and some of the women who Maura and Maeve had helped deliver.

Ardan asked Maeve to dance. They had never danced together before but they were compatible. They danced several times. Maeve was wearing her blue dress. She looked like the night sky; her eyes were bright. Ardan would take a moment here and there just to look at her. They made a gorgeous couple with her black hair next to his auburn hair. His dark brown eyes shone as he smiled at his betrothed.

King Cathal was speaking privately to Brian so Betha had Catherine all to herself. In the conversation, Brian told Cathal that he and Maeve had grown up together. Cathal was intrigued.

"Were you the one? She was educated with you? She learned to ride horses with you?"

Brian said, "She first learned here with my wife, Catherine. They were friends before Maeve went to live with her grandmother."

"Who taught her swordplay?"

"That was at my insistence. I had a dream she would need to defend herself, so I demanded she be instructed with me. I gave her my sword."

"Maeve is a beautiful, talented woman. I am surprised you did not marry her."

Brian did not say anything. He was struck silent, so he shook his head excusing himself.

Cathal thought Brian's behavior odd. He turned then to watch Maeve and Ardan dance.

Brian asked Catherine to dance for a slower reel. They laughed but went to the dance floor. Brian did all the steps as Catherine turned about. Maeve and Ardan danced over so they could all dance together. The crowd began to clap as the young people danced, laughing as they did.

Catherine finally stopped, "Unless you want me to go into labor the night before Maeve and Ardan's wedding, we had better sit." Brian took her by the hand, escorting her to her seat. He kept stealing looks at Catherine realizing that she was most beautiful in her condition.

The morning of Maeve's wedding day started as every other morning. Maeve rose, dressed, drank her tea then went in search of Catherine for the morning walk. Catherine was ready so they started down the stairs then out into the sunshine. It was a beautiful morning; the wind was blowing but it was an enjoyable cool breeze. They were discussing the evening before, laughing about dancing but then Maeve wanted to know how Catherine passed the night. Catherine smiled dreamily.

Maeve laughed, "I am not asking that. How did you rest?"

Catherine smiled, "I slept very well. I did not wake until morning."

"You did not go to sleep until morning," Maeve laughed.

"Yes, you are right, but when I did fall asleep, I was peaceful, comfortable. It was the best night's sleep in days."

Maeve smiled as she took Catherine's arm, "I am looking forward to good night's sleep like that." Both women giggled. They were heading in the direction of the stable when they noticed Rylan running toward them.

"What is the matter, Ry?"

"Get back to the manor as soon as you can. Go now."

"What?"

"Go, Maeve."

Before she could turn Dubhlainn was there with his hand on her arm.

"Miss, let us walk," Dubhlainn said to her with a smoothness in his voice.

Maeve looked at Rylan pointedly, "Rylan, please escort Lady Catherine back to the manor."

Dubhlainn and Maeve walked away as Catherine looked at Rylan.

Catherine urged, "Go quickly, Rylan, I am fine here. Get Ardan and Brian. Run."


Rylan ran to the manor bursting into the foyer. A servant standing there stopped him cold.

"You cannot be here," the servant grabbed Rylan, pushing him toward the door.

"Prince Ardan, Lord Brian….I need to see them now."

The servant kept pushing him. Rylan looked around but no one was present. Rylan grabbed the servant as they struggled in the hall.

Rylan began yelling, "Ardan, Brian, help." He yelled louder and louder. The struggle was getting very physical.

Rylan said, "Excuse me," as he punched the servant in the face. The noise from the foyer was heard by the men in the Lord's study. Ardan, Brian and King Cathal ran out the door coming into the foyer.

Ardan grabbed hold of Rylan standing in front of him, "Ry, what's wrong?"

Registering who was in front of him Rylan spoke, "Your brother took Maive. They are probably on horseback. Brian, Catherine is on the walk waiting for assistance. I will get her. Go with Ardan."

Later on they might laugh about who was giving orders but for now the men, including Cathal and Aengus, ran out the manor door with Rylan. They got to the stable to find Colm on the ground with a bloody face but he was yelling to the groomsmen to saddle the horses. Ardan and Brian mounted their horses, as Ardan yelled, "Colm, what direction did he take her?"

Colm shouted, " To the west, the road to Grashner."

Aengus ordered some men to travel with them.

A groomsman helped Colm to his feet. They brought him to the barn to administer to his face. Cathal stood there watching the dust on the road. Suddenly, Betha appeared next to him.

"Is it true? Did Dubhlainn take Maeve?"

"Yes, he did."

"Does she have a weapon with her?"

Colm appeared from the stable, "She usually has a dagger in her boot. That was something I insisted on when she came back to Parrisal from Grashner."

"Let us hope she has it today and did not become complacent living here under the protection of the Lord."

Rylan came back to the stables after a time.

He looked at Queen Betha saying, "Your Grace, Lady Catherine is in her chamber, crying. She is afraid for Maeve, Ardan and Brian."

"Thank you, Rylan, I will go to her."

Cathal squeezed her hand when she turned to him, "You will know as soon as we know, my love."

Betha nodded as she left.

Cathal and Aengus stood together waiting. Aengus thought he too should go to his daughter but he would not know what to say.

He turned to Rylan, "Rylan, go find Maura. If she is at her cottage, not delivering a child, please ask her to visit my daughter."

Rylan nodded as he ran down the road.

Rylan was grateful for the task to keep his mind off his sister. He had heard the rumors while he stayed at the castle. He knew what Dubhlainn did to virgins. He was afraid for his sister; he kept thinking that her wedding day should not be filled with terror. He arrived at Maura's cottage; she was saying goodbye to Tierney as he was leaving for the stable. Rylan explained as quickly as he could what had happened so far that morning. Tierney got his horse as Rylan told him to head west. Maura grabbed her parcel heading for Catherine. Maura was crying as she thought of Maeve; poor girl, she is too young to deal with the lusts of men.

Maura arrived at Catherine's chamber. She found the Queen and Catherine sitting in the room looking distraught. She asked if she might examine Catherine. She determined that Catherine was not in labor but needed to calm down. She poured Catherine some tea as she added an herb to calm her.

Catherine took the tea gratefully but asked, "This is not meant to put me to sleep, is it?"

Maura smiled with tears in her eyes, "Oh no, my Lady, it is only meant to calm you."

She turned to the Queen, "Your Grace, would you like some?"

The Queen smiled, "My dear, I think we all should have some." Maura smiled as she poured two more cups of tea.

Catherine looked at the other two women, "Maeve does not realize how much we all love her, I think. She does not always understand that sort of love. It may be because she lost her mother so early in her life."

"It may also be because the only other people to love her in Grashner were her grandmother and Brian."

"You are right, your Grace, Maeve is very dear to Brian. I never met her grandmother but I have been told they were very close."

Maura replied, "Her mother was a beautiful woman. She was sweet, kind, caring. She loved Maeve and Colm so much. I did not think Colm would ever be able to live with the loss of her."

"And Rylan? He is her son?"

"Oh yes, Rylan has her green eyes; her face…"

As they rode, Brian asked Ardan why his brother would kidnap his betrothed and where would he take her.

Ardan's face was tense; the fury he felt was just under the surface. He shook his head.

"Where would he take her? I do not know. Why did he kidnap her? He intends to rape her."

Brian's face went white. "What? Rape her?"

They heard a horse approaching behind them. Brian turned to see Tierney galloping as fast as he could. Brian yelled to Ardan, "It is Tierney. He knows these hills; maybe he knows where we might search."

Ardan stopped, waiting for Tierney, "Tierney, where would you take a woman to lie with her?"

Tierney was taken aback by this. "Your brother and Maeve?"

"Yes, I must find them. Where would he take her?"
Tierney looked about, scanning the landscape to get his bearings.

"The cave…up that hill."

Ardan cued his horse shouting, "I know the cave. Watch for tracks."
They followed him as he rode.

As they moved up the hill, Ardan jumped off his horse, grabbed the reins pointing out the horse tracks in the dust. The men veered off the road to tether the horses. Ardan ran in the direction of the cave. The others followed him soon after.

As he approached the cave, Ardan could hear voices. He crept up to the mouth standing to the side so he did not cast a shadow inside. He listened, as his brother threatened the love of his life.

"I have done this many times but you have not. I intend to take your maidenhead before my brother gets to you. Maybe he will throw you aside knowing I have had you first." He laughed a low evil sounding laugh.

"Why would you do this to your brother, Dubhlainn?"

"Because he is a swine. He is my parents' favorite. He will be king. He has no visible talents."

Dubhlainn started to move. He had tied Maeve's wrists together so he now loosened the ropes, and told her quietly in a threatening voice, "Remove the ties from your wrists and your ankles. Then take off your garments."

Ardan moved then to where he could see his brother. He noticed Maeve fumbling with the ropes; she was playing for time. Once her wrists were free, she began to play with the ropes on her ankles.

Dubhlainn started getting impatient. "Hurry up, peasant." The name stopped Maeve. She looked at him. She stood then, as she pulled the rope from her ankles, she pulled the dagger from her boot, making sure it was hidden in the creases of her skirt.

"Peasant?"

"Do you really think you are a princess? No, you are a peasant. Take off your clothes before I do it for you."

She stood defiant, staring at him. He walked to her, grabbed the neck of her dress pulling it from her. He threw her on the ground. He stood over her removing his pants, pulling up her skirt as he laughed. Maeve was shaking but as he lowered himself onto her, she stabbed him. She pulled the dagger out stabbing him again. He screamed, slapping her. Ardan came up behind him, pulling him off her. Ardan knocked him in the head with the hilt of his sword. Dubhlainn fell unconscious. Maeve covered her breasts as Ardan helped her to her feet.

Ardan threw his arms around her, "My love, are you all right?" Maeve said nothing; she was still shaking. Ardan removed his cloak, wrapping her in it. Brian and the other men entered the cave. They looked at Dubhlainn. He was bleeding from his stab wounds; the bump on his head was rising.

Ardan gave instructions to tie Dubhlainn's ankles and wrists and throw him on his horse. Take him to the manor, lock him up.

The men did as they were instructed; Brian looked at Ardan as he held Maeve. She was shaking, not speaking. Brian led the men out, starting for the manor.

Ardan continued to hold Maeve. His eyes filled with tears and she noticed. She looked at him but she could not speak. Her fingers wiped the tears from his face as she shook her head. He spoke to her then, "I promise to never let that happen to you again. Please forgive me. I am so sorry."
Maeve frowned as she looked at him. She shook her head.

Ardan was overcome with emotion. His love had been subjected to the evil instincts of his brother. He had stripped her naked so he could defile her. For what? To get revenge on him for non-existing slights. The tears were streaming down his face. He had thought she was safe; he never thought his brother would come to find her. He was too trusting. He needed to be more perceptive of the blackness in people's souls. He held on to Maeve as if she might fly away if he let her go.

Maeve moved back from him so she could see his face. Again she brushed the tears from his face; this time her voice came to her.

"Ardan, I know what you are doing. You are taking on all responsibility for what happened. You have begged my forgiveness. You truly believe this is your fault? Ardan, this is not for you to beg to be forgiven. This was your brother, not you. I do not blame you. I blame your brother. I am sorry; he is your twin brother and I stabbed him."
Ardan looked at her, "Why are you sorry for defending yourself?"
Maeve smiled, "I wonder."

Ardan took her hands, looking into her face he asked, "Maeve, will this ruin it between us?"

Maeve looked closely, trying to determine what he was asking her. "Ruin our love?"

"I love you; I will never stop loving you. Do you love me?"

"Ardan, you are the man I love. I cannot stop loving you."

"Then, will this ruin it between us?"

"Ruin it?" Maeve suddenly had an intake of breath as she realized what he was asking her.

"Ruin it, you mean our desire for each other. You mean my desire and passion for you? No, no, this will not ruin anything between us. We will be married tonight as planned. Then tonight we will lie together for the first time; you will take my maidenhead, only you, Ardan, only you."

He held her again, kissing her, holding the back of her head as she held his face.

"We need to go, Maeve, or we will miss our wedding."
They laughed as they walked from the cave to mount the horse.

Once down the road, they came upon a lone rider. It was Brian.

"I waited because I wanted to be sure that you were both all right."

"Thank you, Brian. My love is resilient. She is strong and proud."

Brian looked at Maeve who smiled, "Yes, Maeve is strong. She has lived through so much; I do not believe there is anything she cannot survive."

# Chapter 45

When they arrived at the manor there was much jubilation as people saw that Maeve was safe. Maeve was telling both Ardan and Brian that she needed to see her father and brother. Then she needed to see Catherine to be sure she was calm. Then she would get ready for the wedding if they would send Maura to her.

Ardan stayed with her as she visited her father and brother. Brian went to see Catherine to tell her Maeve would be along. Maura was still with Catherine, so Brian told her that Maeve wanted to see her as well. Maura said she would wait for her outside her chamber.

Colm shook Ardan's hand thanking him for saving his daughter. Rylan hugged her. Colm hugged her then, as she told him that the dagger was a very useful tool. Colm looked at her.

"Did you have to use it?"

"Oh yes, I used it…twice."

Colm looked over Maeve's head to Ardan who just smiled. Colm shook his head.

Maeve, escorted by Ardan, went to Catherine's chamber. They knocked on the door. Brian let them into the room. Maeve went to hug Catherine each assuring the other one that they were all right. Catherine told her that Maura and the Queen had sat with her to calm her; they were as upset as she was. Catherine took Maeve by the hand, "Maeve, we all love you. Please know that we do."

Maeve was surprised by this; her eyes filled with tears as she hugged Catherine, "I love you. I am here for you."

Maeve went to her room then to prepare for the wedding ceremony, Ardan left her there once Maura came.

Maeve turned to look at Maura. The look that crossed between them was one of knowledge. Maura went to Maeve holding her.

"Did he hurt you?"

"He did not succeed. I am still a virgin."

"How bad was it?"

"He stripped me, lowered himself on me without his pants. I stabbed him."

"You stabbed him? I am glad."

"Why are there men who want to hurt women like that?"

"I do not know the answer to that but from what I hear Ardan's brother is in bad shape. The physician is trying to save his life. He is still unconscious. He lost much blood on the way back to the manor."

"Maura, on your wedding night, were there circumstances that caused you to be unable to enjoy it?"

"You are asking, if what I had been through had caused me to dread my intimacy with Tierney?"

"Yes, did it cause problems?"

"No, what bothered me was his tenderness to me. I did not feel I deserved his love."

"Of course, you deserve his love. Ohhhh, I told Ardan that nothing could come between us, especially this crazy man. Will I feel I do not deserve Ardan? That's not the way I have planned our lives."

"Maeve, you bested your attacker, you deserve Ardan's love; he deserves yours. Stop thinking these horrible thoughts. Let me tell you this, I no longer feel inadequate with Tierney. The memory is fading; we are now united, together, married."

"Maura, thank you for that. Oh, I must get ready. I am getting married."

Betha and Cathal stood near Dubhlainn as the physician showed them his wounds.

"He is still unconscious from the head wound. He has a dagger wound in his side here that has caused damage to his intestine; but the wound that has caused the most bleeding is …."

He stopped then turned to the Queen asking her if she could avert her eyes.

She frowned, shaking her head, "No, Sir, I too will see the damage."

The physician nodded, removing the sheet, "The dagger was thrust at such an angle and with such force that it mostly severed one testicle. I had to remove it to stop the bleeding, stitching the wound."

Betha and Cathal looked at each other solemnly.

Cathal turned to the physician, "When do you believe he will regain his wits?"

"He should revive soon, I believe. I will be here with him when he does."

"Thank you, Sir."

They walked from the room as Ardan came down the hall. They waited for him to reach them.

"How is my brother?"

"He is still unconscious. He has suffered some serious wounds."

"Will he survive?"

"The physician believes he will; at least he believes he will regain his wits."

The three began to walk down the hall. Betha excused herself from the men so they could speak without her present. Once she was gone, Cathal told Ardan the details of Dubhlainn's injuries.

"Father, I am sorry."

Cathal looked at his son, "Ardan, why do you apologize?"

"Dubhlainn is your son also. He is in serious condition. Your heart is sad as is mine."

Cathal nodded and hugged his son then, marveling at Ardan's empathy.

"There is a wedding scheduled. It is time we got ready," Cathal winked at Ardan as they both headed toward their chambers.

The room for the ceremony was lit with candles. There was a roaring fire which made the room warm and inviting. Flowers had been placed in vases near the front. Chairs were lined up for the guests while there was an aisle for the bride to pass.

People began arriving, finding places to sit. Ardan waited at the door greeting his guests. Catherine and Brian were given places of honor in the front row. Rylan arrived with a smile. He looked very handsome in his borrowed clothing. Ardan noticed his resemblance to Maeve. They went into the room to wait. The friar arrived so Ardan stood with him at the makeshift altar.

Colm had gone to Maeve's room. Maura had stayed with Maeve to help her dress but then left to dress also. Maeve opened the door at her father's knock. Maeve took his breath away. He stood there looking at his daughter who smiled at him shyly. He held her hands, then turned her around.

The dress was magnificent. The color brought out Maeve's skin tone; the pink trim along the hemline and train was lovely. There was pink ribbon trim in the neckline which was not as modest as the blue dress Ardan had given her. Her hair was braided but woven into a crown on the top of her head. There were pink roses woven into the braid. Colm could tell she was nervous so he hugged her, trying to sooth her nerves.

Colm whispered to her, "All people are nervous at their weddings; once the ceremony is complete, you will relax. Ardan will be there with you holding your hand. Take a deep breath, Tiny One, it will help."

Maeve's eyes brightened with tears, "I wish Mama were here."

Colm smiled, "She is, Maeve, I can feel her here with us."

Maeve closed her eyes for a moment, standing perfectly still. Her eyes opened wide, "Da, I feel her too. Thank you."

They left the room then, walking down the hall to the staircase. Maeve looked to the room where the ceremony would take place. There were guards standing by the entrance. They arrived at the doorway. It was time to walk down the aisle to Ardan. Maeve could not see him from where she stood in the entrance but her father could. There was a subtle nod between her father and her groom; Colm looked at Maeve, winking. He and his daughter entered the room to walk down the aisle.

When Maeve came into view of the guests, there were many intakes of breath. Many people just smiled. She was stunning. Ardan's reaction to her was one of deep love; he smiled as he watched her move toward him. Her eyes sought his; their connection was so strong many people were taken aback. Maeve arrived at Ardan's side as he took her hand. His eyes did not leave her face.

The friar began the prayers and they stated their vows. Betha and Cathal held hands, smiling. Catherine began to cry while Brian took her hand, kissing her fingers. Maura and Tierney looked at each other, as Tierney winked. Colm watched his daughter's face, still feeling the presence of Finola.

When the ceremony was finished, Ardan and Maeve walked back up the aisle to the corridor. There Ardan pulled her into his arms to kiss his wife for the first time. The kiss was long and deep; Maeve felt her knees weaken but Ardan's strong arms held her to him. They pulled away from each other as their guests came out of the room. Ardan and Maeve headed for the great hall to celebrate as their friends followed them.The newlyweds visited everyone in the great hall as they walked from table to table. The pipes and drums played as people ate and drank. After the meal, Ardan walked to the musicians, spoke quickly, then walked to his bride to escort her to the dance floor. The musicians began to play the same reel the bride and groom danced to the night Ardan and Maeve had stayed at the inn. Maeve began to laugh but again her feet started tapping as she and her husband danced. There was such joy on their faces that some of the guests began to think they had never been to such a happy wedding. The party lasted all night. The guests danced to the musicians' wonderful music. Ardan and Maeve were not in a hurry to leave so they enjoyed the party with their guests.

There was a commotion later in the evening as guests watched the hallway. A servant came in to speak with Brian and Lord Aengus.

Both men left the room to greet a late arrival. In the hallway, Brian hugged his mother but a look of consternation came across his face. Lord Aengus was the gracious host as he gave instructions to his servant to prepare a room for their guest.

Brian addressed his mother, "Why did you not tell us you were coming?"

"I thought I would be welcome here with the birth of my first grandchild about to take place."

"Of course, you are welcome, mother, but we could have had your accommodations ready if we had known."

"What is this celebration taking place?"

"It is the wedding of Prince Ardan and Princess Maeve."

"How lovely! Who is Prince Ardan?"

"He is the son of your friend, Queen Betha, and her husband, King Cathal."

A look of shock and annoyance quickly passed over Mirima's face. "Betha and Cathal are here? Why is the wedding taking place here and not at the castle?"

Brian took his mother by the arm to escort her to her room, "Because the couple delayed their marriage so Maeve could be here with Catherine to help her deliver our child. It was planned then to have a small wedding here and later a larger celebration at the castle so they did not have to wait."

"Maeve? Maeve, the witch's granddaughter?"

"Yes!" With more emphasis he stated,"Mum's granddaughter."

"How is she going to help with the birth of my grandchild?"

"She has become a midwife."

"And she married a Prince?"

"Yes."

"Is he dimwitted? She is nothing but a peasant."

"Mother, hush. He is not dimwitted. Maeve is important to him and to the King and Queen."

"How astounding! She was not good enough to be your wife. Now she is married to a prince."

Brian's face darkened, "What do you mean she was not good enough to be my wife?"

"I made sure of it. I would not have it."

"How did you make sure of it? What are you saying?"

Mirima realized then she had said too much. She shook her head, "I do not know what I am saying. I am tired from the travel. I will just retire."

Brian did not pursue the conversation. He delivered his mother to her room, kissed her cheek, wishing her a good night's rest.

Brian took some time to return to the great hall. He was upset by this conversation with his mother. What did she mean? He went to his bedchamber to pour a glass of wine so he could calm himself. Once he felt better he returned to the hall. He found Catherine. She smiled at him as she whispered, "Your mother is here?"

"Yes, she came unannounced but has made her presence known." Catherine smiled, took his hand as they continued to watch the dancers.

The prince and his bride began their farewells around the hall. Brian and Catherine waited until they approached to convey their surprise.

"We have taken the liberty of moving your belongings to a larger bedchamber on the third floor. This will be your room for the rest of your stay with us."

"How gracious of you both," Ardan smiled as he shook Brian's hand; he placed a kiss on Catherine's cheek.

"Thank you, Brian and Catherine," Maeve gave each a hug.

The newlyweds continued around the hall as Brian watched Maeve. His mother's words bothered him. He did not understand; he had not wanted to marry Maeve. He did not discuss it with his father or anyone. He looked at his beautiful wife, "Darling, it has been a very long day for both of us. Shall we retire?"

"Yes, my love, let us. I am not sure I will get up in the morning if we stay much longer."

"Let us rise before the midday meal though," Brian said as he laughed.

Maeve and Ardan were escorted to their new accommodations by a servant. Their room was quite large. Filled with candlelight, there was a sitting area near the fireplace which contained a roaring fire. Two goblets sat next to a bottle of wine on a table near the window. There were flowers on the fireplace mantle. The canopied bed was in an adjoining room. Their clothing had been placed in the two wardrobes on the other end of the room. After the brief tour, Ardan took Maeve by the hand and poured two goblets of wine as they sat near the fire.

"You look simply beautiful, my love."

"Thank you, Ardan. You look so handsome. Thank you for my wedding dress. It made me feel like a Princess."

"You are a Princess."

"It feels good to sit here with you, the two of us together, alone."

"Yes, we will have many years sitting alone together."
Once the goblets were empty, Ardan rose taking Maeve by the hand. They went into the bedroom.

"Would you like help with your dress?"

"Yes, please, there are many buttons in the back."

Ardan began unbuttoning the dress. Maeve looked into the mirror to see him as he worked. Finally he finished, helping her by lifting the shoulders off her body as she stepped out of the dress. She stood in her petticoats as Ardan removed his clothing. Ardan turned to her lifting the petticoats over her head. They stood in front of each other naked.

"Maeve, you are afraid?"

"I am told that the first time will hurt."

"Yes, it will but then it will be all right."

She nodded as he pulled the covers down, then he lifted her onto the bed. He laid next to her, whispering her name before he began to kiss her. His kisses were gentle at first; then they became more passionate as Maeve put her arms around him holding him close to her. Ardan had always shown Maeve his passion for her through his kisses but now he probed her mouth with his tongue. Her tongue explored his mouth in the same way. This was a lesson in love as Maeve learned quickly what to do. When Ardan mounted her, she was breathless. The first thrust was painful but she was attuned to his rhythm, moving with him. The culmination of their union brought them both to peaks never felt before by either. They lay in each others arms, whispering words of love.

Maeve leaned up on her arm looking at Ardan in the candlelight, "My love, I am bursting with love for you."

Ardan pulled her face to him as he kissed her again, "My Wife, I love you with all my being."

Ardan held her. They spoke softly of living together , sleeping together, having children. Maeve leaned up on her arm again, "Are you sleepy, Ardan?"

"No, love, are you?"

"No, I would like to try it again."

"Try it again?"

"Yes, I think I …"

"You think you what, Maeve?"

"I think I could be better."

"Maeve? You were lovely, but I will gladly 'try it again' though."

"Ardan, I love you. May we try it again?"

"Yes, my love, we may," Ardan laughed low as he pulled Maeve closer.

They tried it again. When they were finished, Ardan asked, "Maeve, do you feel that was better?"

"Yes, I liked it. Do you feel it was better, Ardan?"

"Yes, I liked it too, love. Imagine how it will be with more practice."

Maeve began to giggle as she kissed Ardan. He pulled her face to his kissing her passionately. With that kiss Maeve began to moan. She pulled closer to him; Ardan reacted to this passion from her. He felt he had chosen well, a passionate bride. They practiced again.

The sun was rising when they fell asleep in each other's arms.

# Chapter 46

In the days that followed, Ardan and Maeve began to move about the manor as they had before. Maeve and Catherine walked. Maeve visited Maura making sure they were prepared for when Catherine began her labor. Ardan and Brian rode about the manor seeing to work that needed to be done.

Mirima had a reunion with Betha. The queen was polite but Mirima was hostile and afraid as she was when Betha was near. Betha was concerned about Mirima's health. She asked her if she was well.

"Of course, I am well. I just do not like living alone at my manor. Brian and Catherine came here so I followed."

"I see. You must have friends at the manor to alleviate your loneliness."

"No one I would call a true friend."

"So, you depend on Brian and Catherine to keep you company?"

"Will you not depend on Ardan to keep you company?"

"I rather doubt it, although Maeve and I have begun a friendship that I hope will deepen."

"How did that happen?"

"Maeve is a lovely woman. We have much in common in our interests. When Ardan and Cathal work together, Maeve and I work together. But if I lose Cathal before I leave this earth, I will not depend on my son and his wife to be my companions."

"You do not know that for certain, dear, you may."
Betha smiled at Mirima which made Mirima angry. Mirima excused herself giving the Queen a brief curtsey.

Mirima went in search of Brian but when she found him, he was with a group of men discussing business. She had to leave then so she went to find Catherine. Catherine was resting as Maeve was leaving her room.

"Lady Mirima, Lady Catherine is sleeping at the moment. She will be awake for the midday meal."

"I see." Mirima walked away. Maeve frowned as Ardan came up behind her.

"I have been looking for you, Maeve, are you free for a bit?"

"Yes, I am free at the moment."

Ardan took her hand as they headed up the staircase up to the third floor.

Mirima went to her bedchamber. She sat in the room alone. She thought to herself that she could have done this at her manor. She began to think about Maeve having access to Catherine that Mirima did not have. How did these two become such good friends? They only had that brief stay together in Grashner while Maeve was ill. She was unconscious most of the time. Mirima did not know that Maeve and Catherine were friends as girls. Now Betha said Maeve and she had a friendship. Why does everyone love this peasant?

Mirima had heard that Betha's other son was injured. She thought she would visit him to introduce herself. So she left her room going in search of Dubhlainn. She found the physician examining the man as she entered. The physician threw the covers over his patient as he turned to the intruder.

"What are you doing here?"

"I have come to visit Dubhlainn. I am a friend of his parents."

"This patient can have no visitors at present. He is under sedation. He could not talk to you if he wanted to do so."

Mirima looked at Dubhlainn who was asleep. She shrugged her shoulders as she left the room.

Cathal was coming down the hall to visit the physician as Mirima was leaving.

"What are you doing down here, Mirima?"

"I came to visit your son; I was bored."

"My son is off limits to you, Mirima. He is very ill."

Mirima turned; she continued down the hall to go back to her room. She kept thinking about how rude everyone was being to her. She had not been invited to the wedding. She was not being included here. She went to her room. Mirima sat for a long time; she decided to leave in the morning. That would make everyone feel bad. She went to the stable to tell one of the groomsmen that she would be leaving in the morning so she needed her carriage. The groomsman bowed to her to say all would be ready. She would not tell anyone else. She would just leave.

In the afternoon of the following day, Brian went in search of his mother. She did not answer the knock at her door so he turned the knob, entering. Her room was empty so he went to the stable. He asked if his mother's carriage was there. He was told that she had left early that morning. Brian smiled, thanking the groomsman.

Brian went to see Catherine then.

"My mother left this morning."

"She did?"

"Yes, she said goodbye to no one."

"That is strange."

"It is fine for now but I fear we will hear about it when we go to Grashner."

"That is true. You will hear about it before I do though."

"It has been enjoyable being here except of course for armies being raised, kidnappings of brides and my mother's visit."

"Yes, I am enjoying being here," Catherine laughed.

Maeve went to see Maura. She found her in the garden cutting herbs. Maura looked at Maeve, smiled, and came right to the point, "Maeve, I am beginning to worry. Catherine should have started labor by now?"

Maeve thought as she counted, "She is overdue? Wait, let me count again."

She counted again. She asked Maura, "When did she tell you?"

"Should we go to see her to check?"

"Yes, we should see her now."

The women went to visit Catherine. After much discussion, much counting, and more discussion, it was decided that her labor should be starting soon. And it did; that evening Catherine began her labor. Brian sent messengers to Maura but he found Maeve himself. Maeve was walking back from the stables when he saw her.

"Come, Maeve, Catherine has started her labor."

"I will run to my room first; then I will come."

Maeve got her medicinals from her chamber; she started toward Catherine's chamber when Ardan came to the room.

"Where are you headed, my love," Ardan questioned with a smile on his face.

"Catherine has begun her labor. Please go to Brian to keep him occupied. This may be a very long night."

Ardan's smile faded, "Oh, I was hoping…I will find Brian."

Maeve's hand brushed his cheek, "I know, my love, I was hoping also but I must go. This is why we are here."

Ardan nodded, but he pulled Maeve into his arms, kissing her.

She ran to Catherine then. As she entered the room, Catherine smiled at her, "They are pretty steady but not very strong." Maeve nodded, as she placed her hand on Catherine's stomach.

The next pain came as Catherine sucked in her breath, "That was stronger."

Maura knocked as she entered. Brian and Ardan were in the corridor. Maura motioned to Maeve.

Maeve opened the door, "Brian, come in to see your wife for a bit. It may be a long night, so you need to see her now because you probably will not see her for quite a time."

She moved into the hallway then, and she embraced Ardan, "Ardan, this can be an experience for you to keep Brian calm. If it goes long as we think it will, he will become distraught. You need to reassure him; this is women's work."

242

Ardan looked at her, smiling, "Woman, I love you." She smiled at that as she reentered the room.

Brian came out; he looked at Ardan shaking his head.

Ardan smiled, "Let us have some ale or wine?"

"Ale."

The two men left the women to their work.

The labor progressed normally at first. The pains became stronger as time passed. Catherine was getting very tired. She was having trouble keeping up; she wanted to sleep. Maura discouraged this by wiping Catherine's face to wake her up again and again. Hours passed. The child was in the correct position but it was not coming down the birth canal. Maura asked Maeve to get the physician, so Maeve dashed out of the room. She found the physician with Betha in the
sickroom.

They were keeping an eye on Dubhlainn. Maeve stood in the doorway not wanting to enter. She had not seen Dubhlainn since he kidnapped her; she did not want to see him.

"Sir, Maura requests you come to Lady Catherine's chamber. She has been in labor for hours."

Betha said, "Go, I will stay here with my son."

The physician accompanied Maeve upstairs to Catherine's room. When he examined Catherine he shook his head, "She is exhausted; the baby's head is large. I do not know how she can get it down the birth canal. We may have to cut her."

Maeve looked at him, "Cut her? What do you mean?"

"Cut the child out of her."

"Like you did my mother?"

He shook his head, "I do not see where we have much choice."

Maeve turned, "Maura?"

Maura looked at Maeve but she did not say anything.

She said to the physician, "I do not believe she is open enough, look at her."

The doctor did look. "Give her a little more time…call me if you need me."

The doctor left the room. Maeve said to Maura, "It is time to do what we talked about."

"Do you think that will really work?"

"I think we should try it. Lock the door. I will prepare the solution."

Maeve and Maura began preparing for an idea they had discussed in all the hours of Maeve's training.

"This may not work but here we go."

Maura administered to Catherine. Maeve helped Catherine up to walk with her around the room. The labor continued; Catherine realized her waters had broken as her feet became wet. Once they laid her back down, Maura examined her again. The child's head had crowned but was too large to pass through. Maeve took the knife they prepared, cutting Catherine enough for the baby's head to deliver. Catherine was told to push, which she did, and the child was born.

Maeve held the child as Maura cut the umbilical cord.

"Catherine, you have a beautiful baby girl. Look at her. She is lovely."

Catherine sat up slightly. Maura stitched her rapidly, cleaning her up as she did. Maeve cleaned the baby and passed her to her mother.

Catherine looked at her daughter with tears in her eyes. "Brian and I chose the name Aisling for my mother."

"That is beautiful. It suits her."

Once they had cleaned up mother and child, they cleaned the bed to get everyone comfortable. Maeve went in search of Brian. He and Ardan had fallen asleep at the table where they were seated.

Maeve shook them both, "Brian, come to meet your daughter." Ardan laughed, shaking Brian's hand. Brian ran from the room. Ardan and Maeve walked up the stairs; Maura was just leaving the new parents with their child.

"Catherine is nursing the girl. Brian is so happy; he is pacing, eager to hold the baby."

"I will visit tomorrow to check on them. I am glad we were able to do this."

Maura smiled at Ardan, "Maeve, may I speak to you a moment?"

Maeve turned to Ardan, "I will be right up, love." He nodded and left the women.

Maura looked sad. "Maeve, I am concerned though about future children. I do not think Catherine should have any more."

"Why? She did fine. We saved both of them."

"Yes, but Catherine is very tiny. The child was too big for her; think if she has a boy next time. A boy would be bigger. She might die."

"Maura, what are you saying? That she cannot have another child which means what, no intimacy with her husband? Is that what you are suggesting?"

"Yes, I am."

Maeve began to whisper frantically, "Who will tell this young married couple who so obviously love each other that now they must live together as brother and sister?"

Maura shook her head, "I do not know. They need to be told though. Maybe the physician will tell them."

Maeve's eyes filled with tears as she hugged Maura, "I love you. I will see you tomorrow. Get some rest."


Maeve went upstairs to find Ardan. He was sitting near the fire waiting for her. He poured her some wine as he made her sit. He massaged her shoulders as he could see how exhausted she was. The massaging felt wonderful to her tired body. Once her wine was gone, he brought her to their bed. She undressed moving to the bed; Ardan lifted her then got into the bed beside her. She reached for him then as she started to cry.

"What is it, my love? Everything is all right?"

"No, it is not. Catherine had a difficult time of it. Maura does not believe she can survive another birth. What does that mean, Ardan?"

Ardan knew what that meant as he held his wife to him. She continued crying softly as she fell asleep in his arms.

# Chapter 47

The new arrival was a darling little girl. She resembled her mother. She had blue eyes as did both her parents. Everyone visited to see her. There was much joy in the household.

Lord Aengus took one look at his granddaughter, saying, "She looks like my Aisling. She is well named."

Queen Betha visited, asking if she could hold the child. Catherine let her, noticing that Betha wanted a grandchild of her own.

Maeve's care of Catherine was done since she had fulfilled her obligation to her friend. She and Ardan were talking about returning to the castle. Betha and Cathal wanted to return also but Dubhlainn's presence made it difficult to leave.

Cathal said to the three of them, "I feel that we have stayed long enough but what do we do about Dubhlainn?"

"How is he? Can he travel?"

Betha smiled sadly shaking her head, "No, he cannot travel. He has been burning up. He does not stay conscious all day as yet."

"Is the physician giving him sedation?"

"At times, yes. At other times, no."

"What if we all return to the castle, then send our young physician here to care for Dubhlainn. Once he is ready to travel, we will send a carriage?"

"That is a good solution, Ardan, let me clear this with Lord Aengus. I will speak to the physician as well."

It was decided that the royals would return home. Lord Aengus was sad to see them leave; he had enjoyed his time with Cathal. As they gathered in the foyer to say farewell, Lord Aengus kissed Maeve's hand thanking her again and again for his daughter and granddaughter.

Ardan and Maeve had bid farewell to the little family privately. Maeve had visited Maura and her father. Rylan said his farewells earlier than anyone. He arrived at their chamber before breakfast. They laughed when they saw him but hugs were profuse. They had breakfast together in their chamber. Rylan seemed very sad to see them leave but he knew they had to move on with their lives yet he must stay to help his father.

Ardan and Maeve were riding back to the castle as Cathal and Betha rode in the carriage. Maeve was happy to be back on her horse, riding alongside her husband, her handsome prince. There was a time on the way home that Maeve and Ardan were trotting their horses next to each other.Maeve said to him, "What is everyday life like at the castle? I know when Rylan and I were visiting, we were not participating in the day-to-day life. How will it be now?"

Ardan looked at her, smiling, "I travel for my father quite a bit. He has mentioned to me that it will be important to visit the villages reassuring them that war is not coming. My mother works with her plants every day so what you were doing as you spent time with her was her normal routine."

"How long do you stay away when you travel?"

"It depends on where I am going and what my mission is."

She nodded but said no more.

When they arrived at the castle, Ardan and Maeve found they had a new bedchamber. It was large, comfortable and all theirs. The servants delivered their clothing, putting everything away. It was still early in the day when they arrived so Maeve walked about the grounds; Ardan checked on the horses.

They met later in their room. Ardan discerned that Maeve was deep in thought. He crossed over to where she was sitting as she looked at him.

"Ardan, would it be possible for me to travel with you?"

"I ….I am not certain. My father will need to be consulted; possibly my mother. You are not tired of traveling, my love?"

"It is not a matter of being tired, Ardan, it is that I do not want to stay here without you, at least not yet. I am sure there will be a time when I must."

"Maeve, you have a new life coming but you are not certain yet what that new life is. I understand. I will speak with my father."

"Thank you, Ardan."


Cathal did not want Ardan to leave right away. They spoke at length of Maeve going with him. They also consulted Betha. They thought it would be fine as long as they entrusted several soldiers to go with them. Ardan and Maeve would stay in the castle for some weeks as they planned the villages they would visit. Ardan took Maeve to order some new clothing.

Maeve's daily life was comfortable. She was happy with Ardan, loving him more and more each day. Being with him on the road was the way it had always been with him since the first time they met. She would love the travel; who knows how long they would be able to travel together. Her life with Ardan would be one of love, friendship, adventure, and hopefully children.

Ardan walked into the room while she was thinking of this. He loved coming to their room to find her there. He thought they were achieving a rhythm of communication. They seemed to know each other's minds and wants. She had looked up as he entered. They were happy to see each other although he had only been out of the room an hour.

"Any news, Love?"

"Yes, our wedding celebration is planned for this spring once winter has passed."

"That will make it easier for people to travel."

"Dubhlainn's health is improving. Our physician thinks he will be well enough to travel in a few weeks."

"How is his disposition?"

"The missive did not say. My father gets the impression he is not saying all."

"I wonder how comfortable he is treating Dubhlainn. He is young you said."

"Yes, he is young. He is the son of our physician here. He grew up here; he knows Dubhlainn."

"I see."

"Shall we dress for dinner?"

"Yes, we should. We only have about two hours before it is served. Can you help me with the buttons on this dress?"

"Yes, of course, if you can help me remove this tunic."
Maeve smiled her brightest smile at him; Ardan winked. They proceeded to dress for dinner.

# ABOUT THE AUTHOR

**Marjorie Hemans is a retired English and Theatre teacher. She resides with her husband in Colorado.**

Made in the USA
Middletown, DE
19 February 2018